SECRETS IN THE GLEN

VEILS, VOWS AND HIGHLAND TIES

CLAIRE GILLIES

GREEN ISLE PUBLISHING

Published by Green Isle Publishing

www.clairegillies.com

Paperback ISBN: 978-1-7392452-5-2

Ebook ISBN: 978-1-7392452-0-7

How delicious is the winning
Of a kiss at love's beginning,
When two mutual hearts are sighing
For the knot there's no untying!
Yet remember, 'Midst our wooing,
Love has bliss, but Love has ruing;
Other smiles may make you fickle,
Tears for other charms may trickle.

THOMAS CAMPBELL

1

Lori's wristwatch echoed the erratic beat of her racing heart – an urgent drumroll preceding the life-altering decision she was about to make. Facing the swelling sea, a deep tremor coursed through her body. Nevertheless, she clung to the steering wheel, determined to ignore the persistent ache consuming her.

Today was the day she had to be here.

Waves surged forward, cascading over the sandy shore and assaulting her windshield with a burst of salty spray. Above her, the sky stretched out in a hazy canvas painted with delicate pink wisps. Her gaze swept across the horizon until it settled on the murky green expanse of the sea – the same sea that had already taken so much from her.

With a measured breath, she attempted to calm her racing heart, drawing on the techniques she used during panic attacks. Focusing on something larger than herself, she synced her breathing with the ebb and flow of the approaching waves. It was time, and there was no turning back. After all, it had been her idea. This decision would finally end the pain that had haunted her for so long.

Lori opened the car door and stepped out, her bare feet

sinking into the cold sand. The salty wind ran through her hair, and she smiled at what awaited her, embracing the unknown.

* * *

Rhona made her grand proclamation across the dress shop, her tone dripping with dramatic flair. "You know what they say, Lori," she began, with a sly grin. "It is a universal truth, at least in our little corner of the world, that a single man with loads of money might just need a woman to help him part with it." Her words resonated through the boutique as she continued her chore, a bucket of soapy water resting by her red-heeled sandals. With satisfaction, she scrubbed the front window, lathering it with soap and guiding the wiper in smooth strokes. The usual display of mannequins lay tossed aside, provocatively piled atop one another.

Lori leaned casually on her broom after sweeping away the remnants of dust and fabric from the floor. "Oh aye. Do you think we've stepped into a romantic Regency novel, Rhona?" With a quick, practised motion, she scooped up the debris and tossed it into a hefty black bin liner. "We're living in the twenty-first century, you know, and besides, he's not all that wealthy."

Rhona shrugged, undeterred. "Well, he does own all that land, and he's got that Mr Darcy vibe … you know, a bit grumpy."

Lori couldn't help but laugh at the comparison. "I'll make sure our Mr Darcy knows exactly what the locals think of him!" She emptied the last of the fabric scraps into the black bag, her head turned away from the swirling remnants of lint and threads.

Lori couldn't deny that Callum's recent business venture – crafting luxury glamping pods on a once-secluded, overgrown hillside – had truly taken off. His vision expanded daily, attracting the attention of eager investors. With Alan's help, they had already constructed three pods, and four more were in the works. Initially, Lori had been filled with anxiety, watching their savings pour into this startup venture. However, her faith in Callum ran deep. He had already steered a successful outdoor business and was well acquainted with the challenges that startups could bring. This new venture was different, though, involving contractors, handymen, and a level of complexity far beyond guiding small groups of tourists on kayaking excursions. Taking a deep breath, she reminded herself that this was Callum's venture, and if it wasn't causing him stress, she should follow his lead. Their most pressing challenge at the moment revolved around the question of staffing. They were in dire need of a dependable workforce. She had taken it upon herself to manage the cleaning of the existing properties, which they had already advertised online and had guests coming in every other night. However, keeping up with the high turnover had proven to be a formidable task. They were in desperate need of help, but finding suitable candidates was turning out to be a monumental struggle.

They had scoured the local area but couldn't find anyone willing to commit to working the entire summer. Attempts to entice candidates from further afield to stay for more than just a couple of nights had also fallen flat. They had placed ads in newspapers and magazines, and although they received inquiries, the staff turnover remained distressingly high. One after another, the hired employees had departed, leaving Lori and Callum grappling with what to do.

"You're fortunate to have me," Rhona chimed in. "It sounds like all those little laddies and lassies were having a meltdown over how remote it is up here."

"They're not exactly kids, Rhona. They're young adults,

in that awkward phase between high school and college." She was already itching to change the subject. She had been tasked with overseeing staffing, and the results thus far were far from satisfactory. "It's baffling, really. You'd assume that 'the Highlands' would be self-explanatory in terms of its tranquillity. But it seems none of them could handle it. The last girl even arrived by train, loitered at the station, and then hopped back on the next one – she didn't even make it to the glamping farm!"

To Lori's ears, it now sounded like some kind of festival where long-haired hippies indulged in weed, though they hadn't officially named the place yet. Callum's focus was primarily on the design aspects – the placement of trees, the type of kitchen sink each property should have, and similar details. For the time being, they had simply been referring to it as the glamping farm, even though it bore no resemblance to an actual farm, except for the occasional stray sheep wandering the hills.

"I don't know," Rhona mused. "I think people are drawn to the romantic idea of living in the Highlands. But the reality is quite different. Not having easy access to hummus or couscous can apparently push some people over the edge!"

Lori cast a meaningful glance through the window, her thoughts elsewhere. Rain gently streamed down on the other side, and then suddenly, heavy hailstones pelted the pavement, bouncing off the street with a sharp clatter.

"What on earth?" Rhona threw her hands up in disbelief. "This can't be right – it's way too early for hailstones. We're still expecting our Indian summer!"

Lori narrowed her eyes at Rhona, concern deepening. In Scotland, when the summer fell short, folks usually banked on a late summer to make things right. Lori, well-versed in this local quirk, knew the weather forecast didn't always catch on to this recurring phenomenon.

"It's an omen," Rhona whispered, leaving fresh fingerprints on the newly washed window.

"Just because we haven't had much of a summer, that's hardly a reason!"

"And the shop – there's hardly been a soul!" Rhona scoffed. "I wouldn't even think of giving this place a spring clean in the summer, but it's been so quiet out there. What else can we do?"

"It can get quiet sometimes!" Lori retorted, trying to rationalise the situation.

"No, it doesn't. We're in the Highlands of Scotland, Lori. Summertime is always bustling! We can't even catch our breath – the roads are clogged with tourists, and the shops are overflowing! I mean, when was the last time you got stuck behind a camper van on the roads?" Rhona raised an eyebrow.

Lori simply shrugged, not wanting to engage in an argument.

"Trust me, there's something amiss," Rhona declared with a gasp. "We might not even get our Indian summer!"

"You really think so?" Lori raised an eyebrow, her curiosity piqued.

"I'm telling you, Lori, this is a bad omen. Freaky weather, no tourists … what's next?"

Once again, Lori shrugged, having little to add, especially when Rhona had already made up her mind.

"They say bad things come in threes," Rhona added, her voice full of conviction.

"Oh, you and your superstitions." Lori sighed. "Please be quiet and stop trying to convert me to your traditional ways. Next thing you know, you'll be placing black cats in our path for good luck!"

Rhona gasped once more. "No, Lori, are you insane? Black cats signify bad luck, not good luck!"

2

Feeling a bit unsettled by Rhona's superstitions, Lori decided to spend the rest of the afternoon with her grandmother to calm her nerves. As she made her way down the lane to Gran's house, she was surprised to find the carpark filled with vehicles. Forced to park on the main street, she muttered to herself as she made her way to Gran's door. She knocked, a habit she had only recently adopted since her gran's recent marriage to Lawrence, and Lori's move with Callum to the glamping park. There was no answer. She pressed her ear to the door and could hear voices inside. She counted to three, just in case, and then opened the door.

The spacious kitchen and open lounge were filled with people, some holding cups of tea, and others with glasses of wine. Lori blinked in surprise, checking her watch – it was still lunchtime. Gran was hosting a gathering without inviting her. Laughter and conversation filled the room, and Lori stood there awkwardly, unable to spot her gran among the crowd.

As she considered leaving, Lawrence emerged from the crowd, his piercing eyes meeting hers with kindness. Despite her sisters' approval of his marriage to Gran, Lori found it hard to relax in his company. He remained somewhat of a stranger, and her initial impressions were far from positive. Their first encounter took place at a community meeting where Lawrence and Gran, initially on opposing sides, engaged in heated arguments witnessed by Lori. Despite their differences, Lawrence brought happiness to Gran's life and had a calming effect on her temper. However, Lori couldn't shake her wariness, still regarding him with caution.

Lawrence rubbed his head and offered a friendly greeting. “Welcome, Lori!” He extended his arms as if to offer a hug but quickly withdrew them, sensing her hesitation. “Would you like a cup of coffee? Tea? Perhaps a glass of wine?”

“What’s going on, Lawrence?” Lori inquired, her question coinciding with a burst of high-pitched laughter that made her flinch.

Lawrence’s face brightened as he explained, “Oh, it’s our little book group. We’ve been hosting it since I moved in.” He cheerfully rolled up the sleeves of his pale blue sweater. “It was really your gran’s idea, but I was more than happy to join in and get to know the locals as a couple.” He nodded a little awkwardly, as if attempting to gently remind Lori of her grandmother’s married status.

“She never told me,” Lori replied, a tinge of hurt in her voice. Gran had always been one to keep busy, and Lori had been so preoccupied lately that she rarely had the chance to see her. If Lori didn’t take the initiative, she might not see her grandmother at all.

Right on cue, Gran appeared, her cheeks flushed with laughter, surrounded by a group of people. The same high-pitched laughter made Lori shudder once more.

“My little Lolo!” She beamed at her granddaughter and planted a kiss on her cheek. “What do you think? Do you like our little book group?”

Lori couldn't help but point out, "There's nothing little about it, Gran," as some members of the group began to say their goodbyes, clutching their books.

Gran air-kissed her departing guests and waved them goodbye with enthusiasm. "Would you like to stay? I'm about to serve high tea."

Before Lori could refuse and slip out the door, the tantalising aroma of freshly baked scones wafted towards her. Her eyes landed on the kitchen counter, which was laden with a mouthwatering spread. Beside which, the kitchen table, covered in a white sheet, was adorned with silver cutlery awaiting the feast. Lori's stomach gave an eager gurgle. She had always adored her gran's cooking and baking.

"I don't want to interrupt," she said weakly, considering the prospect of spending some quality time with her gran and perhaps indulging in a scone with jam. It didn't sound like such a bad idea after all.

"Nonsense!" Gran dismissed her concerns with a wave of her hand and called out to her guests. "This is my granddaughter, Lori. She's not part of the book group, but I'm sure you'll forgive that tiny detail."

The crowd welcomed Lori with murmurs and chuckles.

"How are you, Gran?" Lori asked, her gaze fixed on her grandmother's demeanour. Since her wedding to Lawrence, the older lady had shown no signs of the ailments that the stroke had inflicted upon her. But now that she thought about it, Lori had barely seen her grandmother since the wedding. Between Callum's business and Lori's work, Gran seemed to be occupied – yachting around the bay or spending weekends with friends. Her grandmother's social life had kicked into high gear after marrying Lawrence. Lori was happy for Gran, but she couldn't help but feel a sense of loss. In the early stages of Lori's initial move back home, she'd grown closer to Gran in a way she'd always hoped for. They'd lived together in Gran's house, their family home, which had provided Lori with a sanctuary as she began her business. Over time, they had evolved from simply being grandmother and granddaughter to becoming true friends. Part of her mourned the loss of that closeness.

Lori took a seat at the end of the table, wedged between a large man in an orange wool jacket with a ruddy complexion and an older woman dressed in a black sequin dress. Both were a bit eccentric but engaging. As Lori glanced around the table while helping herself to a scone with a dollop of cream, she realised she didn't know anyone there, aside from Gran and Lawrence, who sat next to each other at the head of the table. That was unusual. Typically, Lori would recognise someone or at least see a familiar face from their small rural village and nearby town. Gran's usual group of ladies, the ones from yoga or the committee, were absent.

"What did you all think of the book?" Gran asked the group, her voice piercing through the lively chatter. Amid mouthfuls of cake, clinking glasses, and the murmurs of delight, a variety of opinions emerged.

"I loved it – an exquisite tale of romance and seizing life's opportunities," declared a slender woman with cropped auburn hair, her freckled arms on full display as she gesticulated.

"What do you mean? Settling for someone you don't love? I found it quite disheartening," chimed in the woman in the sparkly dress beside Lori, her eyes wide with alarm.

"But the sisters, Elinor and Marianne Dashwood, ended up marrying the men they love, the ones they were destined to be with. Right from the start of the novel, it was clear they were meant for each other," the red-headed lady said with a nostalgic smile.

Lori finally recognised the book they were discussing, one she had studied in high school and had watched various adaptations of. She couldn't help but reminisce about her younger, more carefree days when she was an unabashed romantic, long before the years living abroad had hardened her heart.

Gran reached for Lawrence's hand. "I felt so sorry for Marianne. She went through so much."

Lori interjected, "What about Elinor? She endured a lot but couldn't openly share her pain."

The large man beside Lori, dressed in an orange jacket, grumbled, "It was drivel! I could only manage a few pages a night before it sent me into a deep slumber … I guess I should thank it for helping me sleep, as I've always struggled with insomnia!"

Lawrence leaned over the table, his arms clasped together as he continued, "Maybe Marianne could have spared herself all that heartache if she had only heeded the warnings. There's always that inner voice telling you to stop; you just have to listen. Before Marianne encounters Willoughby, there's a scene where she recklessly ignores caution and falls ill due to prolonged exposure to rain. This incident serves as a metaphorical foreshadowing of the emotional turbulence and heartache she'll experience through her involvement with Willoughby." The room fell silent, and Lawrence rubbed his eyebrow with his finger. "The rainstorm symbolises the troubles Marianne will face in her relationship with him and hints at the idea that her intense romantic nature and disregard for practical considerations might lead her into difficult situations. It's a subtle omen, but it's there."

"Oh, please!" scoffed the man in the orange jacket.

Lori shifted in her seat, her mind drifting to Rhona's earlier words about omens. She had never heard that word mentioned so often in a single day. The table fell into contemplative silence, pondering Lawrence's words, until he pushed his chair back and offered to refill everyone's glasses. Lori knew she wouldn't get a chance to have a proper conversation with her grandmother today. She had intended to share some exciting news that was bubbling within her, but, just as had become the recent norm with Gran, it would have to wait for another day.

3

Callum stood in front of their new house, arms crossed, deep in contemplation with Alan by his side. Alan had swiftly become Callum's right-hand man, lending his expertise to all matters concerning the house and their business. The house itself stood out as a striking wooden lodge, seamlessly integrated into the side of the hill. Its sloping roof would soon be covered with grass and lined with solar panels, making Lori chuckle at Callum's whimsical vision of sheep grazing up there. Yet, it was a vision that looked promising, and they hoped it would one day be adorned with wildflowers. Two expansive windows framed the breathtaking view that encompassed nearby islands and the vast expanse of the Atlantic Ocean.

As Lori approached, both Callum and Alan were sipping from bottles of beer. "Well, well, I never! Isn't management a bit lax around here if you're enjoying a drink on the job?" she teased.

Callum greeted her with a kiss, his face displaying a mix of exhaustion and contentment. "We're finishing up for the day, want one?" He extended a beer towards her, and she gladly accepted it. He disappeared into the house for a moment, leaving Lori brimming with pride after him.

"Was it a good day?" she inquired of Alan, who was engrossed in his phone.

"Yes, it was a great day!" Alan sighed. "But damn the mobile reception is terrible around here." He squinted and waved his hand in the air, trying to find a signal, a gesture Lori knew all too well. "Is it really this late already? Tammy might be upset that I'm not home."

"I saw her today at the shop," Lori offered.

"She's got work, but I'm not sure if it's tonight." He frowned. "How did she seem?"

Lori sensed there was more to it than that. Tammy had recently taken up shift work at the local pub, which Lori suspected was a way to keep herself occupied.

"She's fine, except for the usual complaints about the weather," Lori replied. "But really, who isn't grumbling about that lately?"

Alan's eyes remained fixed on his phone. "I hope she's alright."

"You could try over by my car; there's sometimes a signal there," Lori suggested. "If not, feel free to use the landline inside." She pointed towards the house, where an antique dial phone sat on the hallway table, untouched thus far. Lori had hardly been home to use it, given her hectic schedule.

Callum returned, his arm encircling Lori as they clinked their beer bottles together, relishing the view of their house. Meanwhile, Alan moved away, frowning at his phone.

"Looking good," Lori commented.

"You're looking good," Callum said with a dreamy look.

"Oh, really?" Lori arched an eyebrow. "You're quite the charmer, Mr Macrae." She shook her head and rested it on his shoulder. "Is Alan OK?"

"Of course, why wouldn't he be?"

"He just seemed … distracted."

Callum glanced in Alan's direction as he paced around Lori's car, engrossed in his phone. "He's fine."

"He doesn't seem it. Are he and Tammy doing OK?" Lori asked casually, fiddling with the label on her beer bottle.

"Has she said anything to you?"

Lori shook her head. "No, but I just thought maybe we could help."

"We are helping. Alan doesn't need to go back out on the boats. He's seeing his child every day. They're just adjusting, that's all."

Since the inception of Callum's business, he had employed Alan full-time, providing him with a stable income. Lori couldn't help but grimace at the thought of the added expense, but having Alan around had significantly expedited the project, and she now had her own home. Plans were in the works to build a house for Tammy and Alan, but her sister hadn't mentioned much about the arrangement. Callum had also earmarked a plot for Jean and the girls, as well as one for Gran and Lawrence, even though Lori suspected they wouldn't be accepting his offer anytime soon. Still, the gesture meant a lot to her, even if her family appeared somewhat indifferent about being close to her.

Callum turned to take in the view, smiling as he nudged Lori. "Come on, let's not dwell on negativity."

"It's just something Rhona mentioned today …" The words tumbled out, and Lori immediately regretted them.

"What did Rhona say now?" Callum frowned. "That girl talks a lot, often just to get a reaction. Don't pay it any mind."

"I haven't even told you what she said."

"Whatever it is, I'm sure it's just nonsense that's gotten you all worked up."

Lori gazed at him with unease, settling onto a wooden bench nestled against the front wall. A sliding window, ajar, welcomed the gentle breeze into the space. Positioned beneath the eaves of the grass roof, the bench provided sanctuary for Lori, who frequently found solace there each morning, cocooned in a blanket while savouring her coffee, shielded from the elements. Callum joined her, taking a sip of his beer. Their knees touched as they watched Alan, his hand running through his very short hair, a grave expression on his face as he spoke into the phone.

"Did you see the hail today?" Lori asked, her gaze still locked on Alan.

"Yeah, but it didn't last long."

"Didn't you find it strange for this time of year?"

Callum shrugged. "I guess, but nothing shocks me anymore. Just some freakish anomaly. Global warming, you know!"

Lori continued watching him, hesitating. "Rhona said it's an omen."

He fell silent, pondering her words, and then burst into raucous laughter.

"Hey," she interjected, frustrated. "I just wonder … there's no tourists, it's been really quiet here which never happens, and it was snowing in summer!"

"Hailstones." He smiled. "And for all of two minutes."

"It felt longer than that," Lori protested. "But still, something doesn't feel right. We've been doing great – the house, us … everything's coming together. Isn't it?"

"Of course, but that doesn't mean something bad is on the horizon."

Lori bit her lip, unease weighing on her mind.

Callum turned to her, his calm blue eyes meeting hers. "You think too much, Lori Robertson."

"Doesn't everyone?"

Callum chuckled. "Nothing bad is going to happen. We

just got some bad weather in summer. Hey, it's Scotland! If we didn't have bad weather, we'd be very concerned!"

"But all the staff leaving … we've posted ads everywhere, offered good wages, accommodation, and they still leave!"

"Lori, that's not an omen. It's just young folks realising they'd rather be closer to their families than in the middle of nowhere. People underestimate what it takes to live here."

Lori sighed. "Rhona said that too."

Callum placed his hand on her knee, squeezing it. "Well, Rhona and I finally agree on something." He watched her closely, then wrapped an arm around her. "My worried lass, is there something else you're not telling me?"

Lori had secretly been contemplating their impending wedding – or rather, the absence of wedding plans. She didn't want to bring bad luck to their future, and if bad luck was lurking, she preferred it showed itself sooner rather than later. Unable to hide her apprehension from Callum, her gaze betrayed her thoughts before she could suppress them. "I'm worried about the wedding."

Callum laughed. "What wedding?"

"Ours, of course!" Lori retorted, a hint of annoyance in her tone.

Callum shook his head. "You haven't mentioned our wedding since I proposed to you ages ago!"

"It wasn't that long ago!"

"It sure feels like it to me." Callum laughed again, but apparently realising her discomfort, he stopped. "I'm sorry, Lori. You haven't said much about it, and I thought you wanted to wait."

"I did … and now with all this omen stuff, I think I want to wait even more!"

"Then we'll never get married!" Callum teased, then changed tack on seeing her downcast expression. "OK, what I meant to say is we'll get married when it feels right, Lori. I'll go along with whatever you want. I'd even get married on a beach and have a BBQ if that's what you'd prefer."

Lori screwed up her nose.

"But I know it's not your thing," Callum reassured her. "So, whenever you're ready to be my wife – on paper – we'll make it happen."

"I want to be your wife," Lori smiled, her concerns momentarily forgotten.

"There will always be problems … but don't let them stop you from doing what you want. What matters is that we love each other, we're happy together, and we're strong together."

Lori nodded, exhaling. The knot in her stomach unravelled just a little.

Callum laughed once more. "Nothing bad is going to happen. So stop thinking that way, or you'll bring bad luck upon us!" He waved down to Alan, who shouted a farewell and hopped in his van. He sped down the dusty road, Lori and Callum listening to the noisy engine fade away along the winding single-track road.

Lori let her mind be still as soon as the silence returned, and gazed over the loch with rolling hills that extended all the way to the sea. In her opinion, the view got even more beautiful with time, witnessing it evolve through the changing seasons. The lush green that covered the hills, framed by vibrant yellow gorse, was a sight to behold.

Suddenly, the clouds parted, revealing a shard of bright light that illuminated the sea, creating a moody, atmospheric landscape. She often felt like they were the only people in the world, surrounded by wilderness. She smiled at Callum, her tension easing under his touch, as the light grew brighter, revealing the blue sky above them.

"Now, things are looking up already," Callum whispered in her ear. "Don't worry, my love. We'll always have this."

4

Tammy squinted at her cell phone, growing increasingly worried as Alan remained conspicuously late. She fretted quietly to herself, her mind divided as Rory playfully tumbled around on the couch, his gummy smile tugging at her heartstrings. Her beautiful little boy was right there in front of her, yet she was struggling to find a way to escape from motherhood. What kind of a mother was she turning out to be? The thought of prioritising work seemed overwhelming; she felt an undeniable need to be present for her son.

Before she could reach for her phone to call the pub and cancel her shift, Alan finally popped his head in the door, wearing a wide smile on his face. It was a familiar tactic he used when he knew he had some making up to do. Once upon a time, she had found it endearing, but now it just irritated her beyond belief.

"Where were you? I've been calling you!"

"Lost track of time, babe," he responded absentmindedly and scooped up Rory, twirling him around.

"That's not good enough, Alan – especially when I have to work!" Tammy threw up her hands in exasperation. "I can't deal with this now. They were expecting me there, like, five minutes ago!"

"They'll understand. You're a mum, and sometimes things happen." He shrugged, following Tammy to the front door with Rory draped over his arms.

"Yes, but it's supposed to be for things like illnesses, unexpected occurrences … not because my husband couldn't be bothered to come home on time!"

"It's just the pub, Tammy. It's not like they're waiting for you on a space station," Alan retorted. "Although I'm pretty sure half of those old drunks think they're astronauts. It wouldn't hurt them to wait a bit for their next pint."

With her patience fraying, Tammy kissed Rory goodbye and stroked his hair. She reluctantly gave Alan a chaste peck on the cheek.

"Knock 'em dead, love," he cheered, punching his fist in the air before closing the door.

Tammy let out a deep sigh, feeling uninspired and fatigued already. The gentle rain began to fall, and she held her hands above her head to protect her hair. It had taken her nearly two hours to style her locks in a way she had seen glamorous celebrities do: slightly curled, like they'd just rolled out of a luxurious bed, tangled in Egyptian cotton sheets after a nine-hour sleep wrapped around a beautiful man. In Tammy's reality, she would crawl out of bed, hair greasy and slightly tangled, dodging old nappies left on the floor. She was light years away from that sort of luxury. But tonight, she was making an effort, ready to leave the role of Rory's constant caregiver behind for an evening to see the world – or at least the local pub.

She started her car and made the short journey. Normally, she could have walked, but not in this rain or at this hour. She parked outside, looking at herself in the rearview mirror. Her blue eyes stared back at her, but it didn't reflect how she felt inside. Who was she now? She used to be Tammy: fun, larger than life, down to earth, and focused. But she no longer recognised that person. At that moment, she longed to be with Rory, preparing him for his bath, watching him play with his squeaky yellow ducky, and hoped Alan didn't make the water too hot or too cold. Rather than using the thermometer she had placed next to his bath toys, Alan had a way of winging everything, unable to follow any suggestions she made, or habits she encouraged.

Tammy threw her handbag over her shoulder and walked into the hotel, her head held high. She strode past the dreary reception area, marked by a harsh, red sign above the counter that ironically read 'welcome'. It never quite lived up to its name, especially for weary tourists seeking a peaceful night's rest. The hotel wasn't their home away from home. For Tammy, it was simply a place catering to the local clientele. She could hear the murmurs of familiar voices through the frosted glass window, and for some reason, her heart pounded nervously. Why was she so anxious? After all, this job had been second nature to her for years. She'd met Alan here, and even Hector. But she pushed the thought of Hector aside. She shuddered and took a moment to gather herself in the quiet reception area before stepping back into her old life.

Through the door, she found her regulars sitting at the bar. Terry, the cow farmer with a penchant for green jumpers that were tattered at the elbows, nursed a pint of lager. Agnes, his English wife, had come to the area in her youth and fallen in love with Terry. Back when Tammy first started working at the pub, she rarely saw Agnes. However, over the years, Agnes gradually morphed into a constant presence at the establishment, faithfully accompanying her husband nearly every day. There was also Stuart, an elderly man whose occupation had been retired as long as Tammy had known him. He sat at the end of the counter, absorbed in his newspaper but chatting intermittently with the couple, as they often did. Tammy's eyes narrowed as she noticed the waitress, who was just pouring a fresh pint for Terry, and she took her place behind the counter.

"Can I do anything?" Tammy offered, taking off her jacket and hanging it on a peg around the corner near boxes of crisps and peanuts.

"No, you're fine. I just didn't want them to get too thirsty while you weren't here," Kirsty, the waitress, replied. She often made passive-aggressive remarks, reasons unclear to Tammy. Perhaps jealousy played a part. Tammy didn't dwell on it; it wasn't worth the energy. What puzzled her more was why Kirsty opted for waitressing when she eagerly seized opportunities to be the barmaid.

Kirsty took a cash note from Terry and promptly returned his change. Everyone's drinks were replenished, leaving Tammy with the task of restocking or washing glasses. The dinner rush hadn't begun yet. Kirsty wiped the tap's nozzle and offered a subtle "You're welcome. I just saved your late neck" nod to Tammy before disappearing into the kitchen through the swinging door.

"Tam!" Old Stuart announced, slapping the counter. "Long time no see."

"Welcome back, Tammy," Agnes said warmly, her eyes filled with eagerness. "How's motherhood?"

"Oh, great. Rory is doing well."

"Rory! What a cute name! Do you have any photos?" Agnes asked, nodding encouragingly.

Tammy didn't need much encouragement and quickly retrieved her phone, showing off some of the recent adorable photos of Rory. Him eating mango, sitting in his toy car, and rolling on the beach, all with a big, gleeful smile. The pang of longing in Tammy's heart returned, and she wished it hadn't. This was what she wanted, right? To be working again?

Agnes gazed at the photos, her eyes misting. “He is a joy. What a strong-looking lad, so healthy and happy.”

Before Tammy could respond, she realised she knew nothing about Agnes’s family. In all her years working at the pub, they’d had endless conversations, yet she’d never thought to ask about Agnes’s children.

“OK, love, he’s certainly all that,” Terry said with a jovial tone. “Better give that phone back to Tammy. She’ll be keeping an eye on it for any calls from home.” Prying the phone from Agnes’s grip, he returned it to Tammy.

Tammy looked at the last photo on the screen, her heart soaring. She felt better. She would be home to Rory soon. Hopefully Alan would read him his favourite book and put on the sound machine as she instructed him to.

She smiled to herself, unloading the glass washer, until her gaze fell back on Agnes, who remained quiet, looking down at her hands, which Terry held tightly while speaking to Stuart of the usual local affairs.

5

"So, I have news!" Lori clapped her hands together, grabbing the attention of her family.

"Well, good. We thought there must have been a good reason to gather us all in the shop like this," Jean remarked, her tone slightly cooler than usual.

"News? You're pregnant!" Gran's eyes widened as she perched awkwardly on the swivel chair by the front desk.

"Jean, this was the only way I could get everyone together!" Lori crossed her arms. "With Gran's diary crammed with social activities, your work, or Tammy's schedule, we'd never meet anymore! And no, Gran, I'm not pregnant!" Lori clarified. "I'd never get pregnant before marriage." She winced. "Sorry Tammy!"

Tammy began to speak, then reconsidered, closing her mouth again.

"Come on, don't leave us hanging here!" Rhona leaned on the front desk, next to Gran, steadying her as the swivel chair started to spin. "Perhaps before you start offending each of us in turn!" Her hot-pink lips curved into a smile, and she winked at Tammy.

"OK, OK, yes, you're right." Lori took a deep breath. "I

don't know, I've been a little on edge lately … Never mind, that's not what I'm here to say … we've set the date!"

"The date?" Gran sat up unsteadily on the chair. "You mean you're actually going to get married?" She closed her eyes in disbelief. "Thank the Lord, God, Jesus, Mary, and all who sail in her!" She made the sign of the cross on herself dramatically. "I prayed this day would come."

"Gran, you knew we were engaged?"

"I knew Callum had handed you some kind of weed as a wedding ring."

"It wasn't a weed, Gran. It was a four-leaf clover we found together hiking."

"That's a weed," she said flatly.

"I thought it was romantic!" Rhona swooned.

"Thanks, Rhona," Lori replied, folding her arms again. Her announcement wasn't going according to plan. All she wanted was to have a special moment without the usual charades of the Robertson family.

"OK, well, great about the wedding," Jean said as she scanned her phone before shoving it back into her bag. "I really need to get back to work, Lori."

"This is ridiculous! How can we all get a moment together without someone trying to leave!"

"I'm a teacher, Lori, and my lunch hour is over. If some people showed up when they were asked to, then I could celebrate a bit longer," Jean replied, casting an accusing look at Tammy.

"What?" Tammy said defensively. "I needed to get Alan to look after Rory."

"Was that all? Usually, you have a long list of reasons."

"Well, Alan's mum called me too. I had to speak to her before, then there was organising dinner," Tammy explained.

"Face it, Tammy. You are the worst at keeping time," Jean chided, her face flushed as she stood up. "Remember my wedding, Lori? She was the last one to arrive … and you were my bridesmaid! We were all waiting like numpties for the bride's … maid!" Jean shook her head, a little angrier than Lori had seen her in a long time.

"I didn't mean to …" Tears welled up in Tammy's eyes, and Gran gently patted her shoulder.

As harsh as Jean's words were, Lori had to agree with her. If there was anything involving Tammy, she would often give her younger sister a different time than everyone else. Apparently, that technique still needed to be in place, now with even more buffer time.

"Every week when Gran would drag us to church, there was always something – last-minute toilet trips, forgetting lip balm, needing a glass of water!" Jean laughed, waving her hand dismissively. "Anyway, let me know what you need, Lori." She edged toward the door, leaving a rather gobsmacked group behind. "Congratulations!" she said and left abruptly.

"What is up with her?" Tammy whispered. "What a thing to say! I mean, I'm not as bad as she's making out."

Gran and Lori exchanged a look.

"What?" Tammy cried out.

"OK, I think we're getting a little distracted here." Rhona moved towards Tammy. "We're here for Lori's wedding engagement … announcement," she soothed. "Now, Lori, details, please!"

Lori smiled at her friend. "Nothing confirmed apart from the date and the venue. We think a winter wedding might be nice … plus it's the only date they had available and at a discounted price."

"It's not Hector's, is it?" Tammy's mascara had left a mark down her left cheek, her face turning white. It had originally been Lori's idea to have Tammy's wedding at Hector's manor house, the local laird who, in addition to owning acres of land in the area, had also been accumulating much of the female population's attention. Tammy had been included in those numbers, much to Lori's shock.

"No, not Hector's. Given that Callum and Hector don't get along well either, that's the last place we would choose to give any money," Lori said firmly. Callum's history with Hector had been through another of Hector's escapades: Jennifer, Callum's first wife.

"Well, don't keep us guessing!" Rhona's eyes widened. "No, wait … it can't be—"

Lori nodded.

"The Glenlochy?" Rhona sat up straight. "How? It's exclusive!"

Tammy frowned. "Where?"

Rhona grinned. "Only a hidden gem of a castle … quite literally. Hidden from the paupers, and a well-known secret to the toffs! Celebrities are known to get married there. I didn't know where it was located!"

"Not too far away … still in the Highlands!" Lori grinned.

"Well, wherever it is, I'm just delighted you're getting married. You and Callum are meant to be." Gran slowly stood up, stepped over to Lori, and cradled her cheek. "I'm so happy for you both." She chuckled and picked up her handbag. "Now, if you'll excuse me … I have another one of those 'social activities,' as you call it." She waved out the window, where Lawrence miraculously appeared, gazing at the window display.

Tammy stretched her arms above her head and yawned. "Well, that's great news, Lori. Let me know all the deets when you have them." She pulled on a leather jacket, which Lori squinted at on her departure, convinced it had been her own many years prior.

"It's going to be wonderful, Lori!" Rhona said. "Oh who do you think we'll see there? Madonna? Beyoncé? That

Leonardo DiCaprio!" She giggled, but ceased as soon as her phone rang. Answering it, she shouted, "Why did you let him shove it in his ear! What? Right now, you're there! Malcolm, this is just—" She shook her head. "I'm sorry, Lo, I need to go – incident with a chip … or something." She waved, grabbing her coat and bag and leaving without further explanation.

Lori sat down at her sewing machine, sighing. She gazed up at the photo of her mother and thought of the bottle of bubbly in the fridge she had stored for her little celebration. She had hoped things would be different. That her family would be around her to celebrate her good news.

She had yearned to deliver a heartfelt speech and raise a celebratory toast to honour her mother. That morning, she had glanced at the calendar on her phone and had a poignant realisation – it was her mother's birthday. Her hope had been to infuse this special day with a touch of happiness. However, it became painfully clear that not a single soul had taken notice. It was as if her mother's memory had faded into the abyss of indifference. No one noticed. No one even cared.

6

Callum placed the phone down with a satisfied sigh. Another booking for one of the lodges had just come in, and at this rate, he was contemplating adding a few more lodges before the season's end. His original plan of working on expanding their own house alongside running the business might need some adjustments. With talks of their wedding gaining traction, it was becoming apparent that his spare time would soon be a precious commodity. He leaned back in the chair of his makeshift office space and gazed out the window. The vast, uninterrupted view of rolling hills and rugged terrain stretched out before him. This remote location was so secluded that he often thought you could walk ten miles north into those hills and not encounter a soul, except perhaps an occasional lone hillwalker. It reminded him that he should make time for the simple pleasures – like going for a long walk or catching some waves, perhaps. Over the past year, he had been mostly confined to this desk or overseeing the daily operations, both important and tedious, with Alan by his side. His gaze drifted to a framed photo on the bulletin board beside his computer. It captured a joyous moment, taken at Gran's wedding. In that very instant, he and Lori had just sealed their agreement to marry, and their smiles beamed with genuine happiness.

Callum grinned as he admired the picture.

There was much work ahead of him, and he couldn't wait to contribute in every way possible. At least securing the venue was one less concern, thanks to Lori's contacts in New York. He was content, knowing that he would soon marry his first love, a rare blessing in life. Although he couldn't help but acknowledge the peculiar detail that he had been married to someone else for seven years. That chapter was over, and he wished Jennifer well in her new life in New Zealand. Their time together was in the past, and now he had moved on, ready to marry Lori, the girl he fell in love with in high school.

He chuckled to himself and shook his head, overwhelmed by the thought of it all. His reflections were interrupted by the sound of an approaching vehicle. Looking out the window once more, he spotted Alan, who had just parked the van and was preparing to unload various tools.

Slamming the van's door and pulling his cap low over his head, Alan saluted Callum. "Where to, boss?" he called out.

Callum pondered the day's work, unsure whether they should continue with the house or start on another pod. The magnitude of their projects weighed heavily on his mind, and he had already been toiling over paperwork since the early hours. In an uncharacteristic decision, he invited Alan in for a coffee before starting their work.

"I can't believe it!" Alan kicked off his muddy boots by the front door and padded across the wooden floor in grey socks, one of them sporting a hole at the toe. "The sun is actually shining out there, and you're already calling for a break!"

Callum chuckled, flashing a playful grin as he busied himself making coffee. He handed a flowery cup to Alan, part of their vibrant crockery collection, a signature style inherited from Lori's gran, Mary.

Callum leaned against the kitchen counter, facing Alan, who loomed over him even while holding the seemingly tiny cup.

Seemingly sensing a shift in Callum's demeanour, Alan furrowed his brow and asked, "Everything OK, Cal?"

Callum took a moment, savouring the familiar warmth of the coffee before broaching the topic that had been on his mind. "Everything's great. I just wanted to ask you something … Would you be my best man?" He cringed a little; the moment seemed suddenly emotionally charged. His relationship with Alan had always been strong, but playful.

Alan, in his typically relaxed manner, nodded and took a casual sip of his coffee. "Sure, Cal – happy to."

"Thanks, man." Callum nodded to Alan but wasn't sure whether he should shake his hand or offer a hug. They exchanged an awkward pause before continuing their conversation.

"When is it?" Alan asked.

"Winter."

"Good choice! No shinty matches then! It's a while yet, you've got a bit of time to plan."

"Well, not for Lori. She's got her list ready … and I wouldn't dream of organising it around shinty!" Callum scoffed.

"A list? Of course she does." Alan groaned. "They tend to get a bit like that. But as long as they're happy in the end. Luckily, Tammy just went with the flow for our wedding … I actually enjoyed it." He smiled, but his expression darkened quickly. "Apart from that business with Hector," he muttered through clenched teeth.

Callum frowned. "At least it got dealt with."

"Thanks to you! You gave him quite the landing. I just

wish I could've seen the result … would've been amusing to watch him sport a black eye while attending some fancy dinner party in his tuxedo!"

"I wouldn't be surprised if that happened to Hector regularly – I mean, getting punched for his womanising ways."

"Perhaps." Alan shrugged, his tone sharp. "Sometimes I think about it, though. If only it was me who gave him a belt!"

"I couldn't take that risk. He was egging me on too, and if you had … he might've pressed charges."

"He might've done that anyway."

"But I was your best man, and he had wronged me too … with Jennifer."

"Of course, I forgot about her," Alan admitted, his voice edged with emotion.

Despite the heavy topics they were discussing, Callum found himself smiling.

"Well, I'd be delighted to be your best man. Although, I thought you might've asked Francesca to be your 'best lady' or whatever term they use these days. You've known her far longer than me."

Callum shrugged and his lips tightened. "At one point, I might have. But recently, the distance between us has been good. Fran did a lot of silly things last year. She had been so used to me being with Jennifer, then being single all that time … I think she thought I'd be her bachelor friend, always available to help out," he explained, rubbing his neck. "Things got too weird. Lori and her just couldn't get on the same page. I know Fran can get a little possessive over me, in a friendly way. But, Al, I just can't … I couldn't have her be the 'best man'."

Alan grinned. "Well, I'm glad to know I was the second choice!" Before Callum could retreat, Alan smacked his shoulder. "Whatever you need, Cal, I'm here – in business and personal."

"You're a pal, thanks." Callum's voice wavered as he shook hands with his friend. In that moment, he realised just how much he had come to rely on Alan, much more than he had ever considered.

7

Rhona strode purposefully towards the front desk, a stack of bridal magazines clutched in one arm while the other arm balanced a tray of steaming coffee. She dropped the magazines onto the desk with a satisfying thud.

"Oh, I absolutely adore weddings!" She let one eyebrow hitch up, her arms pushed out on either side of her like she was in some Broadway musical. "It's a nice day for a white wedding!" Her voice resonated with a deep, melodic tone, then she pouted, her hands on her hips. "Going to the chapel and we're gonna get marrrrrriiieeed!" Tapping her mouth, she gasped, "I do, I do, I do, I do …" She took a breath, about to launch into more. Lori cringed, waiting for the medley of wedding songs, but Rhona sat down. "That's all I can think of right now."

"Good effort though," Lori said, although slightly relieved.

"Oh, I love this one!" Rhona declared, pointing her purple nail towards a sensuous gown that barely covered the model's bosom. The model reclined on a chair, her skin glistening with sweat, and her legs apart as if she belonged in a seductive perfume advertisement rather than as a virginal bride.

"Can you imagine the look on Gran's face if I showed up to the wedding wearing something like that? She would have a fit, a complete meltdown, an aneurysm on the spot." Lori had no doubt her grandmother would be mortified, rushing towards her, frantically trying to cover her up with her hands or jacket.

Rhona shrugged nonchalantly. "I would wear it for sure."

"Well, we haven't discussed it yet," Lori said, gently moving the magazine aside to get Rhona's undivided attention. "I was wondering if you would be my bridesmaid?"

"Oh, really?" Rhona sat up straight, her eyes widening. "You want me to be your maid of honour?"

"Actually, I just want you to be my bridesmaid." Lori couldn't help but laugh. "I'm not thinking I'll need to nominate different seniorities at the wedding."

Rhona's face fell a little.

"What I mean to say is …" Lori tried a different tack. "I'd like you to be my bridesmaid, just you!"

"But your sisters?"

Lori shrugged. "It seems my sisters aren't particularly interested." Lori's mouth tightened. "They practically rushed out of here before we could even discuss any wedding details."

"Oh, Lo, don't be like that. It was hardly a surprise for them; they already knew you were getting married." Rhona smiled. "They are happy for you and Callum."

"Yeah, well, they didn't seem too fussed either way. Tammy preoccupied with being a mum, and Jean … well, with the same thing, and work. They barely stuck around to hear about it."

Rhona grimaced. "Well, I did the same!"

"But that was a family emergency."

"Still, I'm distracted with kids too." A frown line appeared between her eyes. "It's hard not to be, when you're a mum."

"I don't mean that because they're mums they're distracted. Of course they're distracted. But they just don't seem interested." Lori looked away, considering Gran's lack of effort to meet her too. Just as Lori had decided to stay in Arlochy, her family went back to their own lives. "Anyway, I'm just glad to hear your emergency wasn't anything serious."

"No, Malcolm had just wanted to frighten me. He should know some things aren't serious, but he jumps off the deep end sometimes – he just can be so negative, Mr Doom and Gloom!" Her tight smile exposed white teeth.

Lori touched Rhona's arm gently. "Is everything OK?"

Rhona folded her arms. "Everything's fine. He's just too much sometimes. I don't want to talk about Malcolm." She breathed out, a playful smile gracing her lips. "What I really want to do is get involved in the wedding … get lost in the romance of it all. Is Callum excited about it?"

"Yes, although he doesn't really care about all this stuff." Lori nudged the sprawl of magazines on the table, exhibiting flowers, white dresses, and beautiful models.

"No groom does!" Rhona laughed. "Well, some do, but definitely not the one you're marrying."

"Can you believe it?" Lori asked. "I'm going to marry Callum. I'll be able to call him my husband!"

"I think it's beautiful." Rhona swooned, clasping her hands together. "High school sweethearts, separated by life's distractions, only to find your way back to each other, knowing you had always loved one another."

"Yes, well, he *did* marry someone else, and I *was* engaged to Michael," Lori reflected.

"Yes, well, let's not dwell on those minor details, shall

we?" Rhona sipped her coffee and flipped through the pages. "But there is something not right here … these magazines are all about summer and spring brides! You're getting married in winter!"

Lori nodded, acknowledging the abundance of freshness and vibrancy that leaped out from the pages.

"So, what about holly? Ivy? Maybe Santa could lead you down the aisle?" Rhona joked, "My uncle Dave is his spitting image – the school hires him every Christmas!"

"You're joking, right?" Lori watched her friend shrug. "Well, maybe we could distract a stag off the hills and dress it up as Rudolph the red-nosed reindeer while we're at it?"

"I think you're on to something there." Rhona nodded, flicking through another page, before pointing to another scantily clad bride, at which Lori shook her head disapprovingly.

Lori realised that perhaps Rhona's and her own tastes clashed so much that she would need to ensure everything was agreed upon by her before it was confirmed.

"Are you inviting everyone?" Rhona eyed her friend. "Like Francesca?"

Lori gritted her teeth. Her relationship with Francesca was a complicated one, centred around Callum. After Francesca's previous behaviour, making Lori believe Callum was being unfaithful, it had all become too much for her.

"I don't think so … I haven't thought about who I'm inviting yet."

"Is it going to be a big wedding? Or an intimate one?"

Lori swallowed. "Fairly intimate. The hotel doesn't have too many rooms available."

"Well, you'll need to be ruthless. All those second cousins will need to jog on!" Rhona scoffed, pushing her thumb in the air. "I wish I had that excuse. Our wedding had the whole of the Highlands there."

"Minus me."

"Yeah, well, I can't help it if you were in some godforsaken country, forgetting your own over here."

"It was Australia," Lori said flatly. "But point taken. I was pretty self-absorbed back then."

"Only back then?" Rhona cleared her throat.

"Hey!"

"Oh, you had a lot on your mind then … or maybe you were trying to not have a lot on your mind. Trying to forget a certain young and vigorous Callum Macrae? Poor wee guy was heartbroken for years after you left."

"Well he got over it; he did marry someone!"

"That again! I'm sure it was meaningless."

Lori shrugged.

Rhona frowned. "What, you don't know?"

"I know they ended because of her affair. But he did love her."

"Hmm … well." Rhona shrugged, casting her eyes back to another scantily clad bride. "Why not be the sexiest bride he's ever seen … then he'll be sure to forget about the first Mrs Macrae!"

"No, Rhona!" Lori bellowed. "Where on earth did you get these magazines? Some dodgy alleyway?"

"No, the corner shop," Rhona said defensively, holding the magazine close as if protecting a precious secret. "I thought they had a certain … avant-garde charm."

Lori arched an eyebrow. "Avant-garde? Rhona, if avant-garde is synonymous with borderline scandalous, then sure, these are the epitome of high fashion."

Rhona chuckled, unabashed. "Well, I figured we could bring a touch of rebellious flair to the tranquil shores of Arlochy. Shake things up a bit, you know?"

Lori couldn't help but laugh at the audacity of Rhona's wedding vision. "Shake things up, indeed. I'm sure the good folks of Arlochy have never seen a bridal procession led by Santa Claus."

Rhona grinned, her eyes gleaming with playful determination. "Imagine the headlines: 'Small Highland Village Hosts Unconventional Winter Wonderland Wedding.'"

Lori rolled her eyes. "You're a visionary, Rhona. But let's aim for a wedding that's charming, not scandalous. We wouldn't want Gran fainting at the sight of her granddaughter parading down the aisle with Santa in tow, having a 'ho-ho-ho' moment with tits out and a skirt barely concealing my arse!"

"Fine, fine," Rhona relented. "But mark my words, Lori, a touch of scandal never hurt anyone. It's what keeps life interesting!"

8

I've started swimming," Gran announced, as Lori set down a tray of steaming cups of tea and two slices of cake. Lori had chosen chocolate fudge, but the sight of the thick white frosting on the coconut cake made her regret her decision. Thankfully, Gran pushed the plates together, suggesting they share.

"I'm glad to hear that," Lori said, scooping the light sponge into her mouth. The sweetness hit her tongue, and she relished the chewy coconut shavings. "Have you joined a swimming class? I've heard their water aerobics is excellent." Lori hadn't visited the local swimming pool in Morvaig since returning home.

"Oh no, Lori!" Gran giggled. "You think I mean swimming in a small pool with elderly people, stretching and straining? No, I'm swimming in the sea! They call it wild swimming. The first time was quite a shock, I must admit. And the second, third, and fourth times were just as shocking!"

"I'll bet! Are you sure, Gran? Is that good for your health?"

"Better for my health than sitting on my bum eating

cake!" She raised her fork with a little chocolate cake and gave Lori a knowing glance before taking a bite. "But it's so invigorating. I have a group of strong and fabulous women with me. Sometimes there are more, sometimes fewer, but we always have a good chat while we brave the icy cold water!" She laughed. "Then we put on our coats, turn on the car heaters, and enjoy a flask of tea. It's truly wonderful. We've swum along the pier, and we've gone even further to the far beach," Gran continued excitedly.

"Gran!" Lori gasped. "Please tell me you're not swimming off the western tip."

Gran stopped abruptly, her gaze fixed on Lori. "Darling, it's fine."

"It's not fine. Are you swimming out there, in that dangerous part of the water? The spot you told us never to go to?"

"I never said you couldn't go there. I didn't need to," she replied softly.

"The currents … they're too strong there. You know that," Lori said, pushing away her cake. Sudden emotion overwhelmed her. It had been many years since she had set foot on the beach by the western tip. What used to be a picnic spot for her and her parents now held only heartache. She and her sisters had made a vow never to go there, encouraged by Gran. Or at least, that's what she had thought. "They were taken there, it's not safe. The currents are dangerous!"

Gran looked at her with pity. "Yes, we did think that, didn't we? And we lost such a beautiful spot." She sighed, turning to gaze out the window. Rain lashed against the pane, and a group of people hurried past, huddled together under plastic shopping bags for protection against the fierce weather. A sad smile appeared on Gran's face as she turned back to Lori. "I used to take your father there. We would settle down for a picnic, paddle in the water, and I would watch him build forts."

"They took me there too. We would picnic and swim. It's one of the few strong memories I have left ..." Lori leaned back, the bustling café enveloping her in its lively energy. Unlike her own shop, which often felt deserted, the cafe teemed with customers, each table a snapshot of conversations and shared moments.

Luckily, her old nemesis, Francesca, wasn't working today. But even if she were, Lori knew better than to make matters worse by avoiding her. She had come to accept that Francesca was a part of Callum's life and made sure to be civil towards her, for Callum's sake. Although Callum hadn't spoken of her in some months, she had decided that much. Besides, she couldn't bear to let go of her favourite cafe; it served as a convenient meeting place with her gran, a place that held no distractions.

Stepping into her old family home felt alien. Subtle differences, perhaps, but Gran's once cheery decor had now shifted to accommodate Lawrence's more subdued grey and beige aesthetic. The neutral colours blended with Gran's vibrant household, once filled with pink cushions and a yellow geometric rug that covered the entire hallway. It was like the vibrancy had been dulled, tamed, and muted.

Lori had hoped for a heart-to-heart conversation with her grandmother, but her visits now always seemed to include Lawrence, as if their conversations had become a package deal. This subtle shift in dynamic made Lori's usual trips to her grandmother's house all the more strained.

Still, she'd managed to secure a precious hour of Gran's time, a victory hard-won with the promise of cake from her favourite cafe. Lori once took Gran's constant availability for granted, but life had changed; now, everything had to be meticulously planned or scheduled.

Initially, she had wanted to ask for Gran's help with her wedding, but she decided against it. Gran had already given so much of her time to the family, and Lori wanted her to focus on the things she enjoyed at this stage of her life.

Gran placed a comforting hand over Lori's. "I understand. It was a tragedy, the boat capsizing like that. We didn't know where they had gone. Another impulsive decision from my son," she said, her voice growing taut with emotion. "But Lori, it's not the water's fault. The currents are no stronger there than anywhere else. I know people who swim there regularly, and for fifty years, they've never mentioned anything about dangerous currents." Her grip on Lori's hand tightened. "Perhaps we need to accept that it wasn't the water's fault. Sometimes there are multiple reasons for such tragedies."

"Please, Gran, promise me you won't swim there," Lori pleaded, her head lowered. "I can't … I can't," she muttered.

Gran leaned forward, holding onto Lori's arms. "I won't do anything foolish, I promise you that. But I'm done being afraid. I'm surrounded by experienced swimmers, wise women – teachers, solicitors, churchgoers. There's nothing wrong with that water. It was just something we convinced ourselves of, in order to cope with the pain. But it robbed us of our memories."

Lori shook her head. "I can't go back there."

"You don't have to. But …" Gran looked directly into Lori's eyes. "I will."

9

Lori meticulously dressed yet another mannequin, her third of the morning. Each time she fitted the lifeless figure and took a step back to admire her handiwork, it felt like the outfit clashed with everything else in the window display. Draping a bag over the mannequin's shoulder, placing a scarf around its neck, or securing a brooch – none of it seemed to look quite right. With a sigh of frustration, Lori stood outside, shivering as she peered through the rain-spattered window. The weather had been playing tricks on them lately, refusing to grant even a sliver of the Indian summer they had longed for. Their beloved summer seemed to have vanished before it had even begun.

Rhona, ever the summer enthusiast, was in a state of mourning. The cancellation of their annual Pimm's picnic had left her utterly inconsolable. She had attended the event without fail for the past ten years, ever since its inception. But this year, the cold and rainy weather had mercilessly forced them to postpone and eventually cancel the gathering altogether.

"No … sun … no … Pimm's!" Rhona wailed, her disappointment pouring out in every word. Lori, witnessing her friend's devastation, took pity and insisted that Rhona take the rest of the day off. With no customers in sight and a well-stocked inventory, Lori found herself with some rare free time on her hands. Hence, she had thrown herself into tweaking the window display, though nothing seemed to work.

Lori stood back, arms crossed, and scrutinised the lifeless figures. One mannequin, which sported a stuffed owl on its shoulder, was wearing a scarlet silk gown and a tall tulle headpiece, attempting to exude an air of elegance and sophistication. The other donned a sleek deep-blue tweed trouser suit, with a Panama hat perched jauntily on its head. Lori had been trying to capture the attention of both the wedding market and the racing-season clientele, but her efforts seemed to fall flat.

"What a beautiful display," came a voice from behind her. "Oh wait, is that a real owl?"

Lori turned around to find a woman about her age, wearing a ski jacket and chinos, with beach-blonde hair falling in gentle natural curls around her heart-shaped face. She wore no make-up, but her sun-kissed face didn't need it.

"No, not a real owl." Lori smiled. "It was my niece's teddy … but very lifelike, right?"

"Very." The woman nodded. "It's unusual to find a shop like this in a fishing town." She admired the window, peering inside, and then glanced upwards. It had started to rain. Pulling up her hood, she pleaded, "Can I come in?"

"Of course! Please do!" Lori led her into the warmly lit boutique and closed the door on the dour afternoon. The blonde woman sighed with relief, shrugging her hood down. "Let me take your wet jacket?" Lori insisted, hanging up the sports jacket on a hook by the door. "Can I get you a coffee?"

"Oh, I couldn't ask you to do that."

"Are you kidding? You're the first person I've seen all

day!" Lori edged towards the kitchenette and clicked on the kettle, already preparing their refreshments.

"What a beautiful place you have!" The stranger gazed around the room. Lori saw her from the corner of her eye, looking at a price tag and quietly gasping to herself.

"Thank you." Lori smiled. "Milk?"

"No, just black, please." She bounced on the spot, accepting a cup. "Oh wow, thank you. Nowhere seems to be open … I tried the cafe and the craft shops … everything closed. I was dying for caffeine!" She sipped. "This will be the only one I have today, so I'll savour it!" She closed her eyes, taking a drink.

"What brings you to Morvaig?" Lori inquired, lifting a box of thread spools off the chair by the sewing machine and placing it on the cutting table. She gestured to her new acquaintance to sit, but she refused, so Lori took the opportunity to rest. Her feet ached. She had been cleaning the lodges for Callum every other day, and when she was at the boutique, she'd made it her focus to clean. She stretched her neck with a sigh.

"Are you OK?" the visitor asked with concern.

"I'm just a bit stiff. I haven't really been taking care of myself lately." Lori smoothed a hand across her head and realised another spot was forming on her forehead. With her skin acting up and her limbs aching, she felt far older than her years.

"You need a good stretch. Do you have a routine?"

Lori gazed at her.

"I mean an exercise routine?"

Lori hadn't had a regular fitness routine since her days in New York, when she would walk her commute to the office and occasionally attend yoga or spin classes with her housemate when their schedules coincided. Her days now involved a lot of movement but without any intentional exercise.

"I'd suggest Pilates or maybe yoga," the blonde woman suggested, clasping her cup and warming her hands. "It'll keep you supple, and learning to breathe properly gives your body life again!" She spoke with a serious expression, then her features relaxed. "I'm sorry, bad habit! Always bringing work with me!"

"What do you do?"

"I'm a yoga teacher." She grinned and rolled up the sleeves of her grey zip top. Taking a deep breath in, she slowly bent down. Placing her cup on the ground, her arms loose but laced behind her head, she moved slowly upward with a gentle twist. "Now if you breathe in like this …" She demonstrated. "Then breathe out. That can free you up a bit. But I'd recommend doing this in the morning." Lori was mesmerised, and copied her movements at once.

"Very good."

Lori grinned. "Spoken like a teacher!"

"Guilty!" The blonde woman chuckled, raising her hands. "I could suggest some positions, or better yet, maybe you should check out my channel." She pulled out her phone and scratched her nose. "No signal!"

Lori laughed. "Yup, we're still a bit behind with all that. Let's try by the door."

Her new friend followed her. "Ah-ha!" She showed Lori a video of herself, fresh-faced, legs crossed, wearing white, on an endless stream of videos.

"Oh wow, you're a celebrity!" Lori focused on the number of followers. "You're very popular."

She shrugged. "I guess. I've been doing it for a very long time."

"Sign me up!" Lori pulled out her phone and immediately found the yoga channel. "Yoga with Yasmine! Following!"

"I appreciate it."

"*I appreciate* it. I'll do one of your morning routines."

Lori flicked through her phone, scanning the perpetual stream of videos. "Are you in town for long?"

"A little, seeing family."

"Well, I hope our paths will cross again."

"I'm sure they will." She gulped her coffee. "Thanks for that – I owe you one!"

Lori waved, feeling a sense of determination. She would get into shape for her wedding. It was about time she started.

10

Jean sat at her kitchen table, surrounded by a jumble of papers and textbooks. The evening sun streamed through the window, bathing the room in a warm golden glow. But Jean hardly noticed, engrossed in her frustration with her pupils' work. None of them had been listening to her, and their work showed it. Her love for the job had started to fray at the edges, and she now questioned whether teaching was her true calling.

When she went to the same high school at their age, her teacher, Mrs Gibb, had been a source of inspiration and had opened Jean's mind to the idea of teaching. It looked so effortless back then. The class had been captivated by her stories, tales of travels to distant lands and the people she had met. Mrs Gibb had continued teaching into her retirement, and her stories had evolved into tales of her new passion for hillwalking. The hazards she faced, the tricky terrain, the bothies she would stay in, all by herself. Jean had admired her from afar but had never told her how pivotal she had been in Jean's decision to become a teacher. Now, with Mrs Gibb no longer there, Jean had no one to look up to. Her colleagues were just as stressed as her.

She pushed the papers away, and the distant sound of children's laughter drifted in through the open window. With a sigh, she pulled herself to her feet and followed the sound. Sun streamed through the grubby windows, revealing her neglected home and the beautiful landscape outside. Her daughters, Maggie and Anne, were playing in the evening light, cartwheeling on the lawn.

Behind them, the town of Morvaig could be glimpsed, along with the vast expanse of the Atlantic Sea. Jean squinted to see the distant hills on the horizon, sometimes invisible, but tonight they were highlighted in bright light. The Cuillin mountains on the Isle of Skye. Mrs Gibb had surely climbed those.

What did Jean do? Well, when she wasn't thinking about work, at work, or dreaming of work, she did her weekly food shop and tried to keep her house in order – except for the dirty windows.

Since her recent promotion, she had also been required to act as support for the headmaster, where her organisational skills had been put to the test. Jean didn't know how she could possibly fit in anything other than the typical chores needed to survive. How did anyone have time to do anything?

"Mummy!" Maggie shouted, giggling on the ground.

"Hi, toots!" The fresh air hit her as she walked outside. It smelled sweet, like honeysuckle, and reminded her of snow-capped mountains. A vision of her and her sisters picking wildflowers flashed in her mind.

"Are you still working?" Anne asked.

"Yes, I'm just taking a break."

Anne's downcast face hit Jean hard. "You're always working," Maggie said.

"I need to pay the bills, sweetheart." Jean sighed, sensing she should have left them alone and not disturbed her daughters' playtime. She sat on the outdoor step.

Maggie slumped onto the grass glumly. Anne edged towards the rabbit hutch and pulled out Flops, their recently rescued rabbit that Anne found at the side of the road.

Against her better judgement, Jean had gone along with it and even took him to the vet to get his leg mended. Since that night, Anne had kept him close, vowing to become a vet herself.

Jean leaned backwards, her back giving a creak she had never heard before. Alarmed, she straightened her posture. "What are you doing?"

Anne shrugged. Maggie muttered, "Cartwheels."

Jean arched her head back. "Oh, come on now, girls. Please don't be this way!"

She rocked her feet on the stone step and wondered just how long that gentle warmth would last. Since technically it was summer, and being in the northern hemisphere, their evenings stretched out towards midnight. Jean debated with herself. The sun might disappear soon. Maybe tomorrow they'd return to the strange, cold, winter-like temperatures. Wouldn't it be a waste not to make the most of it while they still could?

"OK, you know what – it's been a long day … an even longer week. Maybe we go somewhere?"

They both looked up at her eagerly, bounding towards her like puppy dogs hearing "walkies".

"I'll take that as a yes then?" Jean laughed and stood up quickly. "Go get your fishing nets!"

The sisters turned to one another.

"Come on – before that sun disappears!"

* * *

They skimmed the rushing burn, catching weeds in the fresh water. Maggie waded in barefoot, her body tense, peering down at the crystal-clear depths below her.

"Be careful, it can get deep in places." Jean had come here many times as a child and knew the deep spots like the back of her hand. In some ways it felt like a lifetime ago that she had stepped into her past, yet now she was here, she could feel that old sense of freedom. "Careful!" She gasped as Maggie wobbled, almost falling into the water, but regained her balance. "It'll be cold in there!"

"My feet are already numb!" Anne remarked, joining her little sister, her curious eyes fixed on where she stepped.

Jean watched from the sidelines, cautiously dry, playing the role of the responsible parent as she should. Not at all how she would have been once upon a time – though she'd not been as adventurous as her younger sister, Lori, who always seemed to sport scraped and bruised knees.

Jean's gaze drifted up to the old stone bridge that arched gracefully over the stream. She'd spent many evenings there, not just during her childhood but also through her teen years, wrapped in Douglas's arms, their eyes tracing the course of the riverbank. They'd explored the entire area, covering Morvaig and Arlochy, seizing those precious few hours they had before Jean returned home to Gran and her sisters. In retrospect, it all seemed so romantic – the world appeared vast and teeming with possibilities. And it truly was. However, when Anne came into their lives as a surprise, everything seemed to settle into a monotony that had stayed with them ever since. Jean had once been full of fun, had loved Douglas and believed he'd be with her forever.

But as time wore on, Jean remained while Douglas departed, leaving her to exist on the fringes, living vicariously through her daughters.

It was Karen who had ignited a spark within Jean,

showing her that life held more excitement than the confines of her stagnant existence.

Now, Jean often pondered Karen's whereabouts, wondering if she ever crossed Karen's mind as frequently as Karen occupied hers.

Maggie pulled out weeds and mud from her net, her eyes shining as she proudly displayed her "treasures" to Jean. "I found so much, Mummy – look at the treasure!"

"I'm sure you have." Jean approached her, cautiously keeping her feet away from the water.

Maggie's smile lit up her face, and it was only at this moment that Jean realised she hadn't seen Maggie smile like that before. Maggie seemed different, and Jean couldn't help but wonder how she hadn't noticed it until now.

"Mummy, it's a fish!" Maggie giggled. "A teeny tiny one!"

Jean peered into the net and saw the small silver-patterned fish, no bigger than her own finger, flipping and flopping in its confined space. Memories of the thrill of finding something in the net, perhaps a tiny minnow or a stickleback, came flooding back. Sometimes she would take them home in a big bucket, hoping to raise them into big fish, imagining setting them free in the wild, ten times their original size. Yet her nurturing skills always seemed to fall short and they died one by one.

"Can we keep it? Please!" Maggie bounced on the spot. "Please, please!"

"Toots, we can't keep it," Jean gently explained. "This is their home. The fish wouldn't survive."

Maggie's face instantly contorted into a pout, a tactic that typically melted Jean's resolve. But this time, she stood firm. She couldn't bear the thought of the fish suffering and ultimately dying in their care. Protecting Maggie from the heartbreak of loss was paramount in her mind.

"No, darling, it wouldn't survive," Jean repeated, her voice tinged with sadness.

"But Anne has Flops. I want something. I have nothing – I'm so alone all the time!" Maggie's tears streamed down her face, catching Jean completely off guard. "I don't have …" she stuttered. "Anyone to play with … Karen played with me, and now she's gone. Everyone leaves … and I'm just alone."

"Nonsense." Jean reached out to comfort her daughter, her throat tightening as she extended a soothing hand. "You're not alone, sweetheart. I'm here. I'll always be here for you."

Maggie shook her head, her anger flaring up. She emptied the net back into the water and threw it down before storming off. Jean stood there, stunned by the intensity of Maggie's emotions. She looked at Anne, who shrugged in confusion, mirroring her own bewilderment.

As Jean gathered the nets and led Anne back toward home, they walked in silence, following Maggie. Their cheerful adventure cut short.

Karen may have left a void far larger than she had ever considered, one that Jean wasn't sure she could fill. Losing Karen had affected them all, and that was something she had wanted to avoid at all costs.

She had to face the fact that Karen's absence wasn't only her loss.

11

The rain hammered against the windowpane, rousing Callum from his slumber. With a groan, he shifted in search of Lori, but she was conspicuously absent. Faint creaking noises drifted from the other room, piquing his curiosity. While he initially slumped back onto the bed, he couldn't find his way back to sleep. So, motivated by intrigue, he ventured out to discover her in the most unexpected posture.

In the middle of the living room, near the bay windows where muted daylight shrouded her, Lori was deep in a yoga pose, her legs gracefully spread apart and hips elevated. Callum felt a stirring inside him immediately. With elegance, she lifted one leg, maintaining perfect balance, then lowered it, completely absorbed in her routine.

He settled down quietly to observe, not wanting to interrupt her concentration, yet finding himself irresistibly drawn to her. Lori appeared nothing short of magnificent, her fiery red curls swept up in an artful arrangement, with delicate tendrils framing her jawline and accentuating her natural beauty. Clad in tight leggings that hugged the curves of her figure, Callum felt his desire increasing.

As Lori eventually turned her head, she caught Callum's gaze and quirked an eyebrow. “Are you going to watch me the whole time?”

Callum grinned playfully. “Well, that depends. How long until I can whisk you away to that bedroom and have my wicked way with you?”

Lori rolled her eyes, a warm smile dancing on her lips. Callum loved that smile. A smile that was just for him, a secret smile between them that had been there since their teenage years.

“I’m busy finding my zen,” Lori quipped.

“I can help you find your zen, if you’d like?”

Lori burst into laughter, her arms falling to the floor. “You are the worst. I’m trying to get back into shape. It was so easy in the city; I didn’t have to try!”

“Why do you need to get into shape? You’re perfect.”

Lori let out a groan, feigning exasperation. “I mean it,” she said, while sauntering closer and placing her hands on her hips. “Callum Macrae, you will say anything to get me into bed.”

“You are beautiful; you always have been to me.” He reached out, tucking a stray curl behind her ear. “Sometimes, I wish I had known you earlier.”

“What do you mean? We knew each other as kids!”

“But it wasn’t until you fell off that bike that day by the river that I really looked at you.” He shrugged. “I was a fool back then.”

“If you could go back now, to that time, would you?”

Callum considered the question. “Maybe. Then I’d have followed you out to Australia without taking no for an answer.”

“Some people would call that stalking, Callum.” Lori chuckled and wrapped her arms around his neck.

“You know … I had planned to ask you to marry me back

then," Callum confessed, a revelation he'd never shared before. He searched her eyes. "I gave the ring away."

"You actually bought a ring?" Lori gasped.

Callum stroked the base of her neck and nodded. "Gave it to some shinty pal before he proposed to his girlfriend and moved down south."

Sorrow flickered in Lori's eyes. "Cal, I'm sorry I hurt you."

"Hey, that happened so long ago." He touched her cheek and traced her chin. "I just thank my lucky stars you're here now, in our house, stretching in such a way it's sending me giddy!"

Lori rolled her eyes. "I think I'll need to do yoga only when you're out of the house." She kissed him, her fingers drumming his back and sliding into his hair. She straddled him and pulled herself up. Callum let out a faint moan and kissed her deeply, holding her high above him.

"My lass, my love," he whispered in her ear, carrying her into the bedroom.

* * *

"Have you thought about how many guests you'd like to invite?" Lori inquired as she bit into a thick slice of white toast generously slathered with butter and marmalade.

Callum poured her a cup of coffee and playfully nuzzled her ear, eliciting a contented sigh from her. It was a sound he'd come to adore, a noise he sought to provoke each time they were in bed together. The kitchen was bathed in a brilliant morning light, cracks of blue sky breaking through the clouds. He couldn't help but gaze out the large window that offered a view of the nearby islands. He marvelled at the fact that he was sitting here with the woman he loved, in their own home, on their own land. His innocent dreams as a young man had become a reality. Reaching for Lori's hand across the table, he caught her eye and was met with that warm smile, filling him with a profound sense of gratitude. He knew just how fortunate he was, and he intended to thank whatever forces had shaped his life.

"My darling, as long as I marry you, we can invite the whole of the Highlands!"

"Well, I don't think we need to do that," Lori said, scrunching her nose and taking the last bite of her toast.

"Then, just family?"

"Yes, and perhaps some friends from far-off places." Lori absently rubbed her hands together to rid them of crumbs. "I've been thinking about my old housemate and Frankie, my previous boss."

"Would they come?"

"Maybe," Lori said, looking down at her notes. "If I give them enough notice. And if they know it's in a Scottish castle, that might be enticing!"

"True," Callum agreed with a nod. "I'd love to meet them and hear what kind of bossy buyer you were!"

Lori raised an eyebrow, a playful glint in her eye.

"Invite everyone, Lori! The more, the merrier!" Callum chimed in cheerfully.

"You might regret saying that." Lori giggled.

He took a sip of his coffee, reminiscing about the small, simple ceremony he'd had when he married Jennifer. The ceremony had taken place in New Zealand, with a BBQ at her family home afterward. It was a small, simple affair near the mountains. It had been so warm that by the end of the day they swam across a lake – an impulse decision of Jennifer's – inviting all the guests to take part. With a wild spirit, she dived into the cold water still wearing her wedding dress. Callum had loved that about her; she pushed him to do weird and wonderful things.

But the older he got, the more he realised he couldn't keep up.

As he gazed at Lori, her concentration etched into her brow as she made notes and highlighted sections in bright orange with a pen, he smiled, feeling an overwhelming sense of gratitude. Then, he couldn't help but ask the question that had been on his mind.

"Lori, are you happy?"

Lori looked up, a hint of concern in her expression. "What's going on? Is everything OK?"

"Yes, everything is fine on my side," Callum reassured her. "I couldn't be happier. But lately, I've been thinking about us, this land, what we're building here, and the legacy we'll leave behind."

"Oh all that!" Her face softened, and she reached her hand across the table. "Of course I'm happy."

A mix of nervous excitement and anticipation bubbled in Callum's stomach. He knew it was essential for them to be on the same page, to understand each other's desires and wishes. The moment had come for him to address a topic that had been weighing on his mind.

"… And about having kids … I wonder if you're still against that idea?"

Lori sighed, setting her notebook aside and taking Callum's hand in both of hers. She looked at it thoughtfully, a gentle smile gracing her lips.

"All this – the house, us working together in your business – we make a great team," she began. "Why don't we say I'm not against anything now? If we end up pregnant, it'll be terrifying! But we'll face it together. We're a team, right?"

Callum could hardly contain his joy. "You mean it?"

Lori laughed, her eyes dancing with warmth. "Alright, but I have one condition, though."

"Whatever it is, I agree!" Callum responded eagerly.

She playfully rolled her eyes. “We’ll see what happens. If it doesn’t happen – well, we’ll cherish what we have together. We won’t force anything; we’ll just be.”

“We’ll just be,” Callum echoed with a nod. From that instant and the rest of the day, he felt on top of the world.

12

As the shop endured another day with minimal foot traffic, Lori spotted the perfect opportunity to treat Rhona to a leisurely lunch, taking advantage of the moment to discuss wedding plans. They found themselves nestled in a quaint hotel overlooking the picturesque bay of Morvaig. Lori expertly poured Rhona a glass of chilled white wine, and, with an air of sophistication, Rhona quipped, "High tea for two, I say!"

"Only the best for you, Rhonz!" Lori responded, ordering an extravagant spread that, given the unusually quiet surroundings, felt like a delightful stroke of luck.

Rhona leaned back, casting Lori an adoring glance and wearing a mischievous smile. "I'm positively thrilled for you and Callum."

"Thanks, me too." Lori chuckled, the wine's warmth slowly taking hold. "Now, since you're my fabulous bridesmaid, I thought we could brainstorm a bit. I've got two dazzling ideas for wedding dresses and bridesmaids' attire."

"Bridesmaids? I thought I was your one and only?" Rhona arched an eyebrow.

"Yes, just a little slip of the tongue!" Lori said, pushing

forward the sketches of her wedding dress concepts. One of them showcased a sleek, 1920s vintage gown adorned with intricate beading around the neckline and draping gently from the arms. Her initial idea was to go bold with a striking green, but she eventually decided that, since this would be her sole wedding dress, classic white was the way to go.

"Oh wowza! Is that what you're thinking of wearing? It's exquisite! Very old Hollywood glamour. I can already envision cascading pearls in your hair. Oh!" Rhona clasped her chest dramatically. "I think I'm going to cry!"

"No, not just yet!" Lori teased, revealing another sketch from behind the first. This design presented an entirely different aesthetic – featuring a full, structured skirt, a snugly crisscrossed bodice, and elegant long lace sleeves. It exuded a Cinderella-like enchantment that Lori had always envisioned as the epitome of a 'proper' wedding dress.

"It's like something from a fairy tale!" Rhona exclaimed, taking a sip of her wine before suddenly choking on it. She hastily coughed into her glass, using her napkin to shield her face. Bewildered, Lori wondered if the dress had triggered a reaction. Before she could inquire, Rhona whispered, "Oh my gosh, it's… it's Graham."

"Graham?" Lori turned to spot a tall, rugged man with a sun-kissed complexion deep in conversation with a waitress. He boasted a head of dark, tousled hair, and as he laughed, Lori managed to catch a glimpse of his handsome face.

"Graham?" She swung back to Rhona, who was now attempting to hide behind Lori's frame, hunched over with uncertainty. "Graham from high school?"

Rhona pursed her lips, her eyes squeezed shut. "Oh my goodness, he looks exactly the same. Holy shit, he's still gorgeous …" Her cheeks flushed. "I don't know what to do. Should I go say hi? It's been ages, and he might not even remember me …"

"No one could forget you," Lori scoffed, observing her friend's unusual disarray. Back in high school, when Lori and Callum had embarked on their teenage romance, Rhona and Graham had had an equally fiery relationship, filled with tension that wouldn't be out of place in a Mediterranean melodrama. Despite the arguments and fireworks, their chemistry had been undeniable, and Rhona was heartbroken when he called it quits. Lori reminisced about the nights spent watching romantic comedies, gorging on tubs of ice cream, and comforting Rhona as she ugly-cried. Back then, Lori had dismissed it as teenage passion, but now, watching Rhona's flustered state, she wasn't so sure.

"Go and say hi, then," Lori suggested.

"Are you crazy? It's Graham Morrison. I can't just go and say hi!" Rhona retorted. "He's, like, a god …"

"Excuse me!" Now it was Lori's turn to arch an eyebrow. "You're an amazing person. Funny, kind, and a smoking hot lady. I will not let you speak that way about yourself. Now, get your fine ass over there and show Graham Morrison what a fool he was to let you go!"

"OK …" Rhona breathed out, nervously biting her lip. Then, in an unexpected burst of courage, she stood up and waved at Graham. But to Lori's horror, and no doubt Rhona's, her hand caught the white tablecloth, sending dishes, teapot, and a platter of cakes tumbling down in a cacophony of crashing china, splashing hot tea everywhere.

Lori cringed as the sound reverberated through the previously serene room, and Graham squinted at them both. Rhona remained frozen by the table, her self-assuredness now nowhere to be found. She muttered something inaudible to herself.

Graham finished his conversation with the waitress and approached their table, a perplexed look on his face. Lori glanced at Rhona, who remained frozen in place.

"Hi?" Graham greeted them with a small wave.

Lori watched in disbelief as her friend unintentionally committed social suicide in front of the man who had once broken her heart. Rhona's eyes widened as she stared at Graham. Unable to endure the awkwardness any longer, Lori abruptly stood up, exclaiming stiffly, "Oh my goodness, I can't believe I caused this mess! I'm absolutely mortified. I guess all these wedding preparations have put me on edge. Thanks, Rhona, for getting the waitress's attention." The waitress, seemingly taking an extra long time to assess the scene, finally arrived to clean up the wreckage.

"No way, is that Rhona?" Graham beamed, his smile lighting up his face.

Rhona opened her mouth, then closed it, momentarily taken aback. However, as if a spell had broken, she suddenly snapped back into her usual self. "Well, Graham Morrison, if it isn't a blast from the past. How have you been?" She mirrored his smile, and both of them gazed at each other in admiration as Lori assisted the waitress.

"I can't believe that's you, I mean – wow!" Graham shook his head in disbelief.

Rhona, always adept at accepting compliments, responded with ease. "Thanks. Do you live here now?"

"No, just visiting family, well, that and attending a funeral."

"Oh, I'm so sorry."

"It's OK, it was my grandmother ..." Graham's voice trailed off, the sadness evident in his tone. Sensing his upset, Rhona reached out and gently rubbed his arm.

Lori, feeling like a third wheel, edged away from their table along with the waitress, leaving them to reconnect and reminisce without her awkward presence.

She ventured into the foyer, where stone-carved faces adorned the tops of pillars, adding an air of intrigue to the space. In a corner beside a window, a chaise lounge beckoned, and she settled onto its hard and slightly uncomfortable surface, idly watching passing cars. The place had a certain luxuriousness that Lori appreciated, yet she hadn't seriously considered it as a wedding venue. Since Callum's proposal, her mind had been weaving dreams of something more personal, something that resonated deeply with their shared essence. This place held no such connection, making a beautiful romantic getaway seem even more fitting.

As she gazed into the distance, the double doors of the foyer swung open to admit two waitresses, deep in conversation and yet thoroughly engrossed in their smartphones.

"Hello, Lori." A familiar face appeared through the revolving entrance doors. It was her new friend from the other day.

"Oh, hello, Yoga with Yasmine!" Lori greeted her warmly.

"Yasmine will do,"

"I wanted to thank you for those yoga poses you suggested. I've been following your morning and night routines, and they're amazing – I'm hooked!" She held back the full truth, not mentioning the enticing distractions Callum often presented during those yoga sessions. She wasn't sure if it was because they had discussed having children or if she had incorporated yoga into her routine, but her yoga sessions had certainly become more intense.

"That's fantastic! You'll feel the effects almost immediately, I'm sure," Yasmine replied, her voice brimming with enthusiasm.

Lori's eyes sparkled with mischief. "In more ways than one." She waved her hand dismissively. "Anyway, my fiancé and I are hosting a small get-together to celebrate our new house. I figured if we don't do it now, we might never do it! We'd love for you to join us." Lori rummaged in her handbag and handed her a hastily prepared flyer, which bore directions to their home.

"I'd love to," she said, scratching her head as she examined the small map. "Sounds like you're in an interesting spot."

"It's remote!"

"That's hard to imagine, I mean what could be more remote than here?" Yasmine chuckled.

"What do you mean? We're in a hotel! That's positively cosmopolitan!" Lori laughed. "Is it nice staying here?"

"It was, but I can't stay much longer. They've booked it up for funerals, weddings, and such. I wouldn't mind, but I've had to move a few times already. The first guesthouse closed due to a family emergency, and then they moved me here. It's been a run of bad luck."

"Can't you stay with your family?" Lori asked, recalling her mention of being in the area for family reasons.

"They don't have room. At this rate, I might need to move on."

Lori's eyes lit up. "How about this? We have a vacant lodge that'll be ready for use by the day after tomorrow once I've given it a thorough cleaning." Due to the ongoing staffing shortage at the glamping farm, she was keen to free up a lodge. She had struggled to keep up with the quick turnarounds, juggling cleaning and bookings alongside her current responsibilities while Callum handled the rest of the business. "Why don't you come to the party, and afterward, I can take you to the lodge?"

"Thank you! You're a lifesaver." Her new friend seemed genuinely appreciative.

With a warm farewell, Lori left to search for Rhona, hoping to salvage what remained of their high tea and perhaps finally make some progress in the quest for her wedding dress.

13

The day of the party rolled around much faster than Lori had anticipated. Despite her diligent planning, there were always unexpected hiccups that demanded her attention. This time, it was the need for extra chairs to accommodate the gathering of Robertsons and Macraes. Well, almost Macraes, as Callum's mother was off visiting his sister in Canada. Lori couldn't help but feel a pang of sadness that she hadn't seen much of Callum's family since her return to the Highlands. They tended to keep to themselves, focusing on their travels during retirement. While Callum seemed unfazed by their distance, Lori wished he had more familial support. She shook her head to chase away those thoughts and added 'chairs' to her ever-growing to-do list.

In the meantime, Callum was grappling with the BBQ, hauling it out from the shed, and examining it with a mixture of determination and uncertainty. Lori admired his unwavering optimism, even though her inner sceptic was convinced that any BBQ attempt in the Highlands guaranteed rain.

"Are you sure you want to do a BBQ?" Lori asked doubtfully.

"Absolutely! It's an Indian summer, and I've hardly used this old girl," Callum declared, affectionately patting the BBQ's lid. Lori knew he'd kept it in his shed when he lived alone, collecting dust. She doubted he'd ever even fired it up.

She glanced skyward, noting the dense, impenetrable clouds threatening rain. There was no way they'd make it through the evening unscathed.

Tammy's compact car pulled up, and she emerged, dressed in a woolly, green-knit jumper over a red knee-length cotton dress and red sandals. Lori greeted her sister with a smile. "You look great, but you know Gran will have something to say about your outfit."

Tammy, unloading bags from her car, froze in place. "I thought it was blue and green that should never be seen …"

Lori cut in, suddenly unsure. "I thought it was red and green?"

Tammy waved her hand dismissively. "Gran and her fashion rules."

"You know Gran, always upholding some fashion commandment."

"And equally eager to break them!" Tammy chuckled while juggling two plastic bags.

"Not when it comes to fashion!" Lori feigned shock before planting a kiss on her sister's cheek and leading her inside, leaving Callum to ponder the enigma of the BBQ.

Inside the house, Tammy gushed, "Wow, this place is stunning – so open, so bright. It's got a Gran-esque vibe."

"Really?" Lori glanced around the open-plan kitchen and living area that was filled with vibrant jewel tones – a purple rug by the front door, turquoise and yellow cushions on the sofa, and a collection of colourful teacups in the kitchen.

Maybe Tammy was onto something. "Actually, it might be more colourful than Gran's now. She's muted herself a bit."

"She hasn't muted herself." Tammy gasped. "What a thing to say. She's just compromised."

"But she hates monochrome and bland … yet her house is losing its vibrancy."

"And it appears to be coming over here," Tammy scoffed. "How many cups and saucers have you pilfered from Gran's?" Her eyebrow raised playfully.

"She gave them to me!"

"Sure she did!" Tammy rested her hands on her hips. "Now, what's next? Should I start chopping veggies or prepping appetisers?"

Lori froze. "I … I didn't get appetisers!"

"What?" Tammy's eyes widened.

"Callum's handling the BBQ. That's his department!"

"But people will be queuing up, hungry, waiting around the BBQ. What if it doesn't light? What if Callum burns things? What if there are vegetarians, vegans …" Tammy rattled off, not stopping to take a breath.

Lori simply shrugged. Not the most experienced cook in the world, she had hoped to entrust the food to Callum while she focused on ensuring everyone's glasses remained filled.

"Alright," Tammy agreed, slipping off her jumper and heading to wash her hands. "I'll take care of the food preparations. Maybe you can check if we have enough alcohol, if everything is chilling. Make some juice. Get everything ready so you're not faffing around when people arrive."

"I don't faff!"

Tammy raised an eyebrow, her gaze landing on Lori's current attire. "You're not wearing that, are you?"

Sulking, Lori retreated to change her clothes, swiftly taking a shower and meticulously taming her curls with mousse. She opted for a cobalt blue chiffon dress that gracefully brushed the floor, trying to evoke a sense of lingering summer, even though their inability to visit the beach during the season weighed on her mind. Upon her return, she discovered Tammy retrieving trays from the oven, each decorated with plates brimming with tantalising bite-sized treats whose contents eluded Lori.

Tammy gritted her teeth, a hint of guilt crossing her face. "I may have gone a bit overboard," she said. "I peeked into your fridge and noticed yogurt, so I whipped up some dips. And when I saw pastry, I couldn't resist making cheesy swirls." Turning to Lori, she continued, "You sure have expensive taste, Lori – organic veggies and deli cheese."

Lori felt a pang of defensiveness. "I just appreciate good food," she asserted.

Tammy sighed, acknowledging the truth behind Lori's statement. "Well, it's lucky that I could work with what you had. But seriously, you guys must be spending a fortune on groceries. Don't you end up throwing a lot away with just the two of you?"

As Lori pondered her past habits in New York, where dining out was the norm, and her more recent life with Gran in the Highlands, where meals were consistently prepared for them, she questioned her food choices. She loved having a well-stocked fridge, even if it meant occasionally tossing items that had gone bad. Wasn't that something most people did?

Tammy rearranged the food on the dining table and meticulously polished the glasses, placing them neatly on the kitchen counter. It all looked delightful, and Lori couldn't help but admire her sister's dedication. Lori grinned. "You're really good at this!" she said.

Tammy nodded, her lips curled into a modest smile. "I like keeping busy and being helpful. Whenever the pub is short-staffed, I pitch in with food prep."

Lori's scepticism seeped into her voice. "Tammy, this is so much more than what you do at the pub."

Tammy simply shrugged, her nonchalant attitude undisturbed.

Gran and Lawrence arrived at the door, both dressed in matching soft floral prints. Gran wore a navy jacket over a pale blue dress adorned with beige and brown flowers, while Lawrence sported a similar style shirt paired with brown tweed trousers.

"Well, if it isn't the happy couple, our newlyweds!" Tammy exclaimed, rushing toward them before Lori could register her actions. Gran beamed and kissed Tammy's cheeks, with Lawrence following suit. Lori patiently waited for them to enter the house properly.

But before she knew it, Maggie and Anne also appeared at the doorway, capturing everyone's attention. Gran embraced the girls with a delighted sigh. It was apparent that she hadn't seen them in quite some time, much like everyone else when it came to Gran, Lori thought. Jean trailed behind them, her demeanour appearing slumped. She was clad in casual jeans, a white T-shirt, and a blazer, and Lori was certain Jean had just come from work.

Before Lori could offer everyone drinks, Tammy had already taken charge, circling the room with a tray. Soon, more cars arrived, and the sound of engines filled the air as new faces joined the gathering. The crowd included Callum's shinty teammates, friends from neighbouring businesses near Lori's boutique, and others whom Lori hadn't realised she'd invited.

Callum's father nervously emerged, clutching a bottle of red wine. Determined to put him at ease, Lori made a beeline for him. It was her chance to finally have a conversation with him since their engagement had been made public.

"Mr Macrae, welcome to our soiree," Lori greeted him, taking the bottle. "Would you like a drink?"

She guided him to the crowded kitchen counter, where many people stood, engaged in lively conversations that grew louder by the minute. Walking alongside Callum's father, who never requested to be addressed by any name other than Mr Macrae, Lori still couldn't find her groove with him. He was pleasant enough, but he remained guarded, never revealing too much information or emotion. She wondered if it stemmed from his days in the army or if the Macrae family somehow looked down upon her own. Her parents were not professionals in the same sense as he was. As they strolled, Mr Macrae cast his eyes around the house, which he hadn't seen since they showed him the plans many months prior.

He nodded. "Good, good. Comfortable. Happy?" he asked, turning to Lori.

"Oh, yes, very happy!" Lori replied, beaming. She escorted him outside where Callum was taking charge of the BBQ, the epitome of the man of the house, holding a beer in one hand and tongs in the other, deftly flipping fish he'd caught from the loch. He laughed and exchanged banter with his mates, and as Lori looked up, she spotted a miraculous break in the clouds, allowing the sun to illuminate the scene.

Mr Macrae made his way toward Callum, with Lori trailing behind, feeling somewhat defeated and uneasy.

"Son." Mr Macrae nodded and positioned himself near the BBQ. Lori noticed other men subtly edging away.

"Dad," Callum replied, his smile unwavering. "What do you think of the house?"

"Very good. You still have a few things to finish off, though. The veranda needs more cladding around the side."

Callum chuckled ever so slightly. "Sure, Dad."

Lori left them to their conversation and returned to her hosting duties. Suddenly, Rhona emerged from a group of shinty boys, waving at Lori. Playfully swatting a man's arm, she flicked her sleek bob and sauntered confidently toward her. "This party is amazing, and those salmon bites are to die for!"

"Salmon what?" Lori squinted, until she noticed Tammy holding up two trays filled with intriguing food. Before she could respond, she felt a presence behind her, and Rhona gasped.

"Hi." Graham Morrison stood tall, dressed in a white shirt with a couple of buttons undone at the collar. Lori could sense Rhona swooning beside her, or at least, the faint screams of her ovaries.

"Graham, hi," Rhona stammered.

"You remember Graham?" Lori interjected, stifling a laugh. "Callum ran into him the other day."

"Thanks for inviting me. What a party – what a place! I haven't been down this way in forever!" Graham's words cut through the chatter, his eyes sweeping across the room with a broad, infectious smile.

"Callum and you used to come fishing here, didn't you?" Lori added, sensing her friend's temporary speechlessness.

"Yes, and who would've thought he'd own this spot now. He's done well for himself!" Graham grinned at Lori. "Congratulations on your engagement too." He took a glass from the tray as Tammy passed.

After a few moments of chit-chat, Rhona's fixed, starstruck expression gradually began to shift. Graham beamed at her. "You look amazing, Rhona. It's like you've gotten younger!"

"Oh, Graham!" Rhona's face flushed.

Lori excused herself, intending to find Tammy, but she was intercepted once again. A hand grabbed her arm, and she spun around to find Yasmine. The woman unzipped her fleece jacket, revealing a black lacy dress that seemed somewhat uncomfortable for her.

"You made it!" Lori linked her arm with her friend's, leading her around the bustling house. They each took a glass of wine, and Lori showed her the view over the loch.

"Are you OK?" Yasmine asked, her gaze focused on Lori.

"Just feeling a bit jittery. Hosting a party with everyone here all at once is a tad overwhelming. I guess it's like a dress rehearsal for the wedding!" Lori laughed, leaning on the veranda and casting a glance at Callum, who remained engaged in conversation with his father. She couldn't help but smile as she noticed his posture was unusually straight, diligently serving food onto plates held by mingling guests.

Yasmine stood close by, visibly trembling.

"You're cold!" Lori noted. "Let's go inside."

"It's not that I'm cold, just a bit nervous."

"Nervous? About what? Don't worry, I won't leave you alone to fend for yourself, Yasmine."

"It's not that. And I should have said, Yasmine is my brand you see and…"

As Lori shifted her attention, she noticed Callum's father enthusiastically waving at them. His face transformed into a warm smile, and he shouted, "Jennifer!" Callum stood beside him, his gaze fixed on the yoga teacher beside Lori.

14

When Callum spotted her that day by Lori, he was taken aback. It felt like a surprise twist in a badly written rom-com – cue the dramatic entrance of his past. Was this some twisted setup for a *This Is Your Life* special, with Jennifer, his New Zealand ex-wife, taking centre stage? "Come on in, Jennifer, and spill the tea about your past with Callum so Lori knows exactly what she's getting into!"

It seemed as if the entire party had hit pause – the lively conversations, the music, the clinking of glasses, everything stopped, mainly because of his father's uncharacteristically boisterous display. Callum waded through whispering guests, sensing judgmental eyes boring into him. Trying to keep his cool, he gripped his beer bottle tighter, attempting to quell the anger bubbling within him.

Feeling the weight of a hundred eyes on him, he couldn't sort this out with everyone watching. So, putting down his beer, he gently hushed his father. "Where's our DJ?" he interjected, forcing a resurgence of music to break the uncomfortable silence.

He went towards his past, dressed in black, beckoning him wordlessly.

Lori, still confused, turned to Callum. "What's happening?"

"Let's find that out from Jennifer," Callum replied, with a tight smile. "Shall we talk in my office?" He motioned for the three of them to move away, creating a silent bubble of privacy. He needed to keep his emotions in check, wary of the consequences if he let them flare up and keenly aware that any misstep could fuel the town's relentless gossip – something he couldn't afford while trying to regain his footing in life. Before they could reach the door, Callum caught a snide comment from one of his shinty friends. "Good on ya, Cal!"

He knew exactly what they were insinuating, but his current task took precedence. If it wasn't for that, he might've given the lad a piece of his mind for being utterly ignorant.

As the door clicked shut behind them, Callum leaned against his desk, attempting to calm his racing heart, sure that it could be heard over the distant thumping of the music.

"Well, Jennifer?" he asked, reaching for Lori's hand, which lay limp in his grip.

"Well, what?" Jennifer sighed. "Dragging me into your office, it feels like being a naughty school girl."

"Deflecting? Classic Jennifer behaviour," Callum retorted.

"It's Jen. No one called me Jennifer except you and your family. That's not who I am."

Callum sighed wearily.

Jen crossed her arms and positioned herself by the window. Callum's attention shifted outside, catching Tammy and Jean engaged in a serious conversation by the BBQ.

"Are you going to talk to me, Jennifer – Jen?" Callum's grip on Lori's hand tightened, but she remained unusually quiet by his side.

"I'm sorry if this has thrown a shadow over your party. I was hoping for a civil conversation—"

"You don't think I'm being civil? You show up at our engagement party to do what? Relive the past? What were you thinking? How did you think that was OK? No call, no email?"

Jennifer smiled. "It's not all about you, Cal. I have my reasons for being here – I have friends to visit, a goddaughter. Also, I was led to believe it was just a house warming."

Callum let out a weary sigh. "OK, you came here … to my house, because?"

"Your fiancée invited me." Jen's gaze flitted restlessly to Lori, then around the room, never settling on anything, least of all Callum.

"You have to leave," Callum demanded.

"Cal, I need somewhere to stay … Lori said I could use one of your lodges …" Jennifer's plea lingered in the air, her eyes darting between Callum and Lori.

"You expect us to help you? You barge in here, disrupting my engagement …" Callum corrected himself. "*Our* engagement! And now you expect us to cater to your needs?" Bitter laughter escaped his lips. "You haven't changed a bit, Jennifer."

"Please, I need somewhere to stay. I have things to do, and I can't find any place around here … I have a funeral in two days …"

"Why is that our problem?" Callum sought support from Lori, but her gaze avoided his, leaving him torn and stranded.

Jen ran a slender hand through her straight hair, the strands cascading like silk as she tucked it behind her ear. The graceful curve of her neck was exposed, and for a moment, it captivated Callum's attention. She had always done that – a habitual gesture he remembered all too well. His gaze wandered to the delicate gold necklace adorning her throat, a small heart pendant that he had given her years ago on their anniversary. Surprisingly, she still wore it, a reminder of their shared history.

Lost in memories, Callum was drawn back to reality when Jen pinched the bridge of her nose in frustration.

"Look, let's start again, shall we? I'm sorry. You're right – I didn't think this through. I came here for family reasons. Then I met Lori. She's lovely, by the way." Her lips pressed together, and her eyelashes fluttered towards Lori, as if seeking forgiveness. "I'm sorry it ended up like this … I didn't realise you were together. All of this is a shock to me too!"

Callum tightened his grip on the table's edge, his other hand firmly holding Lori's. "You thought you could just waltz in and not see me? You've moved back to New Zealand! This is my home – you can't just disrupt everything!"

"Don't be dramatic, Callum," Jen retorted, her eyes glinting with defiance. "You don't own this place – it's a free country."

"Technically, I do own this land you're standing on right now!" Callum stood up, his voice filled with anger. "It's best if you leave."

"Oh, please," Jen scoffed.

"Should I escort you out?" Callum stood up taller.

"You wouldn't. And I don't think your father would appreciate that," Jen countered.

"You're so conniving!" Callum's voice reverberated, his palm landing heavily on the table.

Lori abruptly broke her silence. "Stop!" She threw her hands up, releasing Callum's grip. "Would you both just stop it? This is a disgusting way to talk to one another."

Callum's stomach twisted, his attention bouncing between Jen and Lori. He couldn't bear Lori's tone, the way she looked at him. This was not her. *This was not them.* They needed to free themselves of this situation before they were dragged along on whatever game Jen was playing.

"Clearly, you both have a lot to work through." Lori gestured, a plea in her eyes. "This can't be a part of our life. It needs resolution. It needs healing."

"But we're over, Lori. Jennifer will go back to New Zealand and be out of our lives."

"It's Jen!" Jen shot back.

"Yes, but there's unfinished business, Callum. You both need peace … it's the only way."

"This doesn't impact us, Lori."

"I think it does, Callum." Lori stood her ground. "I can't marry someone still embroiled in bitterness from their last relationship … You haven't moved on."

"I have … I have with you!" Callum cried.

Lori shrugged. "I don't want to marry you if this is not resolved."

Callum looked from Lori to Jennifer; his future to his past. He had been so sure of everything. Now everything felt scattered, unclear, and most of all, unsettling.

15

Tammy strode into the empty hotel foyer, once again finding no one at the welcome desk and no guests mingling. When she passed through the swing door to the pub, the same familiar faces greeted her: Terry, Stuart, and Agnes. Kirsty, the sassy waitress, shook a towel over cups and placed them high with extra crockery. Tammy glanced at the large clock. It was just past 7 p.m. Her shift had only just begun, but Kirsty made her feel late with a sneer. Oh, how Tammy wanted to pull her stumpy topknot. And her old self would have, but ever since becoming a mother, that fiery temper had been tamed – except when it came to protecting her precious Rory. She understood now the fierce instincts of a mother, just like those nature shows she watched from time to time.

"Thanks, Kirsty," Tammy said through gritted teeth. "Aren't you needed in the kitchen?"

Kirsty's rolled eyes and loose mouth suggested she had better things to do, and she huffed away from behind the bar. Tammy let out a sigh; this was becoming ridiculous. She needed to address the tension with her co-worker, to create a positive atmosphere at work where she could actually enjoy coming in. Rather than the gloomy and hostile vibes she endured every time she walked through the swing door.

The patrons paid them little attention, chatting about some fete or show coming up, and seemed to Tammy far more animated than she had known them to be.

"The ceilidh is always good, though my dancing days are long gone. I love sitting back and watching them play, especially when that accordion kicks in!" Stuart, the jolly old man, folded his newspaper and placed his spectacles on top of his head.

"I love dancing!" Agnes said fondly, interlacing her hands behind her glass of wine.

"We won't be able to make it this year, though, love. Remember? I'll have the combine harvester that week, so it's all hands on deck!" Terry frowned at her, momentarily taken aback.

"Oh, yes, of course!" Agnes quickly corrected herself, her smile returning. She caught Tammy's eye. "How have you been, Tammy? And how's your little boy, Rory?"

Terry and Stuart went back to discussing crops and the best technique of moving cows.

Tammy beamed. She loved talking about Rory. "He's doing fantastic! He's babbling up a storm now, trying to imitate everything we say. He's such a funny little guy."

"Any more photos?" Agnes leaned in, curiosity dancing in her eyes. Tammy sensed Agnes's husband, Terry, stiffening beside her, but eagerly retrieved her phone from her pocket. The camera reel was bursting with snapshots of Rory's precious moments. She selected the latest photo, capturing Rory's mischievous grin as he stared back at the camera, his mouth stained with berry juice. Each day, Tammy and Rory spent their time picking brambles in the nearby wood. Whenever she thought she'd filled the tub with enough juicy berries, Rory's chubby hand would dive in for more, making her refill it over and over again.

After the week was out, she had amassed buckets of the fruit, all set for her homemade-jam-making extravaganza. Her kitchen had already witnessed the creation of a delectable custard bramble cake and purple meringues. Now, apple picking was next on her agenda, and she had her sights set on Alan's parents' quaint orchard at the end of their garden. She knew they wouldn't mind watching Rory while she gathered the fruit they had little interest in.

During Rory's early days, Alan's parents had been attentive, bringing Tammy nourishing meals during her recovery and delighting in cuddling Rory while she took a much-needed bath. However, lately, she hardly saw them unless she made the effort to visit. Baking with Rory and preserving jars of chutneys for the winter felt like the perfect excuse to reconnect.

Agnes handed the phone back to Tammy, a whimsical sparkle in her eyes.

"Are you alright?" Tammy frowned.

"Oh, yes, splendid."

"You just seem out of sorts …?" Tammy regretted her words almost immediately. Why would she say such a thing? She didn't know what was "in sorts" for Agnes, apart from polite small talk that they would indulge in.

"Well, we all have our low days … but overall, I'm good. Actually, I'm the happiest I've ever been." Agnes maintained eye contact with Tammy, her hand seeking Terry's. He took it, still deep in conversation with Stuart about machine rentals. That simple act stirred a longing in Tammy's heart, a connection she no longer shared with Alan. Perhaps there was a time when they did, but reaching out to him now would likely go unnoticed, buried under his computer game obsession. Rory had become her singular focus, and with her return to work, Tammy sensed that she and Alan were merely coexisting.

Her heart ached for Rory. Just the thought of him while at work brought a pang. Shouldn't she feel the same for Alan?

Post-shift, she'd often risk waking Rory up just to glimpse him sleeping by the ajar door. Yet, most nights, she was content without seeing Alan, slipping into bed without conversation.

Marriage initially brought immense relief after Alan forgave her for that brief fling with Hector. Tammy once believed Alan was "the one" – the stuff of romance novels and movies. She had invested everything in their relationship. But now, what was she supposed to do?

Pouring another drink for Agnes, her thoughts continued to wander. As Agnes delved into conversation with her husband, Tammy sought solace on a bar stool. Her fingers fluttered across her phone's screen, browsing social media awash with images: friends frolicking on picturesque beaches in vibrant bikinis, savouring colourful delicacies, and show-casing their seemingly perfect, loving families.

Tammy quietly entered through the front door, and was greeted by the dimly lit hallway. She tiptoed past Rory's room, the door to which was already slightly ajar, and paused to peer inside. The room was bathed in a soft, calming light emitted by Rory's blue bunny nightlight. His tiny body lay peacefully, facing away from her as he slept soundly on his belly. A smile tugged at the corners of her lips as she listened to his gentle snores. With a contented heart, she gently closed the door and made her way to the kitchen, craving a simple pleasure – cheese on toast and a cold beer.

The evening had been busy, and she'd spent most of her

time assisting Kirsty, who was disgruntled and overwhelmed, both behind the bar and in serving meals. Tammy had even dared to share her menu suggestions with the chef as their shift came to an end. She had approached the small, shaved-headed man with a friendly smile, trying to bum a smoke from him under the street lamp.

"Hey, do you ever consider jazzing up the menu?" she'd asked, hopeful and enthusiastic. However, the chef's gruff response quickly doused her excitement.

"Tammy, you stick to the bar, and I'll stick to the kitchen," he barked, pointing a finger at himself. His abrupt dismissals intimidated many, but not Tammy. She was determined to get her suggestions heard, though she knew she had to be more diplomatic if she wanted to make an impact.

"Fair enough," she replied, suppressing her disappointment. "But, just a thought … What if we made our own cranberry sauce for the Camembert starters? It would elevate the dish to a whole new level." She'd hoped her suggestion would resonate with him, but he'd waved her away dismissively, treating her like an annoying bug.

She crept into her small kitchen and found Alan fast asleep on the couch on the far side of the lounge. His mouth agape as he snored, a video game was still playing on the screen, and a controller was loosely gripped in his hand. Empty beer bottles littered the floor around him. Tammy's mind wandered back to the early days when playing video games together had been a source of joy, a way to connect. But lately, it seemed like Alan's main focus was on gaming, drowning his evenings in beer and neglecting their relationship. A loud snore escaped Alan's lips, momentarily interrupting his slumber. His mouth closed briefly, only to resume its rhythmic symphony of snores. Tammy sighed, shutting off the game console before retreating to their shared bed. She left ample space for Alan, even though she knew he was unlikely to join her. A small part of her hoped he would stay on the couch for the night.

As she settled into bed, her mind wandered, conjuring up menus and delicious treats. Sweet pastries, homemade cheese tarts, and thick slices of cake danced through her dreams, briefly whisking her away from the everyday reality of being a wife and mother.

16

Lori had spent the early morning engrossed in her work, shaping a delicate robe-style garment with skilled hands. With precision, she cut out the pieces from a lovely pink cotton fabric, adding flair with a vibrant, floral-patterned ribbon around the collar. Hemming the robes had consumed her entire morning, her focus intense and unwavering until Rhona walked into the shop.

She dropped her bag on the desk hastily, approaching Lori with a furrowed brow. "Hey, you OK, Lo? I was worried. You didn't respond to any of my texts."

With a sigh, Lori gently set the fabric aside, its soft texture slipping through her fingertips. "Sorry," she whispered, her voice barely audible. She couldn't express her thoughts or feelings, not even to herself. "I've been slightly distracted."

Rhona leaned over the table, her elbows resting on the pink cotton Lori had been working on. She wasn't going to leave without a more detailed explanation. Lori took the fabric from underneath Rhona, lovingly smoothing her hand over it and placing it beside the sewing machine. "I don't know what to tell you. I've been dealing with the clean-up after the party, managing lodge guests, and trying my best to avoid Callum. It has been a bit consuming."

Rhona offered a reassuring squeeze to Lori's shoulder. "No one saw this coming. I mean, Jennifer being here in town! If I had known, I would've warned you, but I thought she left for New Zealand after the breakup."

"You and everyone else," Lori replied wearily. "She's just here temporarily for family stuff. I couldn't care less about her, honestly. I'm feeling a little low and tired." Sinking back into her chair, she looked up at Rhona. "Let's talk about something else. How's Graham? He seems pretty into you. Does he know you're married?"

Rhona's eyes widened in surprise. "Are you kidding? Of course he does!"

"Is he married?"

"Yes, no woman was going to let him slip through the net! Don't worry, Lo, I'm not some husband-stealer." She straightened her back, her look sincere.

Lori managed a smile. "Just be careful, OK?" She was all too aware of the perils of engaging in flirtatious behaviour. A past encounter with a photographer had nearly caused a rift between her and Callum.

Rhona perched on the cutting table, visibly frustrated. "Believe me, I am. But what's bothering me is how clumsy I become around him. Remember at your party? I spilled red wine on myself, and I hadn't even had a drink!" Rhona squeezed her eyes shut, seemingly recalling the embarrassing moment. "The time after that, when we went for coffee, I tripped and ended up in the lap of some burly fisherman."

"How embarrassing!"

"Not for the fisherman. He seemed pretty thrilled about it all!" Rhona crossed her arms, screwing her nose.

Lori couldn't help but chuckle. "I can imagine he would be. But wait, you went for coffee with Graham too?"

Rhona nodded, flicking her short, dark hair out of her eyes. "Yeah, I had to open the shop the next day, remember? I arrived early in the morning, and there he was, waiting outside. I thought you wouldn't mind if I opened a little later."

"Did he make a move?" Lori asked, her concern growing.

Rhona shook her head. "Nah, nothing like that. He just asked if I wanted coffee."

"So you skipped opening the shop to hang out with your new guy?" Lori teased.

"It was only for like thirty minutes, an hour tops!"

Lori chuckled, finding amusement in Rhona's series of mishaps. "Oh, I can just imagine the scene! Customers walking in, expecting the shop to be open, only to find you gallivanting around, landing on fishermen's laps."

"Come on now, it's not like there's a crowd of people out there. And let's be clear, I didn't sit on their laps on purpose! It was a total accident."

Lori grinned again, enjoying the distraction of light-hearted banter. "Sure, sure, accidents happen. You just need to control yourself around Graham, it seems."

"I swear it's like he's doing this to me! I have no control over myself!" Rhona whispered, her frustration palpable in the empty shop.

"He's bewitched you? Well, I'll be damned. Rhona unable to control her own limbs!" Lori teased.

Just then, the doorbell tinkled, and Callum walked into the shop. He was dressed in a thick Aran jumper and an unzipped waterproof anorak, looking slightly sheepish. He made his way towards Lori and leaned in to give her a kiss, but she turned her cheek, avoiding his lips.

"What a fantastic party, Callum," Rhona said, tidying up some fabric bits, avoiding his gaze and tossing a handful in the trash.

"Yeah, thanks," Callum said, absentmindedly. He shot Lori a puzzled look, sensing that something wasn't right.

"Yes, it was a great party," Lori stood up abruptly, feigning nonchalance as she dusted off a mannequin's shoulder. "The BBQ was nice, and Tammy's starters …"

Callum's eyebrow lifted in surprise. "And that I'm the talk of the town now, with my ex being back and causing a scene in front of everyone?"

"Well, there was that too, but I'm sure everyone's already forgotten," Rhona said dismissively.

"Not around here. 'Worried' locals have been stopping me, asking if I'm still getting married, what with my ex-wife back in town," Callum scoffed, clearly frustrated. "Can you believe it? People enjoy getting involved in anything that doesn't concern them."

"I have no idea what you're talking about," Rhona retorted, briskly moving a box of fabric to the store room.

Callum turned back to Lori, his expression softening. "Wanna walk along the beach?"

Lori couldn't ignore her fiancé any longer, so she said yes, leaving a curious Rhona behind, fidgeting uncontrollably as she repeatedly rearranged the same box.

Callum drove down the road with the windows wide open and the cold air whistling by. Lori noticed the beautiful transformation of the trees they passed, their leaves showcasing a kaleidoscope of colours that whispered the changing seasons. Just before reaching their usual beach destination, Callum's hand gestured towards a turnoff, diverting them from their intended route.

"What are you doing?" Lori's voice echoed with worry as she noticed they were deviating from their well-trodden route.

"I thought we'd head towards the western tip …" Callum replied, a touch of excitement in his voice.

"Absolutely not, Callum!" Lori protested, her hand

reaching out and impulsively tugging at the steering wheel, desperately trying to redirect their course.

"Hey, wow!" Callum's grip tightened on the wheel. "What are you doing? You could cause an accident!"

"I'm not going there, Callum," Lori shouted, her body pressing back against the seat as if attempting to push the van in the opposite direction. She turned her head towards the window, taking deep breaths in an effort to regain control. But then, out of nowhere, that ugly creature that had haunted her during her time in New York resurfaced, gripping her with a force she had never experienced. She couldn't speak, her breath coming in short gasps. For a moment, she thought she had it under control, but then everything around her faded, and she was plunged into darkness.

17

Lori's heart raced as she struggled to make sense of her surroundings. Echoes of distant shouts resonated in her ears, gradually diminishing as she regained her composure. She found herself lying on a sandy beach, the vast expanse stretching out before her, while an angry red sky loomed overhead. Her gaze shifted towards the choppy waters, and there, she saw her parents in a small boat, waving frantically. Panic surged through her as she screamed, warning them of the imminent danger. But the sea swallowed them, engulfing their vessel, only to calm itself moments later.

Water splashed onto Lori's face, jolting her back to reality. She gasped for breath, disoriented and drenched.

Callum's concerned eyes met hers. "You fainted," he breathed.

Lori coughed, her face wet.

"Sorry," he said, showing an empty water bottle. "I had to wake you up. You scared me!"

Confused and still dazed, Lori took in her surroundings. Her hands brushed against the familiar texture of jagged marram grass, while the soft touch of sand greeted her fingertips. “Where are we?” she asked, her voice trembling.

Callum quickly reassured her, his tone soothing. “We're not at the western tip, don't worry! Are you okay? I've never seen you like this before.” He offered her a drink from a flask he had nearby, his preparedness a testament to his outdoor activity company. Lori accepted the sweet tea, finding comfort in its warmth, and rested her head on his shoulder.

“I’m OK,” she finally managed to reply, her voice still shaky.

Together, they surveyed the beach that was so familiar to Lori, a place she often visited for long walks and picnics. But the familiarity of the scene couldn’t mask the weight of painful memories that lingered. “Please don’t take me there again,” she pleaded weakly.

“OK, my love,” Callum whispered, his warm lips pressing gently against her forehead.They remained in quiet embrace, their eyes tracing the rhythmic dance of waves. Time ebbed and flowed, and in the tender embrace of the sea’s soothing lullaby, a comforting solace enveloped them.

“I love you,” Callum murmured, his words barely audible.

Lori’s tired voice responded with equal tenderness. “I love you.” She briefly closed her eyes, exhaustion weighing on her.

Callum broke the silence, his tone gentle. “Perhaps if we just went to the western tip, took things slow … maybe you need to make peace with it. It was a long time ago.”

Lori’s body tensed, the mere mention of the other beach causing her distress. “I can’t go there again,” she whispered, her hand violently tugging weeds out of the sandy earth.

“OK, my love,” Callum whispered, his lips pressing

against her forehead once more, pulling her towards him protectively. She could feel the rapid drumming of his heart, intensifying before he attempted to speak. "Has this happened before?"

"Many times …" Lori reflected, her mind swimming with memories of her panic attacks. Trying to pinpoint the triggers was as confusing as understanding why they occurred in the first place. "New York, mainly, with my job. It was stressful. But I thought I had learned to control it. I had. Maybe there are a few things distracting me, and I didn't keep up with taking care of myself … like exercising. I forgot to keep my mind in check."

"I'm sorry you ever felt that way. It must have been frightening."

She brushed her fingertips over the tufts of grass. "Not really. Well, sometimes." She grimaced, emitting a sardonic chuckle. "I guess I just didn't want to be exposed as a fraud. I was doing something against what my body was telling me to do. I think I knew I was living the wrong life, and it caught up to me."

Callum's gaze remained fixed on her. "And you haven't had an episode since then?"

She shook her head.

"Well, then, there's something about our situation that's triggering it." He frowned.

She managed a smile, despite the exhaustion weighing on her. "I think there are a few things, yes. Like your ex arriving in town unannounced, and planning a wedding!"

"Is your body telling you not to marry me?" Callum's voice was low, his eyes looking down at his left hand which was submerged in sand.

"No," Lori said definitively. "We are meant to be together, Callum. I know that with every fibre of my being."

He pulled her close, his breath mingling with her hair.

"My darling, what are we going to do?" He rested his head against hers for a moment before meeting her gaze.

Lori's heart rate had slowed, and she took in the scene around them – a couple kayaking in the distance, gradually venturing further into the inner isles. She turned her attention back to Callum. "We're going to be kind to Jennifer. We'll welcome her here, show kindness, and mend any cracks between you."

"Why?" Callum asked, puzzled by her suggestion.

"Because it's the right thing to do," Lori replied simply.

"But you don't need to do this. At least I can worry about Jennifer. You don't need to add her to your list of worries."

"We're a team, Callum. We face things together, don't we?"

"We do," he acknowledged.

"Well, then, that's settled," she said with conviction.

"Will you promise me something?" Callum's hand moved from the grass to tenderly touch Lori's cheek. "Promise you'll tell me if things get too much, if you need someone to talk to. I want to be here for you. Tell me if you're stressed, if you feel uncertain, Lori … I mean it, even if you feel like cancelling the wedding."

"I would never cancel the wedding!" she declared with unwavering conviction.

"I'm here to support you. Tell me anything." Callum pulled her close, their bodies intertwining as they embraced each other firmly. Lori realised something then: all this time she had carried the weight of her episodes in silence, her inner battles kept secret from her loved ones – her sisters, her grandmother, everyone. But now, as Callum held her, the world seemed to fade away, leaving only the comforting sensation of his arms around her. She was safe. As their embrace tightened, she felt the invisible walls of isolation crumble around her. It was as if an anchor – one she had unknowingly carried for so long – had finally been severed, setting her adrift in a sea of newfound freedom. He was her rock, her lighthouse, guiding her out of the turbulent waters that threatened to engulf her. He brought her to a place of stability and security, a place where she could finally breathe without fear of drowning.

18

Jean had painstakingly prepared the gym hall for the upcoming event. Rows of empty chairs filled the space, facing a vacant stage. As part of her new role supporting the headteacher, organising functions like this had become Jean's responsibility. Today, it was a talk for the students by a local author. Checking her watch briefly, she quickly arranged copies of the author's book in the middle chair on stage, stealing a glance at its cover amidst the quiet surroundings.

The front cover immediately captured her attention. A woman stood beside a towering cairn, gripping hiking poles. Majestic, snow-covered peaks pierced the sky. It didn't resemble the Scottish landscapes Jean was familiar with, but rather the grandeur of the Himalayas. As much as she'd made the effort in arranging the hall, she hadn't familiarised herself with the book, despite her role as the event's chairperson. With her recent promotion, she had been juggling multiple tasks, struggling to give each one the attention it deserved. Placing the book back on the chair, she reached for her phone, ensuring everything was in order for the imminent arrival of the attendees.

As she conducted the final check, a voice called out from the back of the hall. She turned to find a middle-aged woman with short greying hair standing at the door, radiating anticipation. Jean descended from the stage, extending her hand in a warm welcome.

"I believe you're the author we've been expecting," Jean said with genuine warmth.

"Thank you for having me," the author replied, her hand slightly shaky.

Before Jean could reassure her that the kids wouldn't bite, the bell rang, and almost immediately, the students arrived at the door, eager to miss class for a talk.

As quickly as they entered, Jean wasted no time in welcoming the writer on stage, facing a full hall of sixteen and seventeen-year-olds. She handed over the microphone, relieved to take a momentary break, although she knew she couldn't fully switch off as she needed to chair the question-and-answer session at the end.

She listened attentively as the author spoke. However, her mind couldn't help but wander to thoughts of dinner. Curry? Lasagna? Lately, she had been neglecting her children by getting fish and chips from the local takeaway. They had gone there so often, the staff knew her order by heart.

She needed to break those bad habits, be more proactive, and cook nourishing food that didn't consume her entire evening. Karen was always good at that – having a beautiful meal bubbling when they returned from school. She would pour Jean a glass of wine, lend a listening ear to her day, and offer her own thoughts. But more often than not, Jean just wanted to vent.

"Are you selfish?" The author's words cut through Jean's rabbit hole of thoughts, jolting her back to the present. "Well, I think we're all selfish," the author continued, her voice resonating with conviction. "No matter what we do, we kind of need to be selfish. I couldn't keep going on in my treadmill job, raising a family that I wasn't fully present with. Everything felt taken from me, leaving nothing that was for me. I started resenting everyone, even my own children. I became obsessed with thoughts of how they took from me without seeing or caring how much I gave to them. I was running myself into the ground, deeper and deeper." The author paused, her expression sombre. The students, for once – Jean observed – were silent, listening to every word. "And then one day, I started walking." She shrugged. "It wasn't the best thing I could have done. But I had reached the breaking point. So, I walked to the next street, then the next, until I'd walked outside the city I lived in. Many missed phone calls later, long past my children's bedtime, I finally came back." She held the microphone high, sitting upright, a new confidence on her shoulders. "Do you see these things can happen if you let them fester? I needed to reset. And I did. I'm just lucky I have an understanding husband," she added with a wistful smile.

Jean leaned forward, her curiosity now piqued. How could someone leave their children behind?

"But I didn't stop there," the author continued, her voice growing more impassioned. "What I realised was my body, my own intuition, had shown me just what I needed. So, I climbed mountains … mountains near, mountains far. I kept going until one day I climbed Mount Everest. And even now, I'm told I'm selfish because I, as a mother, left my children to pursue something I wanted to do. It may not matter to you, in your stage of life, but my message here is: What do you want to do?"

To Jean's surprise, the author stood up, approaching the captivated students. With one hand on the microphone and the other holding her elbow, she appeared as a spokeswoman for a TED talk. Even more surprising, one boy stood up abruptly from his chair.

"I want to be a footballer!" he cried out.

A girl stood up. "I want to be an actress," she said loudly, her hand on her hip as her friends giggled beside her. Jean considered shushing the crowd before it turned into a riotous event like an evangelist's or motivational seminar gone out of control.

The author nodded understanding. "What would you do if you could be selfish? Indulge in something that is just for you. It might seem silly to others, but learn from me. Don't become a victim of your own life. You have the power to be happy. So be it. Be happy. You have this amazing place on your doorstep. Explore it more, discover the details that surround you. Understand who you are in your surroundings; that is vital in understanding who you are at the root of things."

With her concluding words, the author smiled, and the crowd of teenagers erupted in applause. Jean clapped too, a little startled at the energy in the room. Glancing at her watch, she realised there was barely any time left for questions. Before the bell rang, she pointed to students with raised hands, hurrying them to ask their questions. In a blur, she found herself shaking hands with the author, who walked out, her head held high.

After the room had cleared, Jean strode purposefully through the echoing hall towards the author's chair, where a book remained. She quickly scanned its contents, a spark of curiosity igniting within her, before carefully placing it in her handbag.

* * *

The day had flown by, and Jean found herself navigating the aisles of the local supermarket, grappling with decisions about dinner. Her mind was scattered, unravelling under the weight of responsibilities. If only she had more time or some extra help, but Douglas was often away, leaving Jean to parent alone. If only she had an understanding husband to assist, perhaps they wouldn't have separated so hastily. Jean pondered the author's declaration of support, but the thought of ever doing something like that to her own kids was unfathomable. If she walked out on them, they'd starve!

She trudged down the aisle, then back up again, none the wiser.

"Mum!" Maggie moaned from behind.

"OK, OK." Jean grabbed soup, garlic bread, and sausages – a quick option that wasn't fish and chips. "Let's go and pay!" she announced, but before she could make it to the check-out counter, she bumped into someone unexpectedly. Karen, her ex.

Karen had a striking new look, with deep-red dyed hair and more make-up than Jean had ever seen on her before. She couldn't help but be taken aback. "Karen? You look so different!" she said, her eyes widening. "I mean, you look great! I'm just a little shocked to see you here … I thought you had moved."

"No, not yet. I'll be relocating to the city to finish off my studies, do placements … you know," Karen replied, her body rigid, her white knuckles wrapped around a plastic bag.

Jean, acutely aware of Karen's recent living situation after their breakup, knew that Karen had moved back in with her mother. The decision to return home had surely added layers of complexity to their already strained relationship. Karen's mother had never been able to accept her daughter's sexuality.

Jean straightened up, ignoring the dull ache in her feet

from the heels she had chosen to wear that day. She ran a hand self-consciously through her damp auburn hair, still feeling the residual moisture from the earlier rain.

Maggie and Anne stood silently behind Jean, their eyes shifting between Karen and the empty shelves. "OK, well, it was nice to see you," Jean said, trying to maintain a polite tone, as if speaking to a parent at school or a colleague rather than someone she had once loved deeply but couldn't envision a future with.

"Bye," Karen replied, still smiling despite the glistening in her eyes. Conflicting emotions played across Karen's face, and she opened her mouth as if to say something. Jean slowly backed away, reluctant to delve into an emotional confrontation, especially in such a public place with locals bustling around them.

As Jean turned to leave, she observed Maggie and Anne hesitating, then their arms tentatively reached out to embrace Karen. The girls clung to her, and Karen reciprocated, holding them tightly before placing a tender kiss on their heads. It was a rare display of affection that Jean had seldom seen from her daughters during her time with Karen.

Jean walked on, opting not to confront the hurt she had caused to three people – Karen, Maggie, and Anne – not to mention the lingering dull pain she carried within herself.

19

Callum rapped his knuckles against the wooden door, stealing a moment to admire the view of the loch behind him. The mist gracefully skimming across the water veiled the small isle nestled within. Two bright yellow kayaks caught his attention as they rested by the water's edge, a leftover perk from his business made available to his guests. Their lodges, discreetly scattered along the hillside, blended seamlessly into the dark landscape in the late morning.

Knocking again, Callum felt his anger simmer. He needed to get this over with. Facing his ex was something he wished to avoid, but Jennifer had to leave. Her presence weighed too heavily on both him and Lori.

The door swung open, and much to Callum's surprise, Jennifer greeted him with a warm smile. Momentarily thrown off, he struggled to recall the purpose of his visit. She had once been everything to him, and for a brief second he found himself slipping back into that daydream.

"Hi," she said, holding the door open. "Perhaps you better come in?"

Callum slipped off his mucky boots at the doormat and

stepped inside, attempting to hide a small hole in his sock. Standing in the compact space between the kitchen and the double bed, he asked, "Are you comfortable?"

"I am. It's pretty lovely. So tranquil," she replied, gesturing towards the kettle. "Tea?"

"No, I better not. I have a lot to get on with." Callum's words held a hint of truth, but were mostly fuelled by his desire to avoid spending any unnecessary time with Jennifer.

"I hope you don't mind if I have one. I'm parched. Been hiking this morning," Jennifer remarked.

"Already?"

"You know me, like to get out and about!" she said, raising an eyebrow playfully and motioned for Callum to sit on the compact couch while she prepared her tea. Callum obliged, perching on the edge of the chair, slightly uncomfortable but aware that it was the best fit for the lodge. Steam from the kettle wafted through the air as Jennifer poured hot water into a small mug. Between tasks, she swiftly tied up her blonde hair, revealing her exposed neck with a familiar freckle just below her hairline – a neck Callum had kissed countless times.

"Oh, is there some food I can buy off you?" Jennifer interrupted his thoughts. "That blasted shop was closed when I went into town earlier. I only have milk and tea bags!"

"They open late on Sundays."

"I'm starving, and it's a bit of a trek to get back in the car and up that dirt track of a road."

"It's hardly a dirt track," Callum retorted, clenching his hands. Jennifer's dismissive tone reminded him of one of the reasons they could never make it work—she brushed aside anything that didn't align with her preferences.

"Well, a little pack of food. You should do that for everyone who arrives. Better yet … a cooked meal, so I don't need to faff with this stove. It's the smallest I've seen around!"

"Let me remind you that you weren't exactly invited here. You forced yourself on me … on my fiancée!" He couldn't hide his frustration.

"I'm not trying to cause a stir in your life. This is not about you. This is about—"

"You?" Callum scoffed, cutting her off. "Yeah, that sounds about right." He had barely arrived, and now he wanted to leave.

"You are so unforgiving. You never forget anything. You hang on to everything, carrying grudges from your childhood into adulthood. Give it a rest, Callum. Lighten up!" Jennifer turned to him, leaning against the sink.

"Why are you really here?" he pressed, cutting through the bickering that would inevitably unfold.

"I told you." Jennifer sighed. "I have business."

"What about your family?"

"They are fine. They can look after themselves for a bit."

Silence hung heavy in the air.

"Look, I don't know what all this is really about, Jennifer. But I came here to tell you to leave Lori alone. She doesn't need this. If you have anything to say, say it to me. Don't drag her into this. It's not fair to her. She has enough on her plate with the wedding and …" Callum stopped himself, realising he didn't owe Jennifer any explanations. "You can stay here until your business is over. As a gesture of goodwill, I'll keep this lodge free until you go. But please, stay away from Lori." He stood up, ready to leave.

"That's what you came here to say? I think we have more to talk about."

"I really don't think we do." He hastily tied his boots, his hands fumbling with the laces as Jennifer watched with a smirk. With determination, he strode down the walkway, leaving the lodge.

"Please, Callum, some food, please," Jennifer called out from the front step, wrapping her arms around herself. "If I'm not here, just leave it on the step."

Callum gritted his teeth and marched back to his house. Looking inside the fridge, he salvaged bacon, butter, and orange juice from his meagre supplies. Lori often ate at the shop, leaving him to fend for himself, resulting in wasted food.

He sniffed at a fancy cheese close to its expiration date and found an unopened small carton of milk. Placing them in an empty box, an idea struck him. What if Jennifer was right? They could provide food for the guests? Create hampers or even tap into the luxury market, offering doorstep delivery of hot meals.

He grabbed a notepad and pen from his office, jotting down his thoughts. It wasn't his lack of business ideas that made him feel stuck; it was finding the time and resources to execute them. He needed help now. He needed workers. He dialled the agency that had previously compiled a list of applicants for him – the ones that had all left before he even got to know their names, leaving the agency on shaky ground. Where were they finding these people? As the phone rang out, he realised it was Sunday, and most places were closed. He grunted in frustration and typed up an email, sending it to as many agencies as he could find online. He had already contacted them all, and not one had provided any viable candidates. Slamming his laptop shut, it was paramount now that he needed to brainstorm how to find the help he needed.

Recognising how long he had been at the computer, he grabbed the box of food and made his way back to Jennifer's lodge. Knocking twice, he left the food by the door. However, before he could retreat to the safety of his house, he heard splashing and turned around. Jennifer emerged from the loch, the water glistening on her athletic frame as she wore a clinging white T-shirt and bikini bottoms that showcased her tanned thighs. She padded back to the lodge, while Callum stood rooted to the spot like a deer caught in headlights. He saw her shiver, a subtle tremor rippling through her body. Then his gaze inadvertently drifted downward, drawn to the tantalising sight of her T-shirt accentuating the outline of her erect nipples beneath the sheer fabric. Heat surged through him, a flicker of desire igniting deep within. With a slight flush creeping up his cheeks, he quickly averted his eyes, coughing awkwardly.

Jennifer grabbed a towel from a large rock near the bottom step and wrapped it tightly around her chest, securing it in place. A mischievous smirk played on her lips. "Nothing you haven't seen before, Callum."

"I've left the food," Callum replied, ignoring her remark. "You can cook it on the stove. There are pots and pans … if you can get it working. But there's also food you can eat right away."

Jennifer sighed in relief. "Lifesaver, thank you."

He spun on his heel, eager to leave Jennifer's presence. "Unless … do you want me to show you how the stove works?"

Jennifer loosened her towel, briefly exposing herself before wrapping it tightly around her chest once more. "I'll figure it out."

Callum nodded and walked away, resisting the urge to steal a glance back, aware that Jennifer was fixedly watching him.

20

"Are you seriously OK with all this?" Rhona raised an eyebrow, handing Lori a cup of coffee. "I mean, she's been here a while now!" She placed a box resembling white powdered Turkish delight on the cutting table.

Lori sighed; Jennifer's stay had gone on longer than she had ever dreamed it would, but she had to trust her gut and hope it would work out in due course. She wanted Jennifer to get all of her jobs done and make peace with Callum for good.

"Of course, Rhona. We've been over this. I just want to be on good terms, no matter what Jennifer is up to. I want to be kind to her."

Rhona nodded, a mischievous glint in her eye as she pinched a dusty pink square and wedged it into her mouth. "Oh yeah, that's a good idea – kill her with kindness!"

Following Rhona's lead, Lori took a bite after the rich coffee danced on her taste buds. The sugar hit her, rose water and pistachios rolled on her tongue, creating a delightful medley of flavours. "Holy crap, those are delicious! Where did you get them? I'll order some!"

Rhona smirked, leaning in beside Lori and snatching another morsel. "More local than you think. Tammy."

"Tammy?" Lori raised an eyebrow.

"Yup, she gave me a hamper. The darling." Rhona pouted. "As a thank you for helping out with Rory."

Lori was caught off guard, unsure of what confused her more – Tammy hand making hampers and not giving her one, or the fact that Rhona was secretly babysitting on the side. Sensing Lori's confusion, Rhona raised her hands. "Tammy would pop in from time to time, maybe wanting to do a wee food shop or even a swim in the pool. I'd be here, and the shop was dead anyway!"

"So she'd leave Rory with you?" Lori asked loudly.

Rhona shrugged. "Anyway, these treats are just a small thank you, or so I believe. She didn't write a card, just had it waiting outside my front door."

"She went all the way to your house?" Lori's eyes widened. "But that's over on the ferry!"

"Shiel Island is hardly an epic voyage over the seven seas! Only a short ride on the ferry! It's not like I see anyone there. You all think life stops at Morvaig!"

"No, Rhona, I for one do not think that!" Lori replied flatly.

"Well, you know what I mean! I get no visitors!"

"Apparently Tammy!" Lori sniped, still unsure of the real root of her annoyance.

"Anyway." Rhona flicked her side fringe. "Let's go back to the beginning. You want to be kind to Jennifer?"

"I sure do. In fact, I think I'll plan a little dinner party or something."

"Well, if you're being all nicey-nicey to Callum's ex, why not bring his ex-friend along too?" Rhona's eyes danced playfully beneath her false eyelashes.

Lori's mouth twitched. "You mean Francesca?"

"Sure," Rhona replied, pressing her lips together in a dubious pout. "If you're doing all this for Jennifer, then maybe it's time to settle the fire with Fran."

"I didn't know you were friends?" Lori asked suspiciously.

"Oh, wheest! I'm not friends with Fran. But I have seen her recently, and she looks … well … not good. Are Callum and her still talking?"

"I don't know. It's none of my business," Lori muttered, pushing the box of Turkish delight away. She didn't want to acknowledge it, but ever since her and Callum's temporary breakup the year before, she had encouraged his friendship with Fran to sizzle out. Lori hadn't talked to Callum about it since, but she had quietly accepted his declaration to not speak to Fran again. Francesca, her old enemy from high school, had never seen eye to eye with Lori. But more recently, Lori may have been uncharitable towards her. She just didn't trust Fran. But wasn't Fran just like Jennifer? In some ways, they resembled each other, Lori had to admit. Shouldn't she just open her heart to everyone and give them a chance?

"Are you saying I need to forgive Fran?" Lori asked, contemplating.

Rhona frowned, crossing her arms. "What did Fran do? Did she sleep with Callum?"

"No," Lori said a little too loudly.

"You just don't like her then?"

Lori opened her mouth, but the words stuck in her throat. That was it. She was jealous of Fran because they hadn't "gotten on" in high school. Everything about Fran rubbed Lori the wrong way, but what was so different about accepting Jennifer? Well, one reason being that Jennifer would go – Fran would be staying.

Still not convinced, Lori pleaded her case. "I don't know

… she took up so much of Callum's mental space. I think he feels responsible for her. She took advantage of him, getting him to do things for her that were over and above. Since they've not spoken, he's not been dragged into her dramas. The last one was a conflict with her landlord!"

Rhona shrugged again, scrunching her nose. "I don't know. I just think if you're going through this whole forgiving thing, if it's on Callum's behalf … he's a big boy, he can work through these things himself. Perhaps you just let everything go?"

"Would you do that?" Lori asked, intrigued.

"Oh god, no. I love despising people!" Rhona laughed. "Gets me through the day!"

Lori watched her friend quizzically. As much as Rhona said otherwise, she didn't seem to harbour any resentments towards anyone, as far as Lori knew, and she seemed genuinely happy. As happy as one could be, living in a community where everyone knew everyone's business.

"OK." Lori stood up straight. "I'm done. I'm going to be the better person."

"What, just like that?" Rhona frowned.

"Yes, why not?"

"OK, great! Now that's over with, we have so much to plan!" Rhona clapped her hands together. "Hen night, bridesmaid dress, and which celebrity I'll snog at your wedding!"

Lori laughed. "You can't plan these things, Rhona!"

"Well, I must. Your wedding is going to be at an exclusive castle where only celebrities and royalty go!"

Lori rolled her eyes. "Sometimes, it's a castle for normal people too!"

"I just need to figure out which celebrity might happen to be there at that time." Rhona tapped a scarlet nail to her chin thoughtfully. "You know Malcolm and I have a name each. If we ever meet them, we can sleep with them."

"Does the celebrity have a say?" Lori scoffed.

Rhona's eyes narrowed. "What do you mean? They'd get a taste of this!" She gestured down her body.

"Sorry, er of course!" Lori grinned. "Who's your celebrity?" She tried to stifle her laughter, but Rhona's expression sent her into fits of giggles.

"It's only in Scotland, mind you." Rhona said, solemnly. "This rule is if they come here. We can't be searching the world for them."

"With a long list of reasons why they should sleep with you?" Lori joked.

Rhona's eyes widened in mock indignation. "Well, perhaps you wouldn't be laughing so hard if you found out your friend and George Clooney had done the deed in the castle's garden shed!"

"What!" Lori had just taken a sip of coffee and sprayed it all over herself.

"Yeah, exactly. If he plans to be there around the same time as your wedding, I'll take a walk around the grounds, and he'll be so enamoured by my wit and personality that he'll take one look at these pins …" Rhona pointed to her legs, encased in black tights and black stilettos.

"Then game over?" Lori asked, grinning.

"Exactly!" Rhona smirked, sauntering sensually towards the front desk. With a playful sway of her hips, she leaned over the desk to retrieve a little black book.

Lori frowned. "Is this your book of previous escapades you're adding poor George to?"

"No, I'm not that ridiculous – this is to plan your wedding! And I don't need to keep a record on paper. I slept with ten men before Malcolm and I got married." She shrugged.

Lori had foolishly taken another sip of coffee. This time

she swallowed before it sprayed over her. "You were with Malcolm pretty young though. How did you manage that?"

"Oh, he got me just when I was getting into my groove. I knew a thing or two just before we met."

"I'm sure you did." Lori winced. "Please can we end the topic there."

"Why? You're so prudish, Lori Robertson! What's the big deal?"

"Because I'm a lady." Lori straightened, her cheeks flushing. "Ladies don't tell."

"Oh jeez, well then that certainly makes me the harlot of the Highlands!" Rhona raised her arm, announcing it to the empty shop. And at that precise moment, both of them realised they were not entirely alone.

Graham Morrison stood at the door, grinning.

21

Tammy knocked on Gran's front door and patiently waited for a response. Gone were the days when she could simply barge into the house unannounced or on her own whims. After bearing witness to Gran and Lawrence's frequent kisses, the thought of accidentally stumbling upon another intimate moment made her cringe; she didn't want to witness something she would later need to un-see.

It was early afternoon, and she assumed Gran was probably out somewhere, swimming, or attending a Pilates class. But just as Tammy was about to retreat to her car, Gran swung open the door, her hair wrapped in a pink towel, though fully dressed.

"Tammy!" Gran exclaimed, opening her arms and pulling her granddaughter into a warm hug, and beaming at her great-grandson, who waddled over to her flower pots on the top step.

"Do you have any plans?" Tammy's smile, though strained, tried to appear genuine.

"Well." Gran glanced at her gold wristwatch. "I have my committee meeting … but that's later. Come in!" She quickly ushered them both inside.

Gran busied herself with making tea and opened a biscuit tin. Tammy quickly jumped in, saying, "We don't need that – I brought my own!" She produced a plastic bag from behind her back. Rory squealed beside them, already distracted by sliding across Gran's floor, with Bracken, the old family dog, sniffing him curiously. Bracken flopped down by Rory's side, and as the baby giggled, he nuzzled into Rory's tiny hands.

"What's all this?" Gran grinned at Tammy, who pulled out several Tupperware boxes with a serious expression.

"This is what I've been experimenting with," Tammy explained, placing some tasters on plates and joining Gran at the table. "You know how I used to work at the bakery? Well, I learned a lot of secrets about how they made things, little tips and tricks."

"I bet you did!" Gran chuckled, her hands on her hips.

"So I've started to see how they do things at the hotel too, and I've been thinking about presenting some ideas to them. But I don't know where to start! Then I had a thought about doing something for Lori's hen party – putting together a banquet to see if I can—"

"That's wonderful, Tam," Gran interrupted, beaming at Rory, who had pulled himself up on her leg.

Tammy bit her lip, knowing that Rory would soon become a whirlwind of energy, likely wreaking havoc throughout Gran's house. She needed to get to the point quickly; she needed to do this now.

"So I've prepared some tasters," Tammy continued, pushing the plates toward Gran expectantly.

"What? Am I supposed to eat all this now?" Her eyes landed on the boxes stacked on the kitchen counter.

"I need advice from the best cook I know!" Tammy pouted, hoping it would get the results it usually did.

Gran squinted at her watch again, grimacing. "Let me

quickly dry my hair, put on some lipstick, and you can come to the committee meeting with me. I know some people who would be thrilled to help taste-test these delectables!"

Feeling a mix of deflation and bubbling anticipation in her stomach, Tammy stayed put while Gran got ready. Rory clumsily padded across the floor, exploring cabinets and drawers, pulling out papers and photographs. Flustered, Tammy stashed keepsakes away, and with relief, Gran appeared soon after, ushering her out of the house.

At the village hall, she was welcomed in a flurry of greetings by several elderly individuals with greying hair. The friendly Mrs Blake assisted her with her boxes, and before Tammy could utter a word, Gran had informed everyone of what was required of each of them. She clapped her hands, assigning tasks with the precision of a drill sergeant, distributing napkins to everyone as if they were soldiers on a mission.

Tammy noticed three men with round bellies immediately gravitating toward the food, and soon the noise of chatter disappeared to be replaced with murmurs of approval or disappointment, Tammy couldn't quite decide. She tried to listen, but couldn't distinguish between the sounds. She set Rory loose on the polished wooden floor, hoping it would buy her some time before she had to leave for his nap.

Gran leaned in toward the group. "Well, what's the verdict from the men-folk?" she mused, taking a deliberate bite of a coconut macaroon.

Nods and words of encouragement followed, and Tammy grinned. She wasn't entirely certain about the food's quality. Alan had always praised whatever she cooked, whether it was a gourmet dinner or a sad frozen pizza with a side of beans on toast. His enthusiasm remained consistent for everything. However, she chose to believe their feedback. Deep down, she understood herself. She recognised the joy she experienced while making them, the love she poured into each crisp tart, each apple strudel, each frosted pink cupcake. She believed that her dedication could be tasted in a single bite. Tammy left the hall feeling light-headed, leaving the remaining food for her recent admirers, some of whom even placed orders for more.

* * *

Tammy arrived home exhausted and plopped Rory on the couch, watching as he immediately slithered off to explore his surroundings. Stepping over the gate that kept him within the illusion of freedom, she sighed heavily and began preparing dinner with a sense of anticipation. Tonight would be different. Despite her earlier culinary endeavours, she had decided to create a special meal for Alan, complete with lit candles, and even throw on a dress and a bit of lippy for good measure. She needed to make a fuss over him, especially since she was in such a good mood herself.

As she cooked, her eyes occasionally flicked toward her phone, hoping for a message from Alan, but there was nothing. He knew Rory's routine; she shouldn't have to remind him. Pouring herself a glass of chilled white wine from the fridge, she took a sip before delving into chopping onions and garlic.

After giving Rory his dinner and a bath, Tammy read him a bedtime story and laid him down in his cot. The house grew quiet as she switched off the light.

Alan still hadn't shown up. Tammy sat at the round table, her head swimming after polishing off the rest of the bottle of wine. By the time he arrived home, the lamb roast she had prepared with so much care had turned cold. Her earlier good mood vanished, replaced with defeat.

“Sorry, Tam,” Alan’s voice broke the silence as he finally entered the room. “Have you been waiting long?”

She stood up slowly, her gaze fixed on her own cold plate of food before her. Without a word, she disposed of its contents in the bin, refusing to look at Alan. With a swift motion, she blew out the candles, casting the room into darkness. Turning on the bright overhead light, she faced him. “It’s OK,” she forced the words out. “I’m going to bed. Enjoy your dinner.” Without waiting for a response, she left him in stunned silence.

As she lay in bed, her mind continued to wrestle with the state of their marriage. The undeniable truth of their rough patch weighed heavily on her. She couldn’t escape the sinking feeling that their once strong connection was slipping away, if not already gone.

As exhaustion settled in, sleep gradually overtook her. In the depths of her subconscious, she clung to a glimmer of hope that things would somehow resolve themselves, that the love they once shared would reignite and guide them back to a place of happiness and understanding. It was a futile hope, but in her vulnerable state, it was all she had to cling to.

22

The long-awaited weekend finally arrived, and all Lori had envisioned was a quiet evening with her tv remote and a bottle of wine. The elusive Indian summer had never materialised, and with the tourist season waning and autumn settling in, she knew her shop would only grow quieter. The idea of jetting off to a hot beach destination had crossed her mind, but with wedding preparations consuming her attention, she had to focus solely on that task. She stretched her neck, with a groan. She needed to take better care of her body, before she would be permanently hump-backed from hours behind a sewing machine.

She stretched her body the way Jennifer had showed her and it relieved some of the ache around her lower back. She breathed out, but a nagging feeling nestled deep within her. No matter where she diverted her mind, something was amiss, especially with Jennifer still loitering in the same lodge, showing no intention of returning to New Zealand. A tightness in her throat lingered even as Lori tried to distract herself with the yoga routine.

Despite Jennifer's continued presence, Lori had kept her word, remaining politely civil whenever their paths crossed –

a fact she was proud of. Yet, an unspoken tension gnawed at her, tempting her to knock on Jennifer's door and address any unresolved issues. She had to continually remind herself that it was between Jennifer and Callum to work through their problems. After all, as Rhona had once wisely pointed out, Callum was not a child and could handle his own issues. Yet, whatever they were discussing, it seemed like nothing was getting resolved.

Still not feeling relaxed and convinced she was doing the yoga moves wrong, she tapped her phone, loading Jennifer's latest video for guidance. There, on the screen, Jennifer saluted the camera from a windswept hillside, gracefully performing her routines among purple heather and craggy rock. A reminder to Lori that she was still there, unmoving, her stubborn presence like moss clinging relentlessly to a rock on that hillside.

She switched off the video, welcoming the pain over seeing Jennifer's perfectly toned body. Then the twinge in her lower back hit again; she grimaced. Perhaps it was time for Lori to pay a visit to Jennifer's lodge, armed with a bottle of wine, and have a heart-to-heart conversation. After all, women had a unique ability to connect and understand each other's difficulties. It was often men who struggled in that department, including Callum. While Callum had no trouble connecting with Lori on a personal level, he often fell short when it came to delving into the depths of someone's needs, wants, and motivations.

She snapped back to reality as Rhona breezed into the shop with her usual exuberance, tossing her black handbag onto the desk beside Lori's elbow.

"Ready?" Rhona quirked an eyebrow, mischief twinkling in her eyes.

"Ready for what?" she shot back, her expression as if she had bitten into a sour lemon. "Nice to see you too, Rhona."

Rhona cleared her throat, and behind her, a group of women emerged, their excitement palpable. "It's time to meet your doom …"

"What's going on?" Lori asked, confusion etching her face. She pushed her chair back, the colour draining from her features.

"I suppose you don't really need the details just yet." Rhona nodded solemnly. "But you knew this day would come, Lori. It's tradition round these parts."

The small crowd behind her erupted in cheers.

"Now, we need your clothes …" Rhona's finger danced in the air. "Who was in charge of clothes?" she asked loudly, snapping her fingers.

Murmurs filled the room as Lori shifted her gaze to see who was present. Local women, women from shops on the same high street, women she knew well, and had trusted.

Jean, manoeuvring through the doorframe, reached Rhona's side. "It was Tammy's job," she whispered, her face flushed with frustration. "I suspected she wouldn't be on time, though." She tossed a baggy grey T-shirt and washed-out shorts at Lori. "Those will take the brunt of it."

"Brunt of what?" Lori glanced down at her burgundy knit dress, horror flashing in her eyes as they snapped back to Jean.

"Lori, put it on – quick before they come and drag you outta here in what you're wearing!" Jean urged, glancing behind her with urgency. "Go!" She clapped her hands, and Lori blindly followed, darting behind the privacy of the wall to the kitchenette, and whipped off her dress. The sounds of the crowd grew louder until Lori's name was called by a man. Feeling as if she had stepped back in time and was the target of a witch hunt, dumfounded, she emerged in her baggy clothes, awkwardly tiptoeing towards them.

"Are you Lori Robertson?" It was Alan, towering above

everyone at the boutique's entrance. A group of men stood around him, one of whom was Callum. If it weren't for his grim smile, Lori's imagination would have taken a dark turn.

"What?" She folded her arms. "What the bloody hell is going on, Alan? Callum?" She scowled.

"Come on, Lori, this is the script – just go along with it – we've all done it!" Alan whispered, nodding encouragingly. "Now, are you Lori Robertson?"

"You know I am."

"And are you marrying Callum Macrae here?"

"Uh-huh." Lori didn't have time to humour them. Whatever was about to happen, she knew she was not going to like it.

"Right then, boys!" Alan waved a finger, and Lori was hoisted into the air by burly men and lifted out of the shop, in a fit of squeals and shrieks around her. She bobbed on top of shoulders for a short distance until she was placed down. Next to her side was Callum, shivering. They were tied to a post in the town square surrounded by plant pots and tourist information signs.

"What is going on?" Lori asked Callum with a groan, her hand finding his. They huddled next to each other in the chilly air.

"Have you never been to a Blackening?" Callum's eyes widened, his nose scrunching as a gust of wind blew through them.

With all her years in different countries, she had missed out on the local marriage traditions. Missed out, or happily escaped …

"What's going to happen?" She cringed, her teeth chattering.

"We'll be grand, just let them have their way … it'll be over quicker," he muttered.

Before anything, Rhona shimmied up to them, producing a silver hip flask from her pocket. “Get this down ya.”

Lori complied, hoping it would settle her rising anxiety. Behind Rhona, Alan and two men held white tubs, wide menacing grins on their faces.

“You bastards better make this quick!” Callum challenged. “I’ll remember this for you!” he threatened, jokingly.

Alan heartily laughed. “My pre-wedding days are over, Callum! You went too easy on me!”

Before Lori knew it, the tub was spilled onto her newly washed hair, covering her face and shoulders. The high-pitched squeal that came out of her shocked even her!

“Be nice to Lori, boys – give me her share!” Callum’s grip tightened as the black gooey concoction flopped down her arms and through her fingers. Whatever it was, it stunk fiercely.

“Very chivalrous!” Rhona appeared again, with Jean, and tipped raw egg over them both.

“Sorry, sis!” Jean squeaked.

All the group around them cheered, and music erupted nearby. Lori squinted at a jaunty fiddle player and guitarist next to them. A strange scene, but one that brought more people to the spectacle, some even coming out of their homes to get a good look. Lori shrieked as she and Callum were pelted with white dust, flour, sawdust, and more.

“OK, OK!” Alan, the ringleader, emerged from the crowd. Lori’s eyes narrowed. “That’s you, may your marriage be long and happy.” He gave a Gaelic blessing, one Lori didn’t know too well, but she got the gist of it. The crowd cheered and clapped; some started barrelling into each other to the music. Alan untied them both and quickly marched away before Callum could grab him.

“Jump! Jump! Jump!” the crowd chanted. Lori turned her

attention behind her, where dark water lapped against the pier.

"Shall we?" Callum wiped his face, but the black tar remained thick.

"I don't know." Lori hesitated, looking back at the crowd.

"We can't go anywhere like this." Callum looked down at himself. "In there is the best thing for us right now."

Not uttering a word but following Callum's lead, Lori clenched her teeth and jumped off the pier into the shock of icy water. Resurfacing, she found Callum bobbing on the surface, arms open in anticipation. Despite her irritation from the public humiliation, Lori swam to him, and they embraced in a kiss, oblivious to the growing crowd on the pier. Suddenly, a few individuals, perhaps overly influenced by alcohol, took a spontaneous plunge into the depths nearby, while the rest merrily continued dancing, cans of lager firmly in hand.

Lori, still in a bit of a daze from her aquatic adventure, found herself draped in a towel and guided barefoot down the jetty by Rhona. Without a chance to bid farewell to Callum, she was ushered into the back of a van where plastic bags concealed its chairs. Girls piled in around her, but Lori couldn't shake the feeling that something was amiss. Plastic bags rustled as Rhona, stationed in the front, distributed cans to the boisterous group over her shoulder. The van jolted to life, its engine roaring as they sped away from the harbour. It was only then that Lori noticed two girls sitting at the back, the last two people she could imagine coming to her hen party. Francesca and Jennifer. Unlike the others, they sat quietly, wearing subtle smiles that didn't match the excitement of the rest of the group.

23

Relief washed over Lori as she sprinted towards Gran's house, eager to escape the clutches of what she had labelled as yet another barbaric Highland tradition. She practically crashed through the front door, greeted by the warm embrace of her grandmother.

"My poor Lolo, are you OK?" Gran inquired, her voice laced with genuine concern. However, before she could scrutinise Lori more closely, she noticed a smear on her own cardigan and let out a horrified shriek. "Lori Robertson, you've covered me in egg!"

Lori, seizing a sausage roll and realising her famished state after the Highland ordeal, retorted with a smirk, "Welcome to my world, Gran!" She raised an eyebrow, settling into the familiar surroundings, and accepted a glass of wine, along with another sausage roll. "Although all this food and wine is helping!"

Rhona scoffed in agreement as the rest of the group converged around the kitchen counter, laden with alcoholic beverages. Gran winced, rubbing her blouse where a stubborn yellow stain had set in. With a tut, she continued, "I'm sorry I wasn't there. I couldn't bear to watch. It's so awful – the smell, the humiliation."

"Thanks, Gran," Lori replied, unimpressed. Knowing her opinionated and respected gran, she mused, "If you had shown up, there might not have been a Blackening. I'm sure Alan would have scampered off terrified!"

Gran's eyes widened at the suggestion. "Oh no, I'd never object. It's good luck. It's tradition!" She nodded, adding, "And Lori Robertson, I do not terrify people – what a thing to say."

"Well, it's true!" Lori defended. "No one would cross you, especially if you wagged a finger at them!"

Gran tutted. "Nonsense! I have never 'wagged' my finger at anyone."

Lori couldn't help but chuckle at the importance Gran placed on tradition – a little word that seemed to allow anything as long as it fell under its umbrella.

Just as Lori was about to grab a chunk of caramel shortbread from a pyramid, Gran shook her head. "OK, that's as much stench as I can put up with. Get in that shower now!"

Lori glanced at Rhona, who disapproved with hands on her hips. "Mary, you know she needs to stay like that …"

"It's tradition, Gran," Lori said, suppressing a giggle by ramming the shortbread in her mouth.

"Not in my house. There's a foul fishy odour; you can't sit down," Gran scolded, wagging her finger at Lori. "In my day, it was chimney soot. Why didn't they use chimney soot?" Gran shrieked at Rhona, who, unfazed by Gran's objection, simply returned to sharing the punchline of her joke with the rest of the hen party.

Stepping out of the steamy shower, Lori found a black dress neatly laid out on her old bed, accompanied by a pair of stilettos and her make-up bag. Grateful that someone had taken the time to gather her belongings, she quickly got ready.

As she made her way to the living room and kitchen, a wave of cheers greeted her. She glanced around and noticed familiar faces from the area, triggering a pang of discomfort. After living in different countries for most of her adult life, it had prevented her from forming any real connections. Rhona's extensive network of acquaintances served as a reminder of the connections Lori was yet to forge. She suspected the presence of everyone was due to her Gran's reputation and Rhona's persistent insistence.

Gran, clapping her hands in delight, approached Lori with pride gleaming in her eyes. "Jean showed me the video on her tiny phone. Jean, you must do something about that crack across the screen." Gran tutted at her eldest granddaughter. "But my goodness, Lori, you leaped off the pier! It reminded me of what you were like as a little girl – always jumping off things at the drop of a hat!" Gran cringed, closing her eyes momentarily. "Anyway, that ordeal is behind us now. I didn't want to know what was coming your way."

Tammy appeared beside them, expertly balancing a tray of glasses filled with bubbly. She nudged Gran, subtly reminding her of the refreshments.

"Ah, yes! Everyone, dig in! Tammy has prepared a delicious spread!" Gran announced. Taking a glass from Tammy and wrapping an arm around Lori, she whispered, "Make sure to make a fuss about the buffet. Tammy put a lot of effort into it."

Lori groaned inwardly, well acquainted with the routine of prioritising Tammy's needs and desires above everyone else's. Despite Tammy's absence at her Blackening and her failure to check on Lori afterward, she seemed singularly focused on the food. And the food was delicious, Lori thought grudgingly as she bit into a homemade pork pie, savouring the crisp and warm pastry.

Francesca, holding a wine glass and dressed in an outfit similar to Lori's, appeared beside her. Her dress featured a necktie and a daring split down to her bosom. With perfectly curled blonde hair and impeccable make-up, she exuded a polished appearance.

"That was one crazy Blackening," Francesca remarked, her mouth twitching as she stabbed a piece of melon with a fork. "The boys really went all out on you, huh? More fish guts than I've ever seen." She deftly chewed the melon, lips shaped in an O, careful not to smudge her lipstick.

"Maybe so." Lori shrugged. "But at least Callum was there with me. We had each other as support." Her voice carried a hint of indifference, yet her dislike for Francesca immediately resurfaced.

"I'm sure the boys are off to their stag party in town by now." Francesca raised an eyebrow suggestively. "This gathering is lovely. Cosy. Like a tea party at my Nanna's house. Just charming." She beamed, taking a slow sip from her glass. Lori could see her lipstick mark on the glass, even after her efforts. "But I can only imagine what they'll be up to," Francesca continued. "I might join them later. Hope you won't be offended. After all, Callum and I go way back," she breezily remarked before walking away.

Old anger flared up within Lori, her grip tightening around her glass. Francesca always found ways to get under her skin, with her whole aura of a man's fantasy – tiny waist and large bust. It was hard for Lori not to see the attraction. But this was exactly what Francesca wanted – to get a rise out of her.

She took a deep breath, reminding herself that Callum had chosen her. She trusted him implicitly, regardless of what Francesca insinuated. Fran might want him to choose her, but he never would. Lori stabbed at the melon, but instead of eating it sensuously like Fran had, she dribbled juice down her chin. She reached for a napkin as Jennifer appeared by her side, startling her. If it wasn't Callum's ex-friend occupying her mind, it was his ex-wife!

"I've never seen anything so barbaric. How are you holding up after that?" Jennifer's sincere gaze locked onto Lori's. Lori was slightly taken aback by her casual attire – jeans paired with a floaty top, yet she still exuded a relaxed beauty.

Gran and Tammy erupted into laughter at something Rhona had said in the kitchen, startling the others, including Jennifer. Lori seized the moment to observe her more closely. Jennifer's hair was effortlessly styled in a bun, her caramel honey skin tone radiated warmth, and a hint of fresh apple blossom lingered around her. Jennifer was a rational woman; Lori could sense that from their first meeting. But why would someone like her, with a thriving business and a loving husband like Callum, jeopardise it all for an affair with Hector? And more perplexing, why did Callum let her go so easily? Even now, many years later, Jennifer remained beautiful, calm, poised, and sensible. It just didn't add up.

Jennifer's gaze returned to Lori, her elegant eyebrow raised in question.

"It wasn't pleasant." Lori crumpled her napkin on her plate, her appetite waning. "But now that I reflect on it … it was sort of sweet."

"Sweet?" Jennifer scoffed. "To have fish guts thrown at you?"

"I suppose you didn't have a Blackening for your wedding?" Lori grinned, trying to lighten the mood.

"No way, nobody around here would dare do that to me. I wouldn't allow it."

"Well, I suppose that's where we differ. I want them to

feel comfortable enough around me to do something like that."

"To throw fish guts on you?"

Lori shrugged. It did sound strange, but she knew what she meant. Having opened a business in the area, marrying a local, and being from Arlochy, she still hadn't felt fully accepted. She moved away from the table, but Jennifer lingered by her side.

"I had hoped we could be friends, Lori," Jennifer said. "I'm flattered you invited me tonight, despite all your friends being here and the fact that I have a history with Callum." She swallowed. Her face was serious, reminiscent of the night she'd shown up for the house party and everything went topsy-turvy. "You've made me feel welcome, helped me out with the lodge. I'm grateful for your efforts to make this easier."

Lori couldn't bring herself to tell Jennifer that she hadn't invited her tonight. She wanted to help her, to work out whatever issue she had with Callum in a civilised way and have her depart for good. But there was something more, Lori could sense it, even if Callum didn't. It was in the way Jennifer lingered around her, in the gestures, not the words.

"Can we grab a coffee tomorrow? Any time that suits you," Jennifer whispered. "I need to discuss something with you."

Lori accepted her invitation, though the upcoming wedding weighed heavily on her mind. With the final deposit payment due at the castle, her thoughts were clouded with countless tasks. Despite the pressing obligations, she found herself feeling stuck, unable to take action. Part of her wondered if she was merely waiting for Jennifer to return to New Zealand or if there was something else holding her back.

Gran chimed her glass, summoning the crowd closer. "Dear Lori, my fearless one. You are a rock to us all, and I hope you and Callum will be very happy!" She raised her glass high, and a moment's cheer erupted from the small crowd. But before they could go back to their conversations, Gran tapped her glass again. "Now, I must say the table service tonight has exceeded anything I could do. Tammy, you have put on the most beautiful display …"

Lori groaned internally; of course, the brunt of the toast would be in honour of Tammy. As if accepting Francesca and Jennifer with open arms tonight wasn't enough, she now had to lavish praise on Tammy – especially hard when her sister had barely acknowledged her the whole evening. As much as she loved her gran with all her heart, she felt as if Gran had always given a bit extra to Tammy, encouraging her selfish ways, which brought her into adulthood as still bratty. And so it went on as Gran explained how Tammy would bake in the kitchen as a little girl in the middle of the night. "I'd wake up to smells of vanilla, thinking I had gone completely mad!" Gran hooted.

Lori downed the rest of her bubbles, feeling suffocated. Pushed into a corner from all directions. She shoved a piece of cake in her mouth, trying to swallow the taste of frustration along with the sweetness. Laughter around her faded into the background, and she found herself yearning for bed.

24

Jean slipped beneath the soft sheets, releasing a contented sigh as the familiar embrace of her own bed welcomed her. The role she'd played as the dutiful sister and friend at Lori's Blackening celebrations had left her wearier than she'd anticipated. Amidst the laughter and festivities, Jean couldn't shake off a subtle pang of emptiness, a disconnection from the moment. She found herself mechanically going through the motions, smiling and nodding, while her mind meandered elsewhere. Now, in the quiet sanctuary of her bed, her mind should have succumbed to the allure of sleep. Instead, an unexplained restlessness kept her wide awake.

With a heavy sigh, she flicked on her bedside lamp and reached for the book lying beside it – the memoir of the author who had enchanted both the kids and Jean during her talk. Though *The Hillwalker* had a slow start, and she skipped a few pages to reach the heart of the story, she found herself devouring the entire book in one sitting. Squinting at her alarm clock, the blurry numbers failed to register. How could she possibly sleep now, after being so immersed? Not after feeling the hillwalker's journey. Desperate for more, she took out her phone to look up articles about hillwalking and bothying. At first, the idea of walking around hills seemed too gruelling and unnecessary; a comfy bed or a movie theatre would have been more her interest once. Yet, with each passing article, a flicker of curiosity ignited within her, propelling her to dive deeper into unexplored territory.

Tired of the persistent emptiness that clung to her like a heavy exhaustion, an overweight cat on her shoulders demanding only the basics – food, sleep, warmth – Jean craved liberation from her stagnant existence. She had grown so accustomed to the weariness that it had become her identity.

She wanted free of her current stuck position, she wanted motion. Not letting life happen to her, but become the person she truly wanted to be. After all, she preached this to her students: to embrace their authentic selves without fear of the world's judgement. Was she as she had feared all this time … just a hypocrite? Did Karen's hurtful accusations reveal a truth about herself she had overlooked? Had she let go of someone who truly saw her, accepting of her faults?

She picked up the book once more, studying the cover. The author seemed to carry more conviction in a single memory than Jean felt in her entire being. The weariness of living a life without any passions had become unbearable. While she loved her girls and found some merit in her work, she couldn't shake the feeling that there had to be more to life.

She reached for her phone again, searching for nearby hiking trails. The Highlands offered numerous options, but she sought more than aimless wandering. She craved a challenge, an endeavour that would allow her to stand atop a summit and revel in the euphoria that so many before her had done.

Ben Nevis loomed in the near distance, the highest mountain in Scotland and all of Great Britain. Many people Jean knew had already conquered it, including Lori, Gran, and Rhona, who did it for a charity event. Memories of their triumphant ascent danced in Jean's thoughts. However, at the time, she had been preoccupied with various jobs, using them as an excuse to sit it out. Why dedicate an entire day to such a climb? Now, Ben Nevis's towering presence called out to her.

Grabbing a pen and notepad from the side table, she began jotting down a list. After rummaging through her cupboard, she found a pair of trainers that were moderately worn. Armed with her backpack and an old anorak she hadn't worn since her teenage years, she stood before the mirror, a surge of energy coursing through her veins.

Jean stood at the base of the majestic mountain, her heart swelling with a blend of awe and trepidation as it loomed larger than she had ever imagined. With a surge of determination, she set her legs in motion, one step at a time, steadily ascending the gradient. The initial climb felt surprisingly easy, and she felt sprightly, creating a rhythm with each step.

However, as she found her stride, guilt crept into her thoughts. Was she being selfish, stealing away this precious Sunday for herself? She had convinced Gran, Douglas, and Tammy to take care of the girls for the day, coordinating their schedules to avoid disruptions to their Sunday plans. She had spent little time overthinking, and had hopped into her car, driving grimly to the starting point.

Inhaling deeply, she relished the crisp mountain air, now tinged with the coolness of autumn. The breeze played around her as she moved higher.

With each stone step, her breath grew heavier, and she

paused to consciously inhale more deeply, willing her lungs to open up. Nose blocked, head stuffy, and light-headedness swirling within her, she continued cautiously. She saluted people coming down from the mountain – red-faced and victorious – while she huffed and puffed.

Did she want that feeling? If she reached the top, would it make her happy or just more exhausted?

Gazing out across the hills on the horizon, glen after glen holding secrets, Jean contemplated the streams below, etched out like jagged sketches. It reminded her of a drawing Maggie had made, a detail she had noticed in her daughter's work. Maggie, creative and easily distracted, could never settle on something for long. Jean had once thought she might pursue writing herself. Reflecting on her own childhood, she remembered carrying her notebook everywhere, creating books for Gran with stapled bits of paper and brightly coloured crayon drawings on the covers. Yet, writing seemed juvenile as she grew older. What could she write that someone would want to read? Teaching studies took precedence, and her own writing became a seemingly pointless exercise.

Hesitating, she gazed at the haziness of the early morning light, recounting the people coming down from the mountain. If they could do it before dawn, surely she could reach the summit at her leisure? She unzipped her bag and produced her old portable cassette player and headphones. She'd discovered it at the back of her wardrobe, and as a lark took it. With new batteries securely in place, she pushed play and popped the headphones on. Miraculously, it played; her ears flooded with Pearl Jam. She laughed, shaking her head.

A few more hikers passed by, to whom she gave a small wave. A man and two women, one trailing behind with laboured breath, overtook her. "See you at the top!" the woman challenged with a smile over her shoulder.

Summoning energy with a final breath and a glance at the pink clouds grazing the hilltops, Jean marched on with determination, whispering to herself, “You will.”

25

Callum slammed the phone down, frustration bubbling within him like a simmering pot. His mother's audacity was almost laughable – inviting Jennifer and him to dinner? It had become a recurring joke, the blatant favouritism his parents showed his ex-wife over his beloved fiancée. But yet, they seemed oblivious to his past pain and his journey of moving on.

So, with a gracious tone, Callum had thanked his mother for the invitation and made it clear that he would only attend the dinner with Lori. The response he received was nothing but silence, followed by a curt goodbye. Callum clenched his teeth, his hands tightly gripping the chair next to his work desk.

He had already emphasised to his mother how unnecessary and unwarranted such an invitation was, especially since Lori hadn't received one. Callum, attempting to cover up their rudeness with excuses of busy schedules, found it hard to accept the reality – they favoured Jennifer over Lori. It was a detail he could never share with Lori; it would shatter her heart.

He did his best to shrug off the irritation, attempting to

label his parents' actions as irrational and illogical. Why would they welcome someone who had caused their own son so much heartache, especially when there was a profound love shared with Lori – love that was undeniably reciprocated?

His parents' behaviour remained an enigma, a puzzle he couldn't quite solve. They remained unimpressed with any achievements – sporting, travelling or starting his own business, it made no matter to them. They'd been expecting him to follow his father's footsteps – climbing the military ladder, adhering to their rigid expectations. But Lori had changed everything. When he met her in high school, she had liberated him from their stifling ways. He'd taken a chance, and refused to succumb to their stagnant existence, determined to lead a life of his choosing.

Glancing out of his office window, he spotted the honeymooners arriving in the carpark. Excitement bubbled within him. Every detail had been meticulously arranged for their stay, and the joy of the surprise they were about to unwrap brought a contented smile to his face. Champagne and delicate rose petals scattered on the bed awaited them, along with a hamper brimming with delightful tastes of the Highlands.

It seemed that beneath his composed exterior, a true romantic spirit was stirring within him after all.

Once he had led the couple to their final destination, his feet took him to a nearby hill, from where he could overlook the vast expanse of the sea. The salty breeze brushed against his face, and even from this distance, the scent of the sea lingered in the air. Callum felt a sense of liberation, as if the very essence of this place resonated within him. It ran through his veins, as essential as the blood that had soaked the land for generations. He couldn't deny the pull he felt, the deep knowing that he was meant to be here.

A soft chuckle escaped him as he pondered his evolving

nature. It appeared he was growing gentler in his old age, as well as having a romantic spirit. From his hilltop view, he glanced at the snug lodges nestled amid the rolling hills. Freshly planted trees and ancient streams wound their way towards the loch. Callum was proud of all his achievements, creating a new habitat, one that welcomed an abundance of birds, breathing life into a once-barren landscape. And it was not only that physical transformation that brought him joy; it was also the impact his lodges had on people. Guests left happy, their spirits soothed and their love for the Highlands deepened.

At the heart of Callum's view, Alan's van zoomed up the single-track road, trailing a swirl of dust. Callum trotted down the hill, eager to welcome his friend.

"Hi," Alan said, unloading tools from the back of the van, with an edge to his voice Callum was all too aware of. He unloaded an extension cable and grass cutters, keeping on top of all maintenance jobs so Callum didn't need to.

"Everything OK?" Callum shoved his hands in his pockets, rocking on his heels casually. He'd noticed over the last few days that his friend had become more inward.

"Yes, Cal. Can a man not just get on without everyone wanting something off him?" He looked Callum directly in the eye, throwing down more equipment.

With the frosty atmosphere, Callum decided to give him his privacy, retreating back to his office, a place that desperately needed his attention.

Dusty boxes had cluttered the space for far too long; it was high time to sort through paperwork, labelling invoices and creating order amidst the chaos. The scent of coffee and musty paper filled the air as he gulped down his third cup, fuelling his determination to restore his office to its former glory.

Immersed in his task, he unearthed a box that seemed

oddly placed. Amidst the clutter of forgotten trinkets, a familiar black velvet box revealed itself. His heart skipped a beat. Carefully, he opened it, revealing the engagement ring he had purchased for Lori years ago. Memories came rushing back, transporting him to a time when innocence and hope fuelled his dreams of a shared future. He vividly remembered showing the ring to Gran, the only person who had seen it before. How had it ended up here, buried amidst forgotten belongings? Had his memory failed him, or had he hastily stowed it away when Lori decided to leave Arlochy for good?

Gently, he traced the smooth band of the ring. He marvelled at how he had changed since those early days, shaped by the experiences that had moulded him into the man he had become. But one thing remained unwavering: his love for Lori. With a determined resolve, he closed the box, safely securing its precious contents. A broad grin spread across his face as he continued organising his office.

Alan's sudden appearance startled him and he sat up, reaching for the box containing the engagement ring. Excitement bubbled within him, eager to share his lucky find with a friend. However, as he presented the ring to Alan, he was met with a downcast and mournful expression. "What's wrong?" Callum asked.

Alan pressed his mouth, breathing through his nose heavily. "Are you sure about getting married, mate? I just don't think you've really thought it through."

Callum chuckled at Alan's solemn tone. "I've thought about it since I was a teenager!" he declared. "I think if I considered it any longer I'll be an old, decrepit man!"

Alan half-heartedly regarded the ring before closing the box with a shrug. "It's nice," he offered, the lack of enthusiasm not lost on Callum. He remembered a time when Alan had been more engaging, exciting, fun. Lately, he had grown more brusque than ever before.

"Let's hope Lori thinks as highly of it as you do," Callum quipped, trying to mask a pang of disappointment. Then, eyeing Alan, he gently probed, "Can I do something? You're not yourself."

Alan fidgeted with an uneven fingernail. "Look, it's nothing to do with here … the work is great."

Always seeking solutions, Callum suggested, "Maybe you should finish here earlier some days and spend more time with Rory—"

"Come on!" Alan cut him off, his voice edged with frustration. "Has Tammy started weaselling in your ear now? It's not enough that she's nagging me every time I am home, without going to my employer too!"

Callum quickly raised his hands defensively. "I don't know what you're talking about. Tammy hasn't said anything, I promise. I just thought …" He frowned. "And don't say that – I'm your pal, not your employer!"

Alan let out a scoff. "Well, my wages come from you every month! Or maybe I'm working for the other Callum Macrae, the better-looking, better-tempered Highlander on the other side of the loch!" He ran a hand over his head, the weight of his words lingering in the air.

With a frown, Callum remained in his seat, confused by the humour his friend had adopted.

"Marriage! Kids! None of it is easy. And if there's one thing that changes a woman, it's kids!" Alan sighed, leaning against the doorframe. "I just wished we hadn't got married sometimes … I feel ever since that happened, I've had a heavy noose around my neck."

"Jesus, man, what a thing to say!" Callum gasped, taken aback by Alan's sudden revelation.

"Look, it's fine … everything's fine." The side of his mouth twitched. "It's just not what I thought. I've never been so pushed and pulled. I feel responsibilities have taken over my life. I used to have fun. We used to have fun."

"We still have fun, Alan," Callum said, confused.

"I didn't mean you. I meant Tammy. She's not happy with anything I do. We used to have enough. Now I don't know if we'll ever have enough." Alan nodded and, without anything further to say, left.

Callum shifted uncomfortably in his seat. The moment of celebration he had hoped for had faded away, the sunset's warm hues now replaced by a shadow cast over their conversation. His mind raced, questioning everything. The uncertainty settled in his heart, knotting into a growing sense of unease.

As much as he wanted to believe in simplistic love, Alan's words lingered in his mind. He loved Lori deeply, but he couldn't help but wonder if history would repeat itself, and he'd make the same mistakes he had with Jennifer.

He gazed out the window, watching the van fade away, a sense of unease lingering in his chest.

26

It had been a somewhat busy day in the shop, and Lori found herself completely immersed in the whirlwind of planning for the upcoming Halloween fair. This time, unlike most local affairs, it wasn't her Gran who talked her into participating; it was entirely Lori's idea. She saw it as the perfect opportunity to put her mind elsewhere and, at the same time, promote her business during the slower months when the summer customers had dwindled.

As she flipped through the pages of her well-worn sketch-book, filled with countless designs and ideas, a tinge of uncertainty crept into her thoughts. The scent of cinnamon and pumpkin spice wafted through the air, courtesy of Rhona, who was energetically putting up Halloween decorations. Cobwebs adorned the shelves, and spooky figurines cast eerie shadows in the warm shop light.

"I'm not quite sure what to make … waistcoats, skirts, coats? Women's buying habits have declined of late – there seems to be no real rhyme or reason to it," Lori mused, her arm propping up her head.

Rhona, ever the lively spirit, scoffed playfully. "You're

mad to start organising anything else … you're getting married soon!"

"Not for a little while yet," Lori said defensively.

"Yeah, but in wedding terms, it's absolutely soon … have you booked the band? The catering?" Rhona raised an eyebrow, momentarily distracted by a cobweb stuck on her fingernail. She waved it around, trying to disentangle it from her person, but it draped around her like a festive garland on a Christmas tree. "You have more excitement on your plate than both of us put together!"

The background music filled the room. The singer's dulcet tone breathed, alongside a piano solo. Rhona closed her eyes and swayed gently, finally dispersing the cobweb and getting back to the window display. "I love this one." Her face gave little away apart from the curve of her lips. "It used to be Graham's favourite."

Lori noticed the subtle change in Rhona's demeanour whenever she mentioned Graham. Then, just as she was sure her friend was lost in a secret memory, Rhona blurted out abruptly, 'Oh ho! You know what … come to think of it … I lost my virginity to this song!' Her cheeks reddened.

Lori asked curiously, "Where?"

"At my house. Mum was away for something in the city, and Karen was at a friend's, I think. We were at a party, the one where Callum serenaded you on the beach. I remember being a little jealous at the time, Callum giving you that undivided attention. I wanted to be in love, and Graham made the effort … he lit candles around my room, put on music," Rhona explained, her face growing darker shades of red.

Lori chuckled, teasing her friend. "Well, I'm shocked … Callum's singing skills turned you on, Rhona!"

"Hey!" Rhona playfully hit Lori on the arm. "Callum is a good-un, but never my cup of tea. Sorry. But I liked how he opened up for you. I wanted that. And I guess I got it with Graham."

"You guess?" Lori grinned, intrigued to know more.

"Well, it was my first time, it's not the most pleasurable time for a girl," Rhona admitted.

Lori understood; her first time with Callum had been similar, but their connection grew stronger over time and so did their lovemaking.

Rhona twirled a pen in her fingers. "That was the only time we …" She raised her eyebrows suggestively, before playfully popping the pen in her mouth, earning a knowing look from Lori.

"I can't help but wonder … what he'd be like now." Rhona sighed, clearly lost in memories.

"Rhona!" Lori laughed, slightly shocked by her friend's openness.

"I know, but that strong chest of his, those arms … he could pick me up and spin me around without me knowing it!" she admitted with a dreamy smile.

"You're a married woman!"

"Don't I know that! To a grumpy farmer who only wants a few Guinnesses at the weekend and a good fart in bed afterward," Rhona exclaimed, making a comical face that made Lori burst into laughter. "You think I'm joking?" Rhona's eyes widened incredulously. "The romance of marriage is so much more interesting than what the reality holds."

"Don't try to talk me out of it when I'm almost in the wives club!"

"Ew!" Rhona screwed up her nose. "Don't say that again; you make it sound like I belong to a cult."

"Well, you know what I mean!" Lori shushed her friend. "I'm happy and comfortable to marry Callum."

"Hmmm." Rhona frowned. "Not really what you wanna hear when someone says why they want to marry you!"

"Rhona! Be quiet! Stop trying to make me doubt!"

"Doubt is healthy." Rhona examined her friend with an inquisitive look and flicked her hand. "I'm just saying, us women change … men don't! Or if they do change, they just get progressively grumpy and quiet." Rhona sighed, playing with a spool of beige thread. "Graham was exciting. I loved who I was then." She threw the thread into a nearby sewing box filled with a rainbow of colours.

Lori bit her lip, not wanting to hear anymore. She knew Rhona was just expressing her thoughts, but wedding doubts were the last thing she wanted to deal with right now. "Are you being serious? Are you having doubts?"

"It's a bit too late for me to have doubts … I already married the guy!" Rhona snorted, then reflected. "No, not really serious. Just been thinking a lot. You know our youngest is starting school soon and it just made me think … I'll have more time to be with Malcolm. I could make more of an effort …" Her red lips twitched nervously. "But then I realised … I don't think I want to. Everything is so doom and gloom over there." She nodded her head in the direction of her home, which was a short ferry trip from the end of the pier. "If it's not about the cows needing milking, vaccinations, or calving, then it's the accounts! Malcolm is so stressed all the time! Sometimes I think if his father didn't leave him the farm we'd be so much happier." She wrung her hands. "I want to be wooed; Malcolm doesn't know the meaning of the word. And for a time, I was happy with it. But now …" She sighed. "It wasn't like that with Graham; he made me feel so—"

Before Rhona could say anything more, Jennifer entered the shop, interrupting their heart-to-heart conversation.

"Hi, are you ready to have coffee?" Jennifer said cheerfully, zipping up her grey speckled top, but Lori noticed her pulling at the sleeves.

Rhona opened her mouth, taken aback, but quickly replaced it with a flash of a smile. "Well, hello. You two are getting along, then?"

Jennifer grinned uncomfortably.

"OK, Rhonz," Lori muttered, picking up her handbag and following Jennifer out of the shop. She took her to the hotel on the hill, as far away as she could be from locals gossiping, but in these parts, there was never a guarantee, and Lori grimaced as she trudged up the steep hill. Lately, she had let her yoga and runs slip, consumed by wedding preparations. Each time she discussed plans with the wedding planner, a new problem arose. If it wasn't decoration limitations or uncertainty about hotel accommodations, it was getting hold of the planners and keeping communication smooth. Lori had been dealing with multiple people at this stage and was becoming more and more anxious about the impending day.

Picking up on her mood, Jennifer asked how wedding preparations were going, but Lori quickly changed the subject.

"How long are you going to stay?" Lori asked, a little too abruptly, but Jennifer smiled.

"A little longer. I have some loose ends to tie up." Her eyes focused on Lori as they sat in the hotel, comfortably seated. They remained still even as their waitress placed coffee and slabs of vanilla cake on the table

"But you have a family? Children waiting on your return, surely? What could make you stay here all this time?" Lori frowned, still annoyed at the whole situation even if she tried to conceal it.

"My family is fine. I need to do this, before anything else happens."

"What?" Lori laughed. "Jennifer, we've put you up in a lodge for weeks now, you and Callum are barely talking, you have a family on the other side of the world, and you're determined to stay here?" She couldn't help but shout; this whole situation was far from simple.

"I have legal matters to attend to, but Lori, you're right," Jennifer said softly.

"Legal matters? Why?"

"Never mind that. I have seen Callum this morning."

"Well that's nice, because I haven't," Lori sniped. She had woken early, determined to get to the shop.

"I needed to know it was safe here, that it was the right decision …" Jennifer trailed off, biting her lip and gazing out the window.

Lori followed her eyes. The harsh, bright white clouds were impenetrable, and the odd seagull floated, gliding on the strong wind currents. Lori couldn't quite see the sea at this angle, but it was there, down below the hill, where the little town of Morvaig grew sleepier as the weeks passed, dragging them into colder winter months.

"Callum and I have more history than you know. The truth is … well, we have a son," Jennifer revealed, her voice heavy with emotion.

The words hung in the air, a weighty silence enveloping their table. The distant clatter of dishes in the kitchen and the faint strains of a pop song on the radio were the only sounds that punctuated the stillness.

Lori's heart pounded in her chest as the weight of Jennifer's words sank in. Her mind racing, she stood up, deteriorated, feeling as if the eyes of the few patrons in the restaurant were on them. This was too much to process in a public place.

"Lori, please sit down," Jennifer implored, but Lori was too stunned to move. Her body felt like it was made of lead, anchoring her hand to the chair while her mind was in turmoil.

Numbly, she finally lowered back down onto her seat.

“I didn’t know how to tell you, but I couldn’t hide it any longer,” Jennifer continued. “You see, my partner and I have been going through a rocky patch, and I needed to understand how Callum’s life was over here if our son needed him, that he’d be there for him.”

The confusion inside Lori only intensified, and her heart ached with the betrayal she felt. “This is insane!” she shook her head in disbelief. “Why are you saying this now? Are you trying to break us up before the wedding? After we took you in, is this how you repay us?”

“No, I don’t mean to break up your wedding, Lori,” Jennifer responded, her voice attempting to soothe the tension. “But I needed to come before things changed, to decide if Callum and his son should know each other.”

Lori’s mind whirled as she struggled to process everything Jennifer was saying. “Wait, does Callum know he has a son?” she asked, desperate for some clarity.

“He does now. I told him this morning,” Jennifer admitted.

That was the final straw. Lori couldn’t bear to listen to any more of Jennifer’s smooth words and manipulative explanations. She stood up, her chair scraping against the floor, and walked away without looking back. She didn’t want to hear Jennifer’s pleas or excuses. She needed to find Callum and sort this mess out.

As she stomped down the hill, her heart pounded in her chest. Her throat tightened, and she swallowed but to no avail. Jennifer’s words sat on her. Heavy. Cold. Uneasiness gripped her. She knew in her gut that everything was about to change.

27

Tammy paced the living room, trying to keep herself composed as Rory sat on the floor, engrossed in a children's TV show that she had just put on as a desperate distraction. She couldn't stand the annoying girl's piercing tones, but anything was better than hearing another round of "Old MacDonald Had a Farm" for the umpteenth time.

Frustration boiled inside her as she checked her phone once again. She had sent Alan countless texts and tried phoning multiple times, and yet he still hadn't shown up. Time was ticking, and Tammy was now officially late for work. She clenched her teeth, suppressing the urge to scream. Was she going to go through this every time she was about to start her shift?

Glancing at the time on her phone screen, she knew there was no other choice. She had to take Rory with her. After leaving a note on the kitchen table and sending Alan one final text, she bundled Rory into his car seat. He seemed happy to go on an adventure with Mummy.

When Tammy walked into the bar, she was relieved to find it relatively quiet, with its usual patrons sitting on their usual bar stools. Kirsty appeared soon after, a tea towel in her hand, her face flushed. She regarded Rory with disdain and raised an eyebrow at Tammy disapprovingly.

"What's all this? You can't bring a baby in here!" she scolded.

"Don't you worry, Kirsty. It's none of your concern," Tammy tried to soothe, but her tone came off as condescending.

"It is my concern! It's in the workplace," Kirsty retorted, placing her hands on her hips.

Tammy could feel the girl's heart race from a distance away, her face getting redder by the second and her forehead sweating. "It's just until Alan shows up. He's running late. You won't notice Rory."

"I think I will!" she scoffed. "And anyway, it's the rules – health and safety means no children—" Kirsty sucked her teeth, and rocked on her heels like a major ordering a platoon.

"Enough!" Tammy snapped, her frustration reaching its peak as she became acutely aware that the three customers, Terry, Agnes, and old Stuart, were thoroughly entertained by the drama unfolding before them. They seemed more interested in watching the barmaids' confrontation than the TV sitcom that played on the screen above the bar.

Kirsty stormed off in the direction of the empty reception, leaving Tammy worried she might make a call to escalate the situation. This was the last thing she needed. How had everything become so hostile and complicated?

Agnes, sensing the tension, offered to take care of Rory, giving Tammy a chance to run after Kirsty.

Agnes's husband hesitated beside her, his face crumpling into a concerned frown. But she swung to life, hopping off her bar stool and scooping up the little boy.

When Tammy found Kirsty with the phone receiver pressed to her ear, she marched over, grabbed it and slammed it down, her anger boiling over. “What is the matter with you?” she shouted, unable to contain her emotions any longer. “Why are you always acting like such a bitch? Whatever did I do to you, Kirsty?”

Kirsty’s mouth twitched with an air of defiance. “You don’t take any of this seriously, Tammy. You look down your nose at all of us.”

“I don’t!” Tammy tried to defend herself, but her thoughts were tangled, and she struggled to find the right words. The truth was that she didn’t feel comfortable in her old life anymore, and she couldn’t fit back into it as seamlessly as she hoped. It was like one of Rory’s puzzles that she continually cleared away, his attempts at moving the pieces that didn’t quite fit.

“Why are you trying to sabotage me? Just be a bit friggin’ nicer, Kirsty!” Tammy shouted, her hand slapping down on the reception desk.

“I am nice. You just never took the time to get to know me!” Kirsty retorted.

Tammy let out a groan of exasperation. “I don’t have the time for anything these days, let alone pussyfooting around you! Just lighten up, girl!” She placed her hands on her hips, her frustration showing.

In that instant, Alan emerged at the counter, the backdrop framed by postcards from past visitors, a detail Tammy had overlooked from this angle until now. “Now you decide to show up!” A surge of rage, unfamiliar and intensified, coursed through her. Despite the temptation to unleash her fury on him, especially with Kirsty present, she resisted, wary of providing fodder for gossip. Instead, she ushered Alan into the pub, determined to keep a semblance of composure.

Agnes was in the backbar, supporting Rory’s hands, leading him around the faded paisley-print carpet. The little boy wobbled, trying to keep his balance, and then with determination went towards the step up to the restaurant area. Tammy watched as he raised his leg slowly, balancing on the step and dragging his other foot behind him.

Not realising everyone was watching, Agnes turned back. "Oh! Is everything alright?"

"Grand, Agnes. You have quite a way with kids!" Alan replied, trying to mask the tension between him and Tammy. He turned to old Stuart and Terry. "Might as well stay for one before we hit the hay!" He settled into Agnes's chair. "I'll have a pint, Tammy," he said, placing a crumpled note on the counter.

Tammy frowned. "Alan, Rory needs sleep. He needs a bath, then straight to bed." She stared at him incredulously.

"He's grand – look, Agnes is looking after him!"

Agnes giggled, perched on the step, holding one of Rory's hands. She stroked his red hair affectionately as he rubbed his eyes, showing signs of tiredness.

"No. It's time for his bed. You were late, Alan. You need to take him home. Now!" Tammy's voice sliced through the air, an edge of steel beneath her firm tone.

To Tammy's relief, Alan scooped up Rory. A tense hush fell over the room as he balanced Rory on his arm and exited without a glance back at Tammy. The charged silence lingered, echoing the palpable tension that hung between them. Things were definitely not good. Not one little bit.

* * *

Tammy parked a little further away from her terraced house that night and walked home in the dark, hoping everyone was in bed and needing the cold air to clear her head. She slowly let herself in, taking off her shoes and padding quietly down the hall, suppressing the desire to look at Rory in bed. But when she arrived in the kitchen, she needn't have bothered to make the effort. Alan's large frame sat at the small kitchen table, his bulk spilling over it as if it were child-size. He drank from a can of lager and watched her intently.

"I thought you'd be in bed," she said, trying to keep her voice steady. She threw her handbag over a chair and shimmied off her raincoat, trying to focus on the mundane task of doing the dishes.

Silence greeted her, and Alan remained rigid in his seat. Tammy sighed to herself and ploughed into washing, wiping, rinsing, and stacking. Alan had never been too interested in housework. The only thing he contributed was making dinner, but since Rory came along, she had taken on the role of a full-time cook. Maybe just as well, she reminisced. He would make such a mess, leaving her with a mountain of dishes to clean up as he drank most of a bottle of wine and played computer games into the night. Although it hadn't bothered her then, it bothered her now.

"I didn't appreciate that behaviour tonight, Tam."

Tammy spun around, her hands gripping the metal basin.

"How you spoke to me in front of everyone. You showed me no respect. After everything I've done for us, and you act like that." He raised his can, his head turned away from her.

"What do you mean? What, the three local drunks at the pub, and Kirsty?" Tammy scoffed.

"That's a bit harsh, isn't it? You liked them. And poor Agnes looking after Rory while you were having some spat with the waitress?" He turned to face her, the muscles tightening around his mouth and nose.

"Kirsty was trying to get me into trouble. She has always hated me. She was about to call the owner and dob me in!"

Alan appeared not to be listening. "It made me think. Perhaps we could get Agnes to babysit? Maybe on the nights you're at the pub?" He pushed his chair back, the sound ripping through Tammy's nerves, convinced it would wake Rory up.

She shook her head, knowing that as nice as Agnes was, she wasn't comfortable having her watch Rory. For many reasons she couldn't put into words, it was a firm no, and she voiced it immediately to Alan.

"It was just an idea. But we could use more help."

"Your parents!" Tammy whispered. "I just wish you'd ask them, rather than leave it to me every time. Don't they want to spend more time with their grandson?"

"We can't expect them to look after Rory, he's a bit of a handful … they're old. I don't want them to feel they have to."

"He's their grandson! You'd be happy for me to ask an alcoholic with underlying depression, but not your parents?" Tammy blinked, folding her arms. "You've gone mad."

"Stop speaking to me like that."

"Like what?" She turned her back to him and started stacking dishes.

"Like I am something revolting to you. You've …" he stuttered. "You've been mean, commenting on everything I do, sniping at what I say, you won't let me touch you."

"The only time you touch me is when you want to have sex, Alan," she snapped, but did not look at him.

"That's not true."

"It is." She felt him suddenly close behind her, his breath on her neck, but nothing more. With determination, she snatched a towel from the counter and began drying a pot. She spun around, calling after his retreating back. "You don't value me in what I do! You think my time is not important. You won't even show up on time so I can go to work! Do you think I want to serve a bunch of drunks until the early hours? No, but we need money to pay this mortgage off!" she shouted, then covered her mouth, her eyes wide. She stood still, waiting for the sharp cries from Rory.

But nothing surfaced. She breathed out with relief.

Alan stayed by the hallway door, his hand soft punching its frame. "Tammy, I don't mind what you do. Just do something that makes you happy." He shook his head. "I'm sick of whatever is going on here. You've been acting crazy, controlling even."

"Someone's got to keep on top of things – if I left it to you, Rory wouldn't be fed and he'd be going to bed at midnight!"

He scoffed quietly. "If you just saw yourself …" He shook his head again, turning to leave.

"What, Alan? Tell me."

"You've turned into such a nag. What does it matter if Rory might miss the odd nap, or get his dinner thirty minutes later one evening? He'll survive. What I just worry about is that *we* won't." He turned on his heel and left. Tammy heard him switch out their bedroom light and the creak of their bed, signalling their conversation was over. She clenched her hands together, her fingernails digging into her palms. How she wanted to scream there in the kitchen. To kick or punch something, to relieve herself as men would do. But she wasn't a man. Instead, she picked up his empty can of lager, threw it in the bin, and wiped the table.

Just when she switched out the lights, her phone vibrated, startling her.

> "Callum didn't come home today. Something is wrong, I don't know what to do."

It was Lori. Tammy reread the message again. Given the late hour, she knew Lori wouldn't have texted if there wasn't some real concern. Without any further contemplation, she left a note on the kitchen table, and texted Alan's phone, knowing he wouldn't look at it until morning. She left the house in the middle of the night, hopping back into her car, leaving Alan to his fathering duties for once. When she started up the engine, she considered that perhaps Lori and Callum had had a fight too. Lori had once helped Tammy, intervening between her and Alan, for which Tammy had thanked her at the time. But now, she couldn't help but feel … if she hadn't married Alan, would she be this unhappy?

Gazing out at the sudden mist that surrounded the car, she switched on the fog lights and slowly directed her car towards Lori's house, leaving behind whatever problems she had with Alan.

28

Jean's eyes adjusted to her phone's blue-screen lighting up. She had drifted off to sleep during a movie, her feet propped up on the couch, still holding a half-empty mug of cold tea. She snatched the phone off the coffee table.

> "Callum didn't come home today. Something is wrong, I don't know what to do."

She put her mug down, allowing the words to wash over her. It was late, very late. The girls had been tucked up in bed hours ago, and her evening had been uneventful, apart from the series of plans she was making for her next hike. The recent triumph of conquering Ben Nevis had already faded into insignificance.

As she fumbled to call Lori, a sense of urgency enveloped her. Straight to voicemail. Panic set in. She glanced at the clock; time was a luxury they couldn't afford. The realisation struck her like lightning – she needed help, and she needed it fast.

Douglas, was her next instinct. She dialled his number,

desperation growing with each ring. Silence. He must be sleeping. Frustration boiled within her. Damn it.

Seated on the edge of the couch, she bit her already short nails, a teenage habit resurfacing under the stress of the moment. She needed to act, an emergency unfolding, but the solution wasn't clear.

A mental debate raged within her – was it fair to call Karen at this ungodly hour? An emergency, she reasoned. She dialled, the phone rang, and Jean felt a mix of relief and guilt as Karen's gentle voice filled her ear.

"Hello, Jean? Are you OK?"

"I am," Jean replied, the somersaults in her stomach increasing. "Karen, I'm so sorry to call you at this hour."

"It's fine," Karen reassured her, the faint sounds of the TV in the background. "I was just watching a stupid movie."

Jean thought of Karen lying on the couch, mirroring her exactly this evening. Perhaps even watching the same show on TV. It was hard to imagine that she was in the same town, in her mother's house, only a few minutes away by car.

"Are you going to tell me what's wrong?" Karen asked calmly, and all Jean wanted was to sit and talk with her again, for her stress over the recent months to melt away.

"I think something's happened to Callum. I can't be sure, but Lori texted me. Something isn't right—"

"You want me to mind the girls?" Karen said at once.

"Yes," Jean breathed, a weight lifting from her.

"I'll be over as quickly as possible." She hung up, and Jean made up an overnight bag. The gravity of the situation pressed on her; her instincts told her this was no ordinary night. When Karen arrived, her kind eyes met Jean's, reassuring her that she had made the right decision to call her after all. Jean wasted no time in getting into her car, hoping her girls wouldn't wake until morning, saving confusion that

Karen was there. Hopefully, she would be back by then, and everything would be cleared up.

* * *

When Jean parked at Lori's, she breathed out with relief. Fog had followed her on the short journey, but had kept its distance to allow her the courage to keep driving rather than park up on the side of the road. Tammy's small car was abandoned in the middle of the drive. *Typical Tammy,* Jean thought. Even in these times, her younger sister didn't think of others, making Jean park in a muddy section.

She traipsed up to the house in the dark, clinging on to the wooden railing to guide her. She climbed the steps with such ease, amazing her past self, who usually would be out of puff at the top. She barged through the door to find Tammy handing Lori a cup of hot chocolate, Lori's head resting on her hand as she leaned against the breakfast counter. The atmosphere was pensive, quiet, much like a room of students waiting to take a test. Jean smoothed her hand over Lori's shoulder and gently rubbed her back, like Gran or their mother used to do when they were upset. Tammy grimaced beside them, pouring Jean a mug too. She produced a handful of tiny marshmallows, sprinkling them on top, before Jean could refuse. She had been against sugar, particularly at night, but as Lori remained slumped under Jean's touch, she may need the extra energy after all.

Had Tammy even bothered to ask Lori about the cause of this upheaval? A glance was exchanged between them, but Tammy's shrugged response only deepened Jean's concern.

"Is Callum still missing?" Jean asked. It was time for the details; they couldn't sit in silence while their middle sister kept her secrets.

Lori nodded.

"Did you have a fight?" Jean probed.

She shook her head.

Jean frowned. "You didn't have a fight? And you can't get hold of him? There could be lots of reasons, perhaps he's out with Alan?" Jean shot Tammy a look. Her younger sister shook her head. What was it with people not answering questions? Her students were the same, never making eye contact and slumping down in their chairs. No one appreciated her, no one even listened.

"She said she's called everyone, no one's seen him," Tammy offered, her eyes downcast.

Jean scanned the room, not sure if looking for clues or for something to do as her mind caught up. A shelving unit with books and framed photos grabbed her attention. Callum diving underwater next to orange angelfish, him atop some snowy mountain wearing sunglasses, Lori and him cuddling on a tropical beach. They had experienced a lot together. Callum was more active compared to most men, unlike Douglas, who played the odd game of football with his mates and spent more time in the pub with them after.

"He's not out drinking? Maybe with the shinty lads?" Jean offered, a desperate attempt to rationalise the situation.

Lori remained silent, and Tammy's headshake only deepened Jean's frustration. Communication, a skill she thought she had mastered, felt elusive in this moment.

"If you've tried everyone, and you feel something's off, then we better contact the police?" she suggested, her mind already on the next course of action.

"She has," Tammy interjected, providing a voice to Lori's subdued mumbles.

Waiting for an explanation, Jean sipped the hot chocolate, and immediately her body tingled with pleasure. The sweet marshmallows blended into dark chocolatey tones, and she drank deeply. The untouched cup in Lori's hands spoke volumes, her focus on the beach photo Jean had been admiring earlier.

"Well what did they say?" Jean pressed, her gaze fixed on Lori.

Lori slowly rose, picked up the framed picture, and spoke hesitantly, revealing a layer of vulnerability Jean hadn't seen before. "They will keep a lookout; they're going to drive around to see if they can find him or anything … suspicious."

"Suspicious?"

"I don't know, Jean! I have asked everyone, called the police, I've been told he should come home, to sit tight and wait for him. But they don't want to know that I know something is wrong. Callum wouldn't do that; he wouldn't keep quiet. He keeps in touch; he doesn't just go missing."

"Who was the last person to see him? You?"

Lori sighed. "No, it was Jennifer."

"Right." Jean pulled out her phone. "Perhaps she knows where he's gone. What did she say they spoke about?"

"Please don't, Jean. I can't talk to her. She's the reason for all this; I can't." Lori's voice grew louder. "He's out there because she used both of us. She has been conniving on so many levels; Callum was right the whole time." Lori slammed her palm down uncharacteristically on the table, her other hand still clutching the photo frame.

"Lori, I'm sorry you have to go through this," Jean approached her sister, resting a hand on her shoulder, hesitating at first. "But you must tell us; only then can we really help."

"You can't help, it's done. All I need is Callum," Lori declared, folding her arms as she faced her sisters. She let out a weary sigh before continuing, "But I guess you better know, before it becomes local gossip."

* * *

Jean and Tammy exchanged a startled glance as Lori's revelation hung in the air. Feeling a surge of responsibility, Jean adjusted her position, planting her feet firmly on the floor. Her mind raced, each detail a puzzle piece in the unfolding mystery. Callum a father?

"OK, well, we need more answers," Jean declared, rolling up her sleeves with determination. "I am going to see Jennifer, speak with her directly. She's here, isn't she? In one of the lodges?" Gathering up her coat and opening her rucksack, she pulled out her flashlight.

Tammy's frown deepened, her hand protective over Lori's. "You can't go there at this time. It's pitch-black outside … the fog! Don't you think she's done enough? What's she going to say that will help us? Lori said she saw him in the morning – he's been gone since then!"

Ignoring Tammy's apprehension, Jean clicked on her flashlight. "Yes, but we can't stay here and wait, can we?"

To Jean's surprise, Lori slowly turned towards her, her grip tightening on the framed photo, but her gaze fixated on her elder sister. "You're right," Lori admitted, her voice edged with determination as she bit her lower lip. "I don't want to waste any more time. We must try."

29

Thick fog enveloped them as they ventured into the unknown, their torchlight piercing the darkness. Lori stuck to the familiar gravel path, keeping in front until they reached the turnoff, where a little green door awaited. Tapping on it, her insides turned like she was in a giant washing machine. The wind had picked up, swirling around them, as if it couldn't decide whether to encourage or deter their quest for answers at Jennifer's lodge.

Slowly, the door creaked open, revealing Jennifer's face blinking at Jean's torchlight. Red, puffy eyes betrayed Jennifer's recent sleep, yet she didn't seem angered by their unexpected arrival. Instead, an anticipatory air surrounded her, as if she had expected their visit. She stepped aside, allowing them to enter the warm and dimly lit living room.

Huddled on the small couch, they sought solace. Jennifer, despite the tension, moved gracefully around the room, casting soft glows with various lamps to dispel the darkness. Yawning, she draped a thick grey dressing gown over her shoulders, tying it securely around her waist.

Despite the situation, Jennifer's nurturing side emerged. She clicked on the kettle, its comforting hum filling the room as she poured tea into four mugs, adding milk and a touch of honey without asking. Lori observed the familiar gestures of a mother, sensing their needs and offering a soothing balm in the midst of turmoil.

Lori clasped her hands together. "Callum hasn't come home. I haven't seen him all day, and he won't answer his phone."

Understanding the gravity, Jennifer clicked her tongue, pouring tea to ease the tension. The room echoed with the sound of sipping tea as they collected their thoughts. Lori's eyes remained fixed on Jennifer, searching for any hint or clue.

Finally, Jennifer confessed, "We had a fight. I shouldn't have let it happen, but he stormed off. I'm sorry about this, Lori. I wanted to speak with you both at the same time, but you were never together when I needed to talk. I couldn't find the time or the words before."

Seated by the log burner, Jennifer, in her dressing gown, ran her fingers through her blonde hair, her gaze fixed on the fire. "He was at his van. He wouldn't come for a coffee or invite me in. He seemed a bit stressed already."

"Did he say where he was going?" Jean asked, crossing her arms, her cup remaining on the coffee table untouched.

Jennifer, eyes fixed on the last log burning, absentmindedly threw sticks into the fire. "After I told him, he wouldn't look at me. He hopped in his van and left. I wouldn't have said anything, Lori, but he didn't want to talk. I needed to tell him. I had to start planning what I was going to do – I need to book a flight home. I need to see my kids."

Lori's hands tightened together, her palms sticky and damp.

"Is this unusual for him? Has he not done this before? Goes away to sort out his thoughts?" Jennifer frowned.

"No, never!" Lori shook her head quickly. "He tells me

everything," she said forcefully, yet her mind raced back to any previous misgivings between them. Had he done this before? When they were going through a rough patch the previous year, and his time spent at Francesca's.

Could he be there now, confiding in his old friend instead of his fiancée?

Jennifer merely shrugged, her expression inscrutable.

"Did he do this when *you* were together?" Lori hesitated before asking, cautious of venturing into unknown territory. She didn't want to acknowledge that Callum had led a whole other life before her. She wished he hadn't, but like her, he had lived, loved, and come back to her.

It was her who had left, after all.

"We didn't have a smooth marriage," Jennifer admitted, her mouth slightly drawn to one side. "We quarrelled and needed time apart before we made back up."

Lori tried to clear her mind, but the image of Callum and Jennifer wrapped around each other, engaging in "makeup sex" emerged in her thoughts. Jealousy simmered just under the exterior, and she struggled to understand why she couldn't let go of his past.

Steering herself back, Lori refocused on the present situation. "Did he say where he was going?" she asked, echoing Jean's earlier question, while Tammy finished her tea, setting the mug on the glass coffee table with a loud clang.

Jennifer shook her head.

"Did you see what was in his van?" she asked instead.

Jennifer blinked, her mouth slightly agape. "What?"

"In his van," Lori clarified. "When he left, did you see what he had in there?"

Jennifer closed her eyes, recollecting their last encounter. "Well, tools … I think there was a box of tools. Lots of clothes," she recalled. "A life jacket … and a surfboard."

Jean turned sharply to Lori. “Could he have gone surfing? Does he do that?”

Lori shrugged. “He does it from time to time, but I went to the beach, and I couldn’t see his van.”

“Well, perhaps we try again.” Without waiting, Jean stood up, followed by Lori and Tammy, leaving Jennifer huddled by the fire, her face pale even against the warm firelight.

They hastened along the path, the first light of dawn tingeing the landscape, dispersing the night's darkness.

Lori stopped in her tracks as she reached the top of the hill, gazing out at the distant isles standing against the dull light. A heaviness fell over her. Jennifer’s words lingered in her mind. Had she and Callum not spent enough time together? They were getting married, but their careers had consumed them both, leaving little room for each other. Wasn’t that normal?

Callum hadn’t been as involved with the wedding preparations as Lori would have liked, but she had taken charge. She was planning it, and any little detail she wanted his approval on, she would run it past him. He had been content with that arrangement, and so had she. Or had she?

Now, with the news of a son, everything felt uncertain. The wedding might need to be canceled. How could they navigate through this? Another obstacle pushing their relationship against hurt, pain, lies, and deceit. This had not been part of Lori’s plan. She had devoted her time to her business, intending to marry Callum and then have children. She had made up her mind; it was how she wanted things to be. But now, it all seemed as if she were adrift at sea again, except this time, instead of Callum being her anchor, she had nothing to hold on to.

Jean squeezed Lori’s arm, pulling her back to the present, and led her back to the house.

Tammy, engrossed in her phone, stood by the door behind

them. She nervously bit her lip before speaking, "That was Gran on the phone. I've been messaging her tonight, keeping her updated on things."

Lori groaned. "Tam, I didn't want to stress her out, especially not in her condition."

"She needed to know." Tammy defended herself. "She thinks of Callum as family. I told her what Jennifer had said."

"We're going to the beach now. Perhaps he went there after I checked earlier," Lori said determinedly.

Tammy grimaced. "OK, but Gran said if he went surfing, he probably went to the western tip."

Lori stared at Tammy in horror. "No, he wouldn't do that. He knows that's where Mum and Dad ..." She trailed off, her voice cracking. "No, he wouldn't do that," she repeated. "He told me we'd never go there again. He promised me."

Tammy nodded, her expression solemn. "Gran said he surfs there from time to time." She added softly, "Gran swims there too."

Time seemed to slow down for Lori. The words Tammy had spoken, the look Jean gave her, and the ground beneath her feet all merged into a blur. The weight of everything became too much, and before she knew it, consciousness slipped away, and she crumpled to the ground.

30

Woozy from her fall, Lori arrived at the western tip, her head resting on the car window. She watched the unfolding scene as she squinted; bright, flashing lights filled the beach – the coastguard boat bobbing on the waves, the sharp, white beam of the helicopter scanning the sea, and police cars parked on the sand. Gran was there, engaged in conversation with a policeman, Lawrence's arm wrapped reassuringly around her. The fog glided over the water like a blanket slipping off a bed.

Unsteadily stepping over the soft sand, Lori made her way toward the blue light.

Gran opened her arms, but Lori didn't embrace her. Instead, she approached the policeman, her anger intensifying. It had been over an hour since the services had responded, but there was still no sign of Callum, or so the policeman gently informed her. Rocking on his heels, wrapped in a bright yellow coat that accentuated his thick build, he stood amidst the scene. Police tape cordoned off Callum's van, parked so close to the sand that Lori worried the sea might reclaim it.

Lori left Gran, Jean, and Tammy to talk, while Lawrence

hovered nearby. Lori wished he would give them space. This was a family matter, and he had no history or real connection with any of them. Recounting the day's events with him held no appeal for Lori; she had no energy for it. Scanning the horizon, she realised she hadn't seen this view for years. After vowing to herself never to return to this very shoreline that took her parents, she found herself again surrounded by police and coastguards. Now, instead of grappling with the sea to retrieve her parents, would she face a similar ordeal with Callum? All she could do was pray that no ambulance would be summoned to carry away another lifeless body. She had seen that once before, and the memory haunted her.

She tried to distract herself with the salty sea spray on her lips. However, it did little to quell the hot tears streaming down her face.

"My Lolo." Gran appeared behind her, wearing a cream beret and a long tweed cape. "Are you OK?" She opened her arms, but Lori couldn't bring herself to embrace her. Gran, once a source of comfort, had changed. Lori had redirected her desire for motherly love away from Gran, investing it in herself and Callum. Gran had moved on, and Lori had done the same. She needed to rely on herself, and she had started to.

She remained fixed to the spot, her body rigid, waiting to hear any news about Callum. The hurt on Gran's face was evident, but it paled in comparison to the turmoil Lori felt inside. She turned her face back to the sea, desperately searching for any sign of him, her heart heavy with uncertainty.

Gran stayed behind Lori as the family stayed at a distance. The roaring sea drowned out everything – the hum of the police car, the boat crashing over the swells, the helicopter overhead. Lori let the water's roar block out all other noise. She felt the waves inch closer, spilling onto her shoes.

Standing there, unmoving, she wondered if she could strike a deal with the sea to release Callum. Could she bargain with the waves and tide, as if making a pact with a mythical creature from the deep?

"I'm sorry, Lori," Gran said beside her.

Lori remained silent, her eyes fixed on the speedboat along the far shoreline, waves crashing over rocks.

"You're mad with me, and you have every right to be. I deserve it," Gran continued.

Without a word, Lori removed her shoes and socks, rolling them up carefully and placing them on the sand. Squinting at the boat, she walked forward, the sea swallowing her feet. Gran followed, trying to reach out, but Lori shrugged her off.

"I can't look at you right now," Lori said.

Silent sobs came from her grandmother, but Lori couldn't bear to listen. She wanted to escape, to untangle herself from Gran's emotions, to be anywhere but on this beach, where she feared hearing the devastating news that her world had been shattered before it had even begun. She felt cursed, destined never to find happiness while those around her enjoyed laughter, family, and purpose.

Gran's sniffles reverberated behind her, fuelling Lori's rising fury. She spun around, her voice desperate. "You have to leave me, Gran, right now! Please, leave me!"

"We need to be together. I am your grandmother. I am always here for you," Gran pleaded, wiping her nose with a tissue and tucking it under her sleeve. Gran's once towering presence seemed to shrink before her.

"You are not here. Not anymore," Lori declared flatly. "You are living a new life. You've decided you want to spend your remaining years with someone else. We don't matter to you now."

"That's not true." Gran stood straighter but was still

smaller than Lori. "You are the most important thing in my life. You're my family."

Lori walked away, and Gran followed.

"It's not enough that you've been keeping secrets from me; now you can't let me grieve alone! Leave me, Gran!" Lori's face flushed with anger.

Her gran frowned. "You are not going to grieve. We are going to find Callum."

"Gran, do you really think they're going to find him after hours in that water?" she erupted. "He's gone, just like Mum and Dad. Everyone goes. And you both made it a little secret joke between you and him. Coming here without telling me! Knowing how dangerous I said it was! But you both came anyway!"

"It's not any more dangerous here than any other shoreline along these parts, Lori," Gran said desperately.

"But still, you couldn't help yourselves. You wanted to laugh behind my back. Well, this is what happens – someone gets killed! Was it worth it, Gran? Mum, Dad, now Callum? Still want to come out here swimming?" Lori spat out the words.

Gran's eyes searched Lori's, and she grabbed her hand firmly. "We will find Callum."

"You don't know that."

The older woman closed her eyes, took a deep breath, her voice wavering with emotion. "I feel it." A gust of wind pushed some of Gran's hair across her forehead, and a chill fell over them. Lori shivered, her body aching all over. Sleep had eluded her; worry had taken hold of her very being. Unsure of what to do – whether to climb the nearby hills and search for Callum herself or stand numbly gazing out at the sea – Lori felt lost.

"I can't lose him, Gran." As Lori spoke, tears streamed

freely down her cheeks. Only then did she realise her bare feet were still submerged in seawater.

"I know," Gran whispered, pulling her granddaughter back towards dry land. Sand stuck to her cold feet. Gran wrapped her arms around her, providing a comforting cocoon. Lori allowed herself to be embraced and for a moment she let go.

The policeman returned with a blanket, draping it awkwardly over Lori's shoulders as Gran held on to her tightly. He offered them tea, but Gran's tone made it clear she wasn't interested. "Thank you, Mr Mooney, but I brought my own." She ushered Lori towards Lawrence's car, where he had spread out a blanket in the opened trunk and was attentively pouring tea into a thermal mug.

"I didn't want you to endure a cup of that policeman's tea. A lovely man, but he has no clue – teabags steeped in water for hours!" Gran tutted, gesturing for Lori to sit down. However, Lori refused, wanting to stay outside in the open, keeping her eyes fixed on the sea.

And then a disturbance broke out in the water.

The distant sound of the helicopter and the officer's radio signalled something happening.

Had they found him?

Lori ran to the officer, who clicked off his radio, his expression serious. "Is he there? Have you found Callum?"

"Sorry, Miss, I can't confirm anything just yet." His radio buzzed again, a sharp voice speaking too fast for Lori to catch all the words. "Received." The officer nodded, waving towards the coastguard boat near the shoreline, before turning his attention back to Lori. "My colleague has found a person along the bay. They are checking if this is Mr Macrae and if he's conscious. I'm sorry, Miss, I don't know anything more at this moment."

Lori bit her lip hard, her heart leaping with each buzz

from the radio. The policeman's bushy eyebrows raised as a different voice crackled through the radio, delivering a message that sent a tremor through her. "We have located the missing person at Polloch side. The individual is barely conscious and appears to be suffering from hypothermia. Requesting immediate medical assistance. Over."

Lori clung tightly to the wool blanket draped across her shoulders, desperately trying to ward off the dread enveloping her. On the cold beach, as a gust of wind ran through her again, she did something she hadn't done in a long time; she prayed, hoped, wished that Callum was safe, but the weight of uncertainty pressed on her shoulders.

31

Lawrence sped down the narrow road in pursuit of Callum. The steady drone of the engine underscored the urgency of the situation. The distant thud of rotor blades caught Lori's attention as they spotted a helicopter circling ahead. Lawrence skilfully parked at the road's edge, and without hesitation, Lori scrambled over a wire fence, her heart pounding. The damp, cool air clung to her skin as she rushed over the lumpy green grass until the stony beach unfolded before her, revealing the coastguard huddled around a figure.

Time seemed to stretch as she stood there, paralysed by the unfolding scene. Gran sensed her distress and held her hand tightly, offering silent support.

And then, there he was. Callum lay on the beach, eyes shut but lips moving. A surge of relief washed over her, but it was tempered by the sight of him – pale and shivering uncontrollably. The coastguard worked swiftly, wrapping him in warm blankets to stabilise his body temperature.

"Callum!" Lori called out, her voice breaking with emotion. The team around him continued their efficient care, preparing him for transportation to the hospital. Secured in a bundle of blankets, he was hoisted up by a coastguard member, lifted by a rope toward the hovering helicopter. Gran stayed close, her hands clasped in prayer. Lori watched intently, holding her breath, desperate to be closer to the man she loved even as he disappeared from view.

Gran held Lori close, providing solace with a motherly touch. "We'll follow behind, my Lolo. Callum will be in good hands."

* * *

In the harshly lit hospital, Lori endured what felt like endless hours on a rigid chair. Gran, always the caring neighbour, went about her usual rounds, offering comfort to elderly patients in the ward. The sterile scent of disinfectant permeated the air, and the low hum of medical equipment added a disconcerting soundtrack to Lori's anxious wait.

"You know, your gran has a heart of gold," Lawrence remarked, leaning against the pale green wall beside Lori, his proximity a reminder of the unfamiliar dynamics in their lives. He chuckled, his greying hair catching Lori's attention, the faintest dark strands resisting the encroaching grey. Up close, she realised he looked a little younger than Gran.

Her thoughts briefly wandered to her late grandfather, a burly man with a rugged appearance that matched his larger-than-life personality. In contrast, Lawrence exuded a refined and genteel aura, a far cry from the rough-around-the-edges demeanour of her grandfather.

"She's always busy," Lori offered, attempting conversation but inadvertently injecting a hint of hostility into her words.

Lawrence's bushy eyebrows raised in surprise. "My dear, that's what keeps her going."

However, Lori hadn't really gotten to know Lawrence yet,

and sitting side by side with him felt awkward. She wondered if she would ever feel as comfortable with him as she had with her own grandfather.

"You and your new life keep her going," Lori retorted, her frustration seeping through. "The wild swimming, the meetings, the soirées."

Lawrence glanced away for a moment before turning back with a soft smile. "Well, perhaps I've added a bit of excitement to her life, but your gran has always been a caring soul, looking out for others. It's just part of who she is. You know that as much as I do." His playful eyes met hers. "She has done everything to make me feel welcome. It's been a bit of an adventure, getting to know each other at this hour in our lives." He paused, his expression changing again. "I just wish you and I …" He stopped, examining his fingers with interest. "I don't have family. Not anymore." Pain clouded his face, and Lori held her breath.

"My daughter. It happened a long time ago now," he continued. "That's the curious thing about pain; it has a way of blurring time, of erasing the years until you find yourself... as I did, a lonely old man. When Mary came into my life, though, I allowed myself to heal. To forgive myself." He shook his head, smiling. "I want you to know, I don't want to come between your family. All I want is Mary to be happy. And I know we aren't blood related or have a shared history. But I really do want to be here for you all. You all matter to me, and the day I married Mary, I swore that I'd be here as a friend to her granddaughters." He grimaced. "Please, anything I can do, just say the word."

Lori considered his words, feeling a twinge of sympathy for Lawrence. He was a pillar of support for Gran, a role Lori couldn't fill as she navigated her own life. She glanced around the hospital, observing the muted activities, the hushed conversations, and the occasional beeping of medical equipment.

A roller-bed emerged down the corridor, a nurse guiding an elderly woman with vacant eyes. They parked the bed at the side of the corridor, the patient staring at the ceiling in silence. Lori hesitated, wanting to offer comfort but unsure of what to say. Gran appeared at the end of the hallway, radiating warmth, and stopped beside the elderly woman. She grasped the woman's hand with affection, sharing a moment of connection.

"Miss Robertson." A nurse interrupted Lori's thoughts, guiding her away from Lawrence's slumped frame and Gran's laughter. The corridor, gleaming under the fluorescent lights, echoed with subdued murmurs and the distant shuffle of footsteps. As they moved into a ward with several beds, Lori's eyes locked onto Callum, lying still. She circled his bed, her heart jolting at his vulnerability. His peaceful yet pale face and long, unruly hair spoke of the ordeal he had endured.

Tucking in the sheet around him, she mumbled to herself, "Callum Macrae, if I catch you doing anything so stupid again, I'll be the one who kills you next time!" The thought of losing him had been uncomfortably close. If the rescue team had been delayed even a moment longer, Callum might not have regained consciousness.

She sat down, her head resting on his chest. "Don't ever leave me," she whispered, listening to his slow but steady heartbeat under the sheet.

"Hey lass," Callum uttered the words in her hair, barely audible.

Lori smoothed his cool head. "I've been so worried about you."

"I'm sorry," Callum whispered, pain etched on his face. "For going to the beach … for not telling you about—"

"Let's forget all that." Lori smiled, unable to resist kissing him on his cold lips, then his cheek, and his forehead, grateful to have him back.

"Lori."

"Callum, please rest."

"But I have a child," he said, the pain evident. "I'm sorry. I didn't want …" He breathed in, regaining his strength. "I didn't want it to be this way. This is not fair on you." He sighed, exhausted. "I don't know what to do."

"It will all be OK." She held his weak hand. "I know it will be OK because we have each other." She crouched beside his ear, smoothing his forehead with her other hand reassuringly. Then the pain left his face, and steady breathing replaced it. She covered her mouth, suppressing the sobs that wanted to erupt from deep within.

32

The morning unfolded with crispness as Jean slipped into her kitchen, a bag of fresh donuts in hand. Rising at an ungodly hour after the ordeal with Callum, she managed to sneak over to the bakery. The scent of jam filled the air as she flicked on the kettle, quietly going about the business of preparing breakfast.

Her stomach rumbled in protest, though her hunger seemed overshadowed by the looming presence of her ex, now in her house. Her ex, who looked surprisingly well and had effortlessly assumed the role of caring for Maggie and Anne without hesitation. It was only fair that she returned the favour, Jean decided, plotting something nice they could do together as a family.

Maybe a day at the beach? Then she promptly dismissed that idea – shivering after her own cold night searching for Callum. A trip to the swimming pool? The weekend beckoned her with possibilities. They could do something on a whim, perhaps a day trip to the city zoo. Something special for the girls' reunion with Karen. Jean couldn't deny how thrilled they'd be to reconnect with their old friend.

Placing two mugs and glasses on the table, Jean set the

scene, almost on autopilot. With each setting, her family of four seemed complete. The dynamic had shifted when they were three, a balance upset that had made them all miserable. Jean had known that, for all her efforts, she couldn't be everything to the girls. With Karen in the picture, they had support. They had someone to cook and plan fun activities, to be the fun parent - everything that Jean seemed to lack. Karen was like a co-pilot in the delicate art of keeping their family together, especially during moments when it felt like everything could crumble at any time.

"How's Lori?" Karen's hushed voice broke through Jean's thoughts, causing her to startle and accidentally pour coffee onto the table. "Sorry!" Karen's smile accompanied her apology, and she swiftly grabbed a sponge from the sink, wiping up the spill. The simple touch of Karen's hand brushing against Jean's arm sent a shiver down her spine, igniting long-forgotten sensations. Memories long buried surged to the forefront, a tantalising reminder of a time when they were more than just two women sharing a kitchen.

As Karen cleaned, Jean stood frozen, her heart racing, her feelings resurfacing after a year of pushing them away. Her eyes traced the movement of Karen's hand, mesmerised by the delicate dance of fingers against the wet tabletop. She wanted more than the life she had settled for. Delicious certainty rose within her and fluttered around her like newly hatched butterflies.

With a small, almost shy smile, Jean handed Karen a mug. "Milk and one sugar," she whispered, the words an intimate secret shared between them.

"You remembered."

"Of course I remember." Leaning against the kitchen table, Jean found herself caught in the familiar and intoxicating allure of Karen's perfume. The scent enveloped her, a symphony of zesty freshness with a hint of spice, a fragrance that had always held a unique power over her senses. She closed her eyes, allowing the aroma to transport her back to moments they had shared, to the warmth of their embraces and the tender whispers exchanged in the dark. "I think about you a lot, Karen," Jean admitted, her voice barely more than a breath. The words hung in the air, like a fragile confession. From just a scent, a floodgate of emotions unlocked, and along with it a torrent of memories, regrets, and what-ifs surged within her, threatening to overwhelm her composure. "Do you think about me?"

Karen's fingers brushed Jean's hand, her touch electrifying. "I think of you often."

Jean leaned into the touch, her heart racing. The events of the night, the near death of Callum, and the weight of missed opportunities – it all hit her like a tidal wave. She took a step closer, the gap between them narrowing until their bodies were almost touching. With trembling fingers, Jean traced a path from Karen's jawline to her lips. A wave of longing washed over her. But as quickly as the moment had bloomed, it shifted. Confusion clouded Karen's eyes, and she took an involuntary step back, breaking the spell.

"What's wrong?" Jean's voice quivered.

Karen's gaze darted around the room, her lips parting as if she was about to speak. Instead, she shook her head, her eyes avoiding Jean's. "I … I'm not sure what's happening," she confessed.

"I think I've made a terrible mistake." Jean's words rushed out, the realisation hitting her like a lightning bolt. She wanted Karen, she wanted to explore what could still be between them, to feel that connection again.

Karen pushed her hand against Jean's chest. "No."

"What?" Jean stopped, her posture stiffening. "But you came over …"

"Yes." Karen sighed. "But that doesn't mean I want us to

be together again. You needed my help. I love the girls, I always will. I thought you knew that." She frowned, forlorn. "You didn't want me, remember?"

Jean bit her lip hard, the sting a grounding reminder. She didn't want things to play out like this. There was too much beneath the surface to ignore. "I'm sorry, I thought you wanted this."

"I did. But you didn't. That's why we split up, Jean." Her voice carried a hint of anger. "I need to go." Karen placed her mug down on the table. "I'm glad everything worked out. With Lori and Callum, I mean."

"Please, Karen, stay a little longer. The girls would be over the moon to have you here," Jean implored. How had her emotions taken such a dramatic turn over the course of the evening? She couldn't let this moment slip away, not when she finally understood what she truly desired.

"I don't think that's a good idea, Jean. It's better if I leave before they wake up. They've been through so much already, all because of their mother's confusion about what she wants in life. You're hurting them too, Jean." Karen turned and left the room, as quietly as she had entered.

Jean slumped into a chair, her hand reaching for a donut. Since her emotions were no longer in control, she devoured the treat in contemplative silence, each bite temporarily soothing her. She wanted to shake herself, to scream at her own hesitations. Everything felt like it was slipping through her fingers, an irretrievable moment in time. Caught up in her thoughts, she absentmindedly reached for another donut, her fingers smudging powdered sugar on the tabletop. The warmth of the coffee cup beckoned to her, and she drained the remaining liquid in a final, decisive gulp.

33

Lori stirred from her slumber, rubbing her bleary eyes. The light filtering through the window cast a soft glow in the room. She had dozed off on Callum, his weighty hand resting on her shoulder. As she shifted, his hand slid off, yet he remained asleep. She watched the gentle rise in his chest, relieved that he was safe and resting.

Gran and Lawrence had left earlier, their departure following the doctor's assurance that Callum was on the road to recovery. The nurses had treated Gran with special attention, her compassionate nature and attentiveness to the elderly patients earning her cups of tea and warm smiles. Gran squeezed Lori's shoulder as she left, her other hand holding Lawrence's.

Lori stepped out of the room, leaving Callum to rest. A hot drink was in order, something to chase away the chill that had seeped into her bones from the previous night's ordeal. The cafe had closed for the night, leaving her to resort to a vending machine. She inserted the coins, and with a series of clatters and jolts, a cup of steaming hot chocolate was dispensed. She shivered involuntarily, the memory of the cold wind and dense fog still clinging to her.

Gran's sensible advice to return home for some rest and a shower had fallen on deaf ears. Lori was resolute in her decision to stay by Callum's side. What if he woke up and found her gone? The thought itself was enough to keep her rooted to her current spot, even as she waited for her hot chocolate to fill to the brim.

However, her solitude was soon interrupted by approaching footsteps. Jennifer, clad in her usual smart sporty attire, her long hair neatly pulled back, approached Lori. Lori instinctively turned away, reaching for the now overflowing cup, only to have the scalding liquid burn her hand.

"Ouch!" Lori cried out, setting the cup down on a nearby table. She winced at the sudden pain, momentarily forgetting her discomfort around Jennifer.

"Are you alright?" Jennifer's voice held genuine concern as she appeared beside Lori.

Lori's response was curt. "I'm fine." She managed to sound more composed than she felt. "Look, Jennifer, it's not a good idea for you to be here. Callum is still recovering."

Jennifer's eyes shifted, her nervous tic of pulling at her sleeves not escaping Lori's notice. She glanced at Lori's cup before meeting her gaze. "Can I join you?"

Lori shrugged, sinking into a chair in the sparse hospital hallway. Despite the late hour, the place seemed eerily quiet, chairs left unoccupied in the dimly lit corridor.

Jennifer settled beside her, her own cup in hand. Lori couldn't help but notice the sense of comfort that Jennifer seemed to exude, even in this tense situation.

"I couldn't sleep," Jennifer admitted, her voice carrying a mix of sincerity and vulnerability. "I checked your house, and I was worried when I didn't find you there."

"The doctors said Callum needed another night at the

hospital," Lori responded, her tone firm. "He had a bad case of hyperthermia. They need to be sure he's recovering before he goes home."

Worry etched across her features, Jennifer inquired gently, "How is he?"

"Better. Exhausted, but better," Lori replied, her gaze still focused on her cup. It wasn't the first time she'd dealt with Jennifer's presence, yet the main issue that had driven her and everyone to the hospital was still unaddressed.

"Lori, I didn't anticipate things turning out this way. I just wanted to talk. I never imagined things would escalate like this."

Lori remained silent, her thoughts swirling. Jennifer's sudden appearance had thrust her life into turmoil once more, and until the heart of the matter was confronted, nothing would truly be resolved.

"I understand all that." Lori finally spoke, her voice tinged with a mixture of weariness and determination. "But what I can't comprehend is why you chose to show up precisely now."

Jennifer's brows furrowed in confusion. "What do you mean? I told you, I couldn't sleep—"

"I mean," Lori said, frustrated, "why come at this time? You're saying it has nothing to do with Callum and me getting ready to marry?"

Jennifer's response was swift and almost indignant. "Absolutely not. Why would you even think that?"

Lori rose from her seat, the weight of the conversation and its implications bearing down on her. "Thank you for coming, Jennifer. But right now, I need to be with Callum."

Jennifer stood as well, her urgency evident as she trailed behind Lori. "Lori, we need to talk properly. I'm going home really soon, and I need to discuss matters with Callum."

Lori continued to stride forward, the corridor stretching

out before her. As Jennifer matched her steps, she kept walking, and soon her companion's footsteps stopped, leaving Lori space to breathe and find Callum once more.

But just as Lori reached Callum's room, a tension-filled atmosphere loomed. Jennifer stood at the doorway, her presence an unwelcome intrusion. Their eyes locked, a silent standoff that hinted at the storm of emotions about to be unleashed.

"Please go, Jennifer," Lori whispered.

"I don't appreciate whatever it is you're accusing me of," Jennifer retorted, her eyes narrowing as an edge crept into her voice. "Whatever it is, you better spit it out, Lori."

Lori spun around, her grip firm as she seized Jennifer by the arm, pulling her away from the room and back down the dimly lit corridor. She spoke in hushed tones, a tense urgency in her words to avoid waking Callum. "Are you out of your mind? Coming here at this hour and demanding my time? All this" – Lori raised her hand – "is because of your actions. If you had just told me and Callum immediately, we could have resolved this quickly. But you dragged it out, playing some game, disrupting everything we had worked so hard for. You come in and pretend to be so much more than what he told me about you."

"What did he tell you about me?" Jennifer raised a curious eyebrow.

Lori shook her head, frustration etched on her face. "Not much – that's not the point!" she snapped. "You have caused havoc. Why wait, Jennifer?"

"Are you planning to have kids, Lori?" Jennifer's tone shifted, her gaze penetrating.

"I don't see what that has to do with you," Lori replied, a touch of defensiveness in her voice.

"This might be Callum's only child. And I know I might

not have broken the news so well," Jennifer said, her words calculated.

Lori scoffed. "That's an understatement."

"But wouldn't Callum want to be part of his son's life? He always wanted kids after all; it would be a shame to deprive him," Jennifer suggested.

"You're despicable," Lori hissed. "Please leave. You've caused enough damage. If he really is Callum's son, then we can work it out."

"It's not that simple," Jennifer backtracked, folding her arms.

"But, of course, we need to have proof he's his son," Lori remarked, her scepticism cutting through the tension.

"What do you take me for? You think I'd lie about something like that?" Jennifer challenged.

"Honestly, Jennifer? I don't know you at all – you could be capable of anything. And with the hurt you've caused Callum, I don't think it's done your character any favours. Now, I must get back to him, please leave, and we'll discuss this another time."

Jennifer reached for Lori's hand, desperation in her eyes. "Please," she said, confused.

Lori shook off her touch, her resolve unyielding, and with a final shake of the head, left Jennifer standing in the corridor.

34

Tammy carefully adjusted the cream ribbon adorning the hamper. Within the cardboard box lay a delightful assortment of treats – banana cake, jars of jam, a savoury quiche, and apple and onion chutney. Each item had been meticulously prepared by her, a collection of her culinary creations that, when combined, emitted an air of elegance that Tammy couldn't help but admire.

This particular lodge marked the final stop in Tammy's distribution rounds; the trusty wheelbarrow she used for the mission stood empty beside her. With a sense of accomplishment and pride, she looked at the hamper one last time before turning to go.

As the door creaked open, Tammy's eyes met those of a young woman, still heavy with sleep, with traces of last night's mascara smudged beneath them. "What day is it?" Her voice was hoarse.

"Saturday," Tammy replied, her own confusion briefly surfacing at finding herself outside a stranger's front door. How could someone not be aware of what day of the week it was?

The woman's eyes widened, and a spark of realisation lit

them up. "Food! How lovely!" Her accent bore the hallmarks of a refined upbringing, likely to have attended prestigious English schools.

Tammy's smile brightened. "It's a small token of thanks for your stay here," she explained warmly. A thought crossed her mind, and she added, "By the way, could I confirm your check-out date? I seem to have forgotten."

Tammy had taken it upon herself to manage the lodgers during Lori and Callum's absence at the hospital. Knowing that her sister's mind had been preoccupied, Tammy willingly stepped in, ensuring smooth transitions between guests. What a surprise her sister would have when she found out that her guests had not only left, but that their bedding and lodges were clean in plenty of time for the next arrivals.

Tammy could compare the lodges, if a little smaller, to the hotel she worked at, where once there was always a flurry of people coming and going. It had been a bustling hub of activity, with a steady stream of patrons. Tammy's involvement, before she'd had Rory, had spanned various roles – from managing reception to cleaning, tending bar, and even offering her services as a short-term tour guide. She had taken hotel guests on excursions around Morvaig town centre, acquainting them with the local sights and sounds.

Tammy's current routine had grown monotonous, lacking the vibrancy and novelty of interacting with new faces. She yearned for movement, for the chance to meet strangers and engage in lively conversations. Instead, her days had become stagnant, her excitement limited to the occasional interaction with Terry, Stuart, and Agnes. More often than not, their well-intentioned chatter about local customs and anecdotes – particularly those involving tractors – had a tendency to drive away any tourists who dared to venture in.

"We leave tomorrow," the young woman stated, her fingers absently tucking a strand of hair behind her ear. "I've left all of this dreadfully late. It's my husband's birthday," she mouthed, the words barely audible. "I foolishly promised him scrambled eggs, but the shop is a few miles away, isn't it?"

"Yes, it's a bit of a bumpy ride to the main road, but once you get there, Morvaig has everything you need – cafes, a supermarket, pubs," Tammy replied, a warm smile playing on her lips.

The woman swallowed. "That's my problem, you see. I don't think we need to see a pub ever again."

A soft giggle escaped Tammy, a bubbling excitement tickling her from within. "Well, why don't I make breakfast for both of you?" she offered, fully expecting the girl to politely decline. To her surprise, the young woman's eyes widened before she quickly accepted and closed the door.

Tammy leisurely descended the lodge's wooden steps and took a moment to look out over the tranquil scene. The lodges were clustered around a small loch, each one nestled into the gentle curves of the hillside. A sense of serenity washed over her as she surveyed the surroundings, a stark contrast to the cramped council house in town that she called home. There, their garden was nothing more than a postage-stamp patch barely large enough for a table and two deck chairs. It was ironic how in the Highlands, she often found herself in close proximity to others, an experience akin to city living, yet without the accompanying amenities.

She took a breath, gazing at the water.

At times, she felt jealous of Alan for having the opportunity to work here, despite his complaints. His demeanour had become progressively grumpier. But how? If she worked here, she would be over the moon.

"Rory," Tammy whispered with a fond smile. The open space had provided Rory ample room to explore and he had crawled out of the wheelbarrow with remarkable speed, his curiosity leading him to examine the weeds clinging to the hillside. A mischievous tug at the plants resulted in a tumble, and his infectious laughter filled the air. He had laughed so much recently, Tammy's heart swelled with pride and love. He was changing so quickly, his baby chubbiness giving way to the spirited, active boy he was becoming. Yet, a hint of sadness lingered. Time was slipping through her fingers, and she yearned to savour every moment of Rory's growth.

She wanted him close to her, so she could watch him grow each day. She wanted to live with ease, with family around her. But what she had was none of those things.

Something was not working. She had barely spoken to Alan since their last fight, and their relationship was strained. She'd expected more from him as a father and a husband, and she found herself grappling with the realisation that perhaps their hasty marriage had not been the solution she had hoped for.

But could she wait around for him? Pull them out from this slump, to pursue what she wanted and take care of Rory the way she wanted?

"What am I waiting for?" Tammy asked herself, her voice barely above a whisper. She cradled Rory in her arms, her eyes fixed on his innocent face as he protested being picked up. Setting him back into the wheelbarrow elicited another round of giggles. She pushed him uphill toward Lori's house, hoping that in Lori's cluttered fridge would be the suitable ingredients to make a delicious breakfast.

* * *

"I've got an idea," Tammy said, her hands rubbing together with a mix of excitement and nervousness. She motioned for Alan to take a seat after he arrived home from his "walk" into town with Rory in the stroller. She knew it was more of a pit stop at every pub along the way, with Alan indulging in the local ales.

Disregarding the faint scent of alcohol that clung to Alan's breath, Tammy cradled Rory in her arms, showering him with affection before gently placing him on the floor, allowing him to explore his surroundings. Flicking on a children's cartoon on the TV, she hoped it would provide some distraction, giving her the chance to lay out her idea.

Alan flopped onto the small sofa, his imposing size contrasting with the petite furniture. "I hear Callum is on the mend. He'll probably need more time at home to recover. I was thinking, maybe I could offer to help him out more in the office," Alan suggested, shifting on the sofa cushions in an attempt to find comfort. He had a knack for looking uncomfortable wherever he sat.

Tammy let out a scoff. "You and paperwork? You're allergic to each other!"

"I could learn," Alan retorted, his tone oddly determined. "He might need extra help, especially when he's stuck in that office all day."

A disbelieving smile tugged at the corner of Tammy's lips. "So, you want to become a paperwork guru all of a sudden?"

"Not exactly," Alan said, his frustration evident as he removed the pillows from behind him, tossing them onto the floor with an exaggerated groan.

Rory squeaked in delight, using the chance to bounce on the discarded pillows. Tammy winced, realising she hadn't cleaned the floor in a couple of days, adding another task to her already overflowing to-do list.

"I just think that if I could handle some admin tasks, it might open up more opportunities for me," Alan explained.

Tammy's mouth opened in horror. "Are you planning to find another job?"

"No, no, not that. But I have to think about our future, right? You keep telling me that," he replied.

Tammy hesitated, well aware that pushing Alan out of his comfort zone often led to unintended consequences. "You've always enjoyed manual work, remember?"

Alan let out an exasperated sniff. "It was just a thought."

Tammy waved a dismissive hand, her focus shifting to Rory as he vocalised his demands for attention. Time was running short, and she needed to express her own plans before Rory's antics became all-consuming.

"What if I offered a cooking package?" Tammy blurted out suddenly, her voice carrying a hint of urgency. Alan nodded in response, and Tammy took it as a sign to continue. "Functions, takeaways – I could prepare meals for people and even deliver them."

She tapped her fingernail nervously against the table, her mind racing to articulate her vision. "Think about weddings – for our own wedding, we had to round up all the locals to bake. And while there are restaurants, not everyone wants to dine out. Sometimes people prefer the comfort of their own homes, where they can enjoy a delicious meal without leaving their own space. Or imagine a romantic meal for two on a secluded beach, complete with a white tablecloth, flowers, candlelight. I could cook the meal to perfection, serve them, and then discreetly leave, allowing them to enjoy a peaceful walk along the shoreline."

"But," Alan interjected, a furrow forming between his brows, "what if they take hours to finish the meal? You'd have to stay there the entire time."

Tammy sighed, her hopes momentarily deflated. "Yes, Alan, some special meals can take time. It's part of the experience."

Alan's uncertainty was palpable. "You'd need proper

kitchen equipment, health inspections, and a suitable workspace. It could be a lot of money upfront, Tam."

Tammy felt a spark of determination. "I can start here, our home. It's small, but I can make it work."

Alan shook his head, his voice taking on a practical tone. "Maybe if you save up first, gradually invest in the necessary equipment. And then once you're ready, you can start the business."

Tammy's enthusiasm wavered, the weight of practicality settling in. She turned to her tiny kitchen, her vision of a culinary endeavour fading slightly.

"It's a nice idea, Tam," Alan reassured her, his attention already shifting to the TV. He had seamlessly turned the channel without her noticing. The sounds of a football game filled the room, and Rory's protest at the change in programming drew Tammy's focus. He waddled over to her, his lip pouting.

She scooped him up, pressing a kiss to his cheek, and turned back to her kitchen with a sigh.

35

"I'm not an invalid," Callum remarked as Lori plumped up a pillow behind his back.

"Oh, I know that," Lori responded playfully, presenting him with a cup of sweet tea. She draped a tartan wool blanket over him, giving it a brief waft before tucking it snugly around his frame.

"I feel like a numpty," Callum admitted, wincing slightly as he adjusted his position.

"Doctor's orders!" Lori held up her hands in mock surrender. "If you want a swift recovery, you've got to follow my instructions." She settled beside him, her presence a comforting anchor.

"You're enjoying this power, aren't you?" Callum let out a weak chuckle as he sipped his tea, feeling the warmth seep through him.

Lori met his gaze, her expression softening. "Callum, we need to be sensible. You insisted on being outside, but we can't take unnecessary risks."

"I just wanted to watch the sunset," he confessed in a hushed tone.

As the last rays of daylight surrendered to the encroaching

night, a gaggle of wild geese appeared, their distant squawks punctuating the air. Callum's gaze followed their V-shaped formation, leading his thoughts into the tranquil expanse of the horizon. The sun had left a small pink watery mark across the sky. He had noticed that colour during his solitary moments on the beach. That colour had briefly pierced through the fog of his thoughts, revealing a truth he had been trying to avoid. The truth about Jennifer, the pregnancy, and the painful choices he had made. He shivered.

Lori's voice gently pulled him back. "We should get you inside, Callum."

"I can't think within four walls," he admitted, his gaze still lingering on the fading sky.

"Well, at least finish your tea," Lori urged, tucking another blanket around him as if to reinforce her point. She settled back beside him, their closeness offering solace amidst the chill.

Callum shook his head, chuckling gently. His irritation gave way to relief that he had Lori on his side.

"Can I get you anything else?" she asked.

Callum thought about suggesting that she stop fussing over him, but he held back, simply shaking his head. "I need to send your sister a thank you, for taking care of the guests. With all the chaos of being in the hospital, it totally slipped my mind."

"It slipped my mind too!"

"You were distracted with me and your own business," Callum pointed out.

"Well, Rhona is always there – I didn't pay it much thought, to be honest. You were my priority."

A stillness settled over them and Callum shifted on the bench uneasily. The weight of the words he needed to say had been pressing on him for the past few days, and he knew it was time to face the music. He had wanted to find the right moment, but as the seconds ticked by, he realised that there might never be a perfect time for this conversation.

He finally spoke up. "I'm sorry, Lori."

Lori turned to him, her blue eyes locking onto his. "What for?"

He let out a sigh, the tension in his shoulders starting to release. "For going to the same beach where your parents died. I knew you never wanted to go there. It was stupid of me, but I just needed to go somewhere different, to clear my mind—"

Lori's frown deepened as she absorbed his words, and she withdrew slightly from his side. Her arms crossed over her chest as she stared out toward the sea.

Callum's heart sank at the sudden coldness he felt from her. He instinctively reached for her hand, hoping to bridge the growing gap between them, but her arms remained tightly folded against her body.

"Why are you lying to me?" Lori's voice was surprisingly steady, her gaze fixed ahead.

Callum's mouth went dry, a feeling of unease settling in his stomach. "What do you mean?"

Lori scoffed, finally turning to face him with a mixture of frustration and hurt. "I know you go there often. Gran told me. You both have a secret pact, not to tell me. And here you are, after all this – pretending to be a good guy."

"I am," he said, his tone defensive. "I am a good guy." He was hoping the words were true.

Lori turned away again, and Callum's heart clenched as he watched silent tears stream down her face. The sight struck him like a dagger, and he drew in a quick, sharp breath. What had he done?

"I didn't want to hurt you," Callum began, his voice soothing as he leaned slightly toward her. The blanket slipped off his shoulder, forgotten in their conversation. "I was protecting you. You couldn't stand being near that place, and I hoped time had healed your wounds. But after the last time I took you there, after your panic attack before we even arrived, I knew I couldn't tell you about it."

Her response was a bitter scoff. "So you and Gran lied to me."

"We didn't lie, Lori," Callum said, a mix of frustration and exasperation in his tone. "We just thought you didn't need to know. The truth is, it's no more dangerous there than anywhere else. I was trying to protect you."

Lori's voice dripped with sarcasm as she retorted, "My knight in shining armour."

"Lori, this isn't about that," he insisted, his tone pleading. "I've apologised – what more do you want from me?"

Her response was a frustrated sigh. "Oh, I don't know, Callum. Maybe for you to stop playing protector all the time."

He shook his head in frustration. "I can't help it if I want to protect you. Sometimes your emotions get the best of you and—"

"What does that even mean?" Lori's eyes welled up with fresh tears. "I can't control how I feel …" Her voice wavered as the tears began to fall. "And how do you think that made me feel? You going to the place my mother and father died? Sneaking away to find solace there and then coming back to me, pretending like nothing happened. How many times have you lied, Callum?"

Callum's anger flared, his patience wearing thin. "It wasn't like that," he snapped back. His frustration surged as he felt Lori trying to control his actions. "You're trying to dictate my life, Lori. You can't tell me what I should and shouldn't do."

"I see that now," she admitted quietly, her shoulders slumping as if a heavy weight had settled upon them. "And now you have a child," her voice wavered slightly, revealing the emotional turmoil she was grappling with, "and I'm trying to be supportive. I just wonder … what other things you've lied about?"

Callum's jaw clenched, his frustration mounting as he desperately tried to find the right words. "I have never lied to you," he insisted, his voice firm and resolute.

"I thought we just established you had," she replied, her gaze now distant as she turned to look at the sea.

A rush of frustration surged through Callum's veins, his hand involuntarily clenching into a tight fist.

"Maybe you always knew you had a child." Lori's words cut through the air, striking at the heart of his fears. "And you kept that from me all these years?"

The accusation hung heavily in the air. "I would never do that, Lori," he pleaded. Then, in a sudden bristle of anger, he snapped, "You Robertsons think the world revolves around you!" His voice, tinged with anger, his heart pounding. "This time, it's my business – my child, my life!" The words were punctuated by a sudden snap of emotion.

Lori raised an eyebrow. "Well, I can see what you really think now, Callum," her words dripping with bitterness. "Maybe it is your life. You don't want to share it with anyone, least of all me!" Her voice trembled. "You're not a good guy, Callum. You're just trying to get your own way with this. You want your own secret life? Go ahead." She stood up and marched away, her brisk strides distancing her from Callum and their unresolved confrontation.

With a heavy sigh, he fished out the little black box that held a symbol of commitment, a future he had so eagerly envisioned. But now, that future seemed hazy and uncertain.

He flicked the box open again, his heart doing a somersault at the sight of the elegant ring nestled within. In a sudden change of heart, he snapped it shut, tucking it back into his pocket. He found himself oddly aligned with Alan's scepticism. The idea of going through with the wedding while this chaos brewed beneath the surface felt like an absurd charade. As the final wedding details were being hammered out, he'd found himself struggling to tap into the anticipated excitement. After all, it was supposed to be his big day. His heart should have been doing the happy dance, but instead, it was caught in a complex tango of emotions.

The decision that had once seemed so straightforward now looked like a fog-covered crossroads. He didn't want to end up adrift and lost in his own life, just as he had been on his surfboard that day. And yet, the idea of putting the brakes on the wedding seemed like a path fraught with its own set of pitfalls.

He couldn't think straight. Surfing was meant to help clear his mind. Instead, his mind was jumbled with more emotions and he found himself lost in the same fog that had pushed him out into the depths that night. Without seeing land, but left freezing on his board. A lonely place he never wanted to be again. But if he stopped the wedding, Lori would never forgive him. He would lose her. He took a sip from the half-forgotten cup of tea Lori had handed him earlier, feeling its warmth chase away the ocean chill. Wrapping the blanket around himself a bit tighter, he gazed over the hills to the sea in the distance, wondering how everything had gotten so complicated. It was supposed to be a joyful time, a celebration of love and commitment. But now, even his most steadfast convictions wavered in the face of the unexpected news.

36

Hey there, sunshine!" Rhona practically leaped into action as Lori entered the shop. The small bell above the door tinkled cheerfully, a stark contrast to Lori's mood. "How's Callum? How are you? I can't believe what you told me over the phone – a son! Well, that's a twist, isn't it? I knew that Jennifer was up to something!" Rhona's words flowed like a rapid river, hardly allowing for a breath between her sentences. "And guess what, if you can believe it, I've actually sold one of those red velvet coats from our online shop! And not to mention, two of your capes went out the door this morning! I'm buzzing – haven't had sales like this in ages!" Her energy was infectious as she followed Lori towards the kitchenette where the kettle was bubbling.

"That's fantastic, Rhonz," Lori replied, attempting to match her friend's enthusiasm but falling a bit short.

Rhona's keen eyes immediately picked up on Lori's lack of verve. "What's wrong?" she asked, tilting her head with a concerned expression. She instinctively placed a comforting hand on Lori's shoulder.

Lori managed a nod. "Callum's OK. But something's

different between us. Ever since I started planning the wedding, things have felt … different. It's like we're not quite the same people anymore."

Rhona nodded understandingly. "Well, a lot has happened in a short span."

Lori sighed with frustration. "There's just too much on my plate. The wedding, this business, Callum's lodges, our house, his son now, and Jennifer is still lingering around!"

"Ugh, that woman!" Rhona's eyes sparked with indignation. "Why won't she just disappear already? She's caused enough damage!"

"I don't blame her," Lori said weakly. "Of course, she wants her son to know his father. But what I can't wrap my head around is why she waited this long to show up! Callum was here all this time, single and pining for her. I'm sure he would've dropped everything to be with them."

"But didn't she remarry?" Rhona's arms crossed defensively, her gaze locked onto Lori. "Maybe she just wanted to give her new husband the role of being the child's father."

"Maybe," Lori mused, chewing on her lip. "I just wonder why she chose now to resurface. And it's not like I should even be thinking this way, but part of me wonders if it's a financial motive."

Rhona's eyebrows shot up. "You mean, like, trying to secure everything Callum has for the child?"

Lori shrugged helplessly. "I'm not sure about the legalities, but her sudden appearance seems rushed and last minute. Something about it just feels off. She claims she didn't know we were together or getting married."

"Do you think she's lying?" Rhona's voice dropped to a conspiratorial whisper.

"I think something's missing," Lori said, her gaze fixed on the kitchen wall. She wracked her brain, attempting to recall the conversations with Jennifer, but nothing came to her. "I just couldn't stand talking to her any longer. This whole situation has turned everything upside down. I mean, maybe Callum has a son … or maybe he doesn't! How are we supposed to trust her?"

Rhona's eyes widened in speculation. "What if she's here to sabotage the wedding?" She grinned with a hint of drama. "Honestly, this whole situation feels like we're in the middle of a soap opera!"

Lori's stern look cut through Rhona's levity. "This is serious, Rhonz."

"Right, sorry." Rhona cleared her throat. "Why not have an honest talk with her?"

Lori's shoulders slumped. "I've tried. She's not telling us everything. She's turned our world upside down. I'm just furious about it. But more than anything, I feel powerless. This is Callum's situation. And how he's handled it … well …" Her voice trailed off, a pained expression shadowing her face.

"How has he handled it?" Rhona busied herself with the teapot, her focus surreptitiously locked onto Lori's face.

"He's not facing it head-on. He's avoiding Jennifer. It's like he can't bring himself to confront her … It's like he's …" Lori's lip quivered, and unbidden tears welled up. "It's like he still loves her."

"No, Lori." Rhona's voice was firm. "He loves you. He's just confused."

Lori shook her head, her teeth pressing into her lower lip. "If he really loved me, he would've dealt with this situation instead of letting Jennifer linger here."

"Well, to be fair, it was you who insisted Jennifer stay," Rhona pointed out, raising an eyebrow.

Lori had indeed asked Jennifer to stay until she and Callum resolved their issues, but those issues had only deepened and remained unresolved.

"He's been running away from things," Lori said at last. Rhona thrust a cup of tea into her hand, and the warmth seeped into Lori's cold fingers, providing some comfort. "We had a fight yesterday," Lori admitted, gazing at the swirling brown liquid in her cup, as if searching for answers in its depths. "We never fight."

Rhona leaned back against the fridge, her fingers clenched at her side. Lori couldn't help but notice the fading remnants of a recent bottle of fake tan on her friend's fingers. Rhona's usually adorned fingers were bereft of their usual collection of rings. Lori's curiosity got the better of her, and she let her gaze drift to Rhona's neck, half-expecting to see her wedding band on a chain. But today, there was nothing. No jewellery, and very little make-up on compared to her usual getup. "Every couple fights. It's when you start to sleep in separate beds, that's when it's a concern," Rhona said with a nod, a knowing glint in her eyes.

Lori's confusion was evident. "What?"

To Lori's surprise, Rhona let out a chuckle. "Oh, your expression is priceless. Don't worry, Lori. Malcolm and I have been on separate paths for a while now. Something inside me just snapped last month when I found myself awake for the umpteenth time due to his snoring. I thought to myself – what the hell am I doing, sacrificing my sleep next to a man who doesn't really care anymore?"

"I'm so sorry," Lori blurted out, her mouth working faster than her brain. "You never said anything, and here I am blabbering on about my own problems."

Rhona simply shrugged. "It's easier to focus on other people's issues sometimes. Honestly, don't fret. Some things simply reach their natural end."

Lori's eyes widened. "And Graham? Have you heard from him?"

Rhona's gaze briefly dropped to the floor before meeting

Lori's with a small smile. "Graham left last week. Went back to his family." Her smile turned wry. "He has a wife and kids, you know. Didn't stop him from suggesting he wanted to have an affair."

Lori choked on her tea. "What? What happened?"

"Well, I let myself entertain the daydream for a bit. We even shared a few kisses. But deep down, I knew I couldn't."

"Because of Malcolm?"

Rhona nodded solemnly. "Because of my kids. And let's be honest, Malcolm hasn't looked at me with that kind of longing since we conceived our youngest."

Lori's mental calculator went into overdrive, piecing together the timeline. "But that's … it's been years!"

Rhona's grim smile spoke volumes. "Years, yes."

Lori was dumbfounded by her friend's revelations. "You've been dealing with all of this and still managed to be there for me?"

Rhona's gaze softened. "Lori, we all have our struggles. Relationships are complicated."

"But did you ever want to … with Graham, I mean?"

A flicker of a smile played on Rhona's lips. She leaned slightly over the counter, as if to share a secret. "Of course I did. I've fantasised about it more times than I can count."

"So, why didn't you?"

Rhona's mouth tightened, her features serious. "Because I knew I'd be the one blamed for breaking up a marriage. And beyond that, he has kids. I couldn't bring myself to be the reason they'd have a broken home. As much as I wanted to, I just couldn't."

"So you're staying in an unhappy marriage?" Lori's voice held a mixture of concern and disbelief, unable to fathom the idea of enduring a loveless relationship.

"For now, yeah," she replied, her voice carrying a hint of

resignation that didn't quite match the fire Lori was accustomed to seeing in her friend.

Lori straightened, her resolve firming. The thought of Rhona, her strong and vibrant friend, trapped in a relationship devoid of love unsettled her deeply. She took a step forward. "There must be something we can do?"

Rhona's usually composed exterior wavered, her face revealing a vulnerability she rarely showed. A single tear escaped her eye, tracing a path down her cheek, a wordless admission that her connection with Malcolm wasn't as simple as she had let on.

"I never did say to you." She breathed out, her voice tender. "I'm so glad you came home. We were always great pals, weren't we?" A wistful smile played on her lips. "It's meant a lot to have you in my life again. No matter what happens, I have friends near."

"Rhona," Lori whispered, moving closer towards her, "I'm here for you. Not just as a friend but as family." She wrapped her arms around her friend. "Whatever happens, I'm here."

37

Jean parked her car by the side of the road, surrounded by a cluster of rowan trees with branches swaying in the breeze. She unloaded her cargo – a tent and three backpacks – onto the grass. Anne remained in the front seat, her sullen mood evident as she flicked a page in a teen magazine. Loud pop music played, a high-pitched female voice floating outside the back window, making Jean wince. Meanwhile, Maggie walked through the undergrowth along the path Jean had chosen for their adventure.

The recent rescue of Callum had cast an unexpected shadow over her children's spirits, an unusual, subdued air enveloping them. It wasn't until their father's call the previous night, cancelling their anticipated weekend plans, that the gloom seemed to intensify. Anne's reaction, in particular, surprised Jean; usually her little shadow, Anne had always been her constant companion, even guiding Maggie on proper behaviour. Jean had watched her oldest daughter blossom recently, her limbs growing longer and even hitting the same height as Jean. But Douglas's absence this weekend, with the possibility of extending further, had hit them harder than Jean expected. Even though she had the girls full-time, her friendly agreement with her ex-husband allowed Douglas to have the girls whenever he could. But work intervened, something Jean understood but her girls struggled with.

Jean tied a jumper around her waist, laced up her walking boots, and pulled on a baseball cap before hurrying her girls to get ready. Deciding on a camping trip, something they'd never done before, was spontaneous. With good weather on the horizon, Jean seized the chance and unearthed a stored tent from the attic. A Christmas present that had only been collecting dust over the years, Jean just hoped it wouldn't collapse before their eyes.

They left the car behind and ventured onto the hillside, following a vague path worn by animals over time. Jean had heard of this specific walk, with the promise of a bothy at the end of the route - a little hut where she and the girls could spend the night, if it wasn't already occupied by other hikers. But with no signs and barely a track to follow, she pressed on, hoping they were headed in the right direction.

Sun hit her skin, warming her, and she breathed in the heather that surrounded them, its flowers covering the hillside with purple vibrancy. Turning to check on her daughters, she saw them trailing slowly behind, their faces downcast. Maybe a camping trip was too ambitious. But she wanted more outdoor experiences after her own recent walks, and trips she could take her daughters on. She found that with each step, her head cleared.

At the back of her mind, a pile of students' papers sat waiting for her return home. She would have made that her priority, but since Douglas's last-minute cancellation, Jean was determined to focus on other things.

"Mum, how far is it?" Maggie said with pain, as if they had been walking all day, and not only left the car mere moments before.

"Not far," lied Jean. "Oh look!" She pointed in the sky to a bird of prey that circled above them. "What do you think it is?"

"Just a buzzard," Maggie replied unenthusiastically.

"People say they've seen seals and dolphins here. We're heading toward that tip down the hill." Jean pointed along the shoreline.

"We've seen those before." Maggie sighed.

Anne lingered at the back of the group, her silence carrying an unusual hostility for her typically even-tempered demeanour. Jean tried to maintain a smile, watching for wildlife, and silently yearning to comfort her eldest. However, something held her back.

As they walked, the landscape transformed into rolling hills stretching out before them. Jean delightedly pointed out fluffy white clouds in the blue sky, likening them to playful animal shapes, though her attempts were met with silence from her companions trailing behind. Once, they would have eagerly joined her game, but now they seemed lost in their own thoughts.

The path would occasionally vanish, only to reappear again, prompting a quick glance at the map as Jean guided them through a narrow glen. Long yellow weeds swayed in the breeze, while a gentle river meandered past them. Jean tucked the map away and soon found herself lost in a meditative state, allowing the sounds of birds and the rushing water to distract her, though old thoughts of Karen resurfaced.

Memories of her disastrous encounter with Karen lingered in her mind. She tried to divert her thoughts, but the emotional residue persisted, casting shadows over her attempts to focus on the present.

Amid the barrage of apologetic text messages she had fired off that fateful day, Jean had managed, to some extent, to shift her perspective. Yet, as she pondered the complexities of her feelings, a cascade of questions flooded her mind. Did she genuinely yearn for a rekindling with Karen, or was it a mere tug of fleeting lust? The answer eluded her, shrouded in the ambiguity of her emotions. The proximity of Karen had a curious effect – catapulting Jean's feelings and desires to dizzying heights, only for them to dwindle in her absence.

The idea of reviving their relationship felt rushed and daunting. Jean shivered at the thought, exhausted by the chaos of love and lust. Single life had its challenges, but after years of relationships, she yearned to enjoy her own company, free from the inevitable departure of a partner.

They walked further through a desolate landscape, until a pair of glassy eyes peered at Jean through the weeds, prompting her to halt suddenly. Her daughters almost bumped into her. A young stag observed them, its antlers curving like the branches of a rowan tree. Jean smiled at her girls, only to find Anne engrossed in her phone and Maggie nonchalantly chewing gum while picking at her blue nail polish. Neither seemed to register the majestic creature before them. Jean frowned but continued walking across the glen, aware of other pairs of eyes dotting the landscape, silently tracking their journey.

The trek led them through mud, uneven terrain, and a woodland before opening onto vast fields of barley swaying in the wind. Amid Anne's sighs and Maggie's groans, they finally paused on large rocks to rest. Jean bit into her ham sandwich and gazed at the expanse before her, captivated by the graceful dance of the barley stalks. Maggie noisily munched on a packet of crisps, and Anne nibbled on an apple. Jean had never seen similarities between her girls before. Anne, orderly and recently turned vegan, with the diet of a thirty-year-old; Maggie, messy, loud, and scrappy. And yet, as Jean looked at them now, they mirrored each other's glum expressions with a shared pout.

She consulted the map once more, her fingers tracing its lines, and with determined encouragement managed to motivate her girls to move forward. Unbeknownst to her, a pebbled beach and their bothy lay at the end of the barley fields. With a sigh of satisfaction, Jean spread her rucksack and tent on the grass, removed her sweaty socks, and tentatively stepped onto the rocks, heading towards the water. Maggie performed cartwheels on the grass while Anne sat on another rock.

"Come in for a paddle, girls!" Jean called out with a laugh, but her words were met with indifference. She allowed the clear water to splash against her ankles, and for a brief moment, her mind focused solely on the horizon. For the first time, she felt a deep sense of peace.

She had spent the better part of her life not knowing herself. She still didn't, not fully. But walking, exploring new corners, had opened her eyes, and she looked outside herself. She could taste the salt spray, and feel the coldness enveloping her, her feet turning slightly numb. She smiled to herself, then turned back to the bothy, with her girls in view.

Anne retrieved her phone and, after a sigh, slid it back into her pocket. Probably no reception in a place like this, Jean thought, relieved.

"Everything OK?" she asked, settling down next to Anne on a rock.

"Yeah," Anne mumbled, shuffling slightly.

"Well." Jean smiled. "I thought we'd check out this bothy and see if it's suitable for three adventurous gals like us!" She clapped her hands, then pulled up her reluctant daughter and led her towards the cottage.

The green wooden door creaked open, and sunlight flooded the dark interior. A window on the far side revealed a sink, and on the back wall stood a fireplace. Everything appeared clean – a surprise, given that this spot was regularly used by campers. Low benches on either side of the fireplace could serve as their beds. Luckily they had no real need for the tent, they had more than enough space to themselves.

"What do you think?" Jean inquired.

Anne shrugged. Jean took it as a "yes, Mum, it's a wonderful spot for the night, let's do this!" – a sentiment Anne might have openly expressed a year ago. She clapped her hands again and began unpacking. Her first task was the fire, for which she had stashed away firelighters. While her girls foraged for dried driftwood, Jean worked on making the space as cosy as possible.

As night descended and the sun melted into the sea, they sat in silence, watching the sunset by a bonfire. "Beautiful," Jean breathed, but received little response from her girls. Their dinner had consisted of instant noodles and bread toasted over the fire. Jean was pleasantly surprised by how delicious it all tasted compared to her usual cooking at home. The fire crackled, and Jean silently congratulated herself. She had stepped outside her comfort zone, trying something she had never thought she would enjoy. She just wished her girls felt the same.

"Something bothering you?" Jean asked, careful not to spoil the day.

Her question was met with silence.

"Girls, you'll see your dad again soon. Maybe next week."

"Yeah," Maggie responded, her eyes briefly meeting Anne's before turning toward the flickering flames. Her voice, though quiet, carried the weight of unspoken longings. "It's not just Dad," she admitted.

"Maggie, shut up," Anne snapped, her sharp tone catching Jean off guard. She had never heard Anne speak to Maggie that way before.

"I miss Karen. And Dad. And … and you," Maggie

finally confessed.

Jean furrowed her brow, then chuckled. "But I'm right here, Toots."

Maggie shrugged.

"I've been putting you girls first. I'm cutting back my hours at school – I'll be home earlier. I know it's not perfect, but isn't it better?" Jean asked, a hint of heartbreak in her voice. After speaking with the headmaster, she had managed to carve out a little more time for herself than she had thought possible. She had made every effort, adjusting her work schedule to prioritise her girls, but it seemed to fall short. Why was it always her making the sacrifices, and why did it still feel like it wasn't enough?

"You're gone too," Maggie stated. "On walks all the time now."

Jean exhaled. "Toots, I just need a little time for myself."

"Are you seeing someone else?" Anne's sudden question jolted Jean back to the present, the accusatory tone slicing through the air like an unexpected gust of wind.

Before Jean could answer, Anne crossed her arms defensively, scuffing the ground. "You're distant. I heard Karen leaving our house the other morning. Are you back together with her?"

Jean's mouth opened, her mind racing. "What do you mean?" She had never truly shared with her kids about Karen, disguising her as just a friend.

"Karen was your girlfriend. But you broke up. So, are you getting a new girlfriend?"

Jean couldn't find words. How had her girls picked up on the fact that Karen was more than a friend? She had worked so hard to keep that part of her life hidden. "Are you suggesting I'm going to bring someone new into the house?"

"No, it's just that you're distracted," Anne stated.

Jean frowned, trying to find the words. "I'm sorry, girls.

I've been trying to work out what makes me happy."

They both looked at her with sad eyes.

"And you both make me happy," she quickly added. "But I feel like I can't be my best self. I've needed to work out what it is I want." She tried a different tack. "You see, you'll get older and you'll leave – then what will I do? When that time comes, I want to be prepared. You girls are everything to me."

"You've been different recently," Anne said, reflecting.

"I have?" Jean replied, her voice betraying a hint of confusion. She searched her daughters' faces, hoping to discern the emotions beneath their expressions.

"Yeah." Anne shrugged. "Happier I guess, that's why we thought there was someone else …"

"No … no one else. I'd tell you if there was. So you know about Karen?"

Anne rolled her eyes and Maggie scratched her chin, her legs swinging off the big rock she sat on.

"Maggie's friend has two dads, and I'm old enough to know about gay people, Mum," Anne said, as if she were discussing something as trivial as dinner compared to the subject Jean had been avoiding for so long. She had wanted to protect the girls from any potential negativity, and she thought she'd swept it under the rug. But what if she did meet someone else? What then? Would she hide it again and hope no one noticed whether it was a woman or a man?

"I'm sorry; I should have trusted you both more. I see that you're both much more responsible than I ever was at your age." Jean gazed at the flames crackling into the gloomy night air. Her girls remained seated on the other side of the fire, and she bridged the gap to sit between them. Wrapping an arm around both of them, they looked out over the water gently lapping, the tide receding. The sky had become sprinkled with bright, shiny jewels, one of which moved slowly like a satellite or aeroplane, as Maggie pointed out to them. Jean squeezed their arms, taking in the scent of the fire and the cool night surrounding them.

Extending her arm, feeling the heat but still at a safe distance from the fire, Jean was filled with an overwhelming love for her girls. They were strong, independent, and making her prouder with each passing day. They were also girls who still wanted their mother around, even though she knew deep down that it wouldn't last much longer.

"I'd like to make a pact," Jean began, "that I will tell you if I ever find someone. But I don't think I'm ready; Karen hit me harder than I thought." She paused, still unsure whether to discuss too much details with her daughters. "It's taken me a bit of time to really adjust. But I will tell you if that moment arises, and you both tell me if there's anything you're hurting about or want to ask me. I want you to ask me anything. Don't stay in the dark anymore. I kept you both there, and I'm sorry for that now."

She opened her hand flat, and Maggie reached out over it, then Anne over that. Jean placed her other hand on top of theirs. "And I'd love some company on my walks. If you want to join your old mum, we can go off exploring." She squeezed their hands, and they giggled. The heaviness evaporated around them.

Reaching into her backpack, she pulled out a bag of marshmallows. "Now, who's up for toasting these little delights and making a game out of spotting shooting stars?"

As the sweet aroma of caramelised sugar wafted through the air, Jean leaned back, joining her daughters in gazing at the stars. The crackling fire, the gentle lapping of water, and the comforting warmth of her daughters' presence surrounded her. In that moment of serene simplicity, she found a reassuring certainty that, perhaps, she was indeed walking the right path.

38

Tammy waved goodnight to the last straggler in the pub and locked up behind them. She had been waiting for this moment all evening. The restaurant and bar area, now bathed in dimmed light, belonged to her alone. She could feel that her time here was drawing to a close. She had been contemplating it for a while, but tonight she was sure of it. Tomorrow, she would hand in her notice and embark on a new chapter in her life.

Throughout the evening, she had engaged in a lively exchange of text messages with Callum. His job offer for his lodges had served as a confirmation that it was time for her to embrace something fresh. The glowing reviews from recent lodgers praising Tammy's culinary skills and exceptional customer care had made the decision even clearer. Callum had called earlier, eager to have her join his team, and Tammy had enthusiastically accepted. The promise of better pay and increased creative freedom was too enticing to ignore.

While the specifics of her role were yet to be confirmed, Tammy knew she would be responsible for cooking, cleaning, and assisting customers during check-in. Callum had expressed a desire for her to come prepared with ideas the next day.

She poured herself a white wine spritzer and inserted a coin into the jukebox machine. The first sip brought a realisation – it had been too long since she let loose. With a delighted grin, she danced around the empty pub, losing herself in the music.

* * *

"What did you say?" Alan rolled over in bed in the dull morning light, his tired eyes blinking back at Tammy. "You're handing in your notice?"

"After all the exciting news I've told you – that's the bit you hang on to!" She groaned, already annoyed. She had barely slept the night before, contemplating the best way to tell Alan about her new position, but it was clear, even in his tired state, that he was not pleased.

"But … Rory?" Alan croaked.

"Yes, I'll work it out. I might even be able to have him there while I work. People are pretty cool with kids, Alan. The pub, on the other hand, wasn't somewhere I could take him."

Alan frowned. "But what if it doesn't work out? Callum employing both of us – shouldn't we have other options? I mean, what if the business goes under? Whereas people will always use the hotel."

"Alan, nothing is certain in life. Any business can fall apart. But do you really think Callum is the type of guy who wouldn't make something a success? He's barely started the business, the land is still a work site in spots, but he's already getting customers. Who knows where this will lead? And I get to cook." Tammy felt her stomach flutter with excitement and she couldn't help but smile.

"Well, you said you're going over today? You can work out the details, see if it's really what you want to do," Alan remarked, his tone carrying a note of caution.

Tammy let out a breath, but before Alan could pick up his phone to scroll through his messages, she gently placed a reassuring hand on his arm. "Alan, we have to help each other out. Can't you see I'm excited about this? You used to support me, lift me up. Now, you want me to be content with very little."

His eyes conveyed a hint of weariness as he responded, "You used to be content with our life. Not anymore."

"I want more," Tammy asserted.

He sighed, shaking his head.

Tammy, feeling a surge of impatience, demanded, "What?" Her tone was sharp, cutting through the emotional tension that hung in the air.

"When we married, I thought you knew what I could give you. It seems you won't need me soon. I can't keep up with you, Tam; you've changed," Alan admitted.

She pushed herself out of bed, the creak of the mattress mirroring the strain in their relationship. "Maybe I have changed. What's so bad about that? You've stayed the same, actually worse … you're going backward. You think since we got married, that that's it – no more trying, our lives are over. Well, we have to work at this."

"It shouldn't be work. We love each other," Alan countered, his tone pleading.

"OK, Alan, don't make any effort and see how that works out!" Tammy scoffed, her frustration boiling over. With a decisive motion, she threw herself into the shower, the sound of running water masking the subtle sound of her exasperated sighs. She needed to wash away Alan's negativity that had seeped into her everyday life.

As she fretted in the shower, she wondered what she would become if she continued down this path.

* * *

Callum waved from the nearby hill beside his and Lori's house, the wind tousling his hair as he diligently pulled out weeds. With Rory slung over her shoulder, Tammy approached, meeting him halfway in the heather. Seeing him up close, it struck her how much smaller he appeared, his eyes heavy with exhaustion, making it difficult for her to find the right words.

"How are you doing, Callum?" she inquired, carefully setting Rory down, the chill wind cutting through her like a blade. Callum knelt beside his nephew, extending his hands to marvel at Rory's curiosity, seemingly ignoring her question.

"He's grown so much since I last saw him. Time goes by quickly for children," he remarked with a hint of sadness, still engrossed with Rory. "I'm sorry I haven't been here for him enough. I hope I'll see him more; I'd like to be a good uncle. Better than any of the men in my family were," he added bitterly.

Touched by his honesty, Tammy knelt beside him. "Is everything OK, Callum?"

"Oh, yes, just feeling a bit sorry for myself," he admitted, his gaze remaining fixed on Rory. "It's special to see them grow." He smiled at the little boy, who beamed back.

Tammy glanced at the house. "Is Lori home?" she asked.

"At the shop," he replied.

She surveyed the hill, the view taking her breath away each time. From this vantage point, the hills and small trees concealed the lodges, except for one that she could just about spot with a bit of neck-craning. A cheerful yellow light radiated from it, accompanied by a trail of smoke wafting from its chimney.

Excitement coursed through her. "Can we talk about the business?"

Callum laughed, slowly standing up, allowing Rory to explore every rock and clump of heather. She licked her lips, contemplating fetching the folder from her car, filled with photographs and magazine articles, along with her laptop containing the inspiration she hoped Callum would support. However, she decided not to waste any time and dived right into her ideas.

She discussed hampers and custom meals, proposed romantic themed evenings, and even suggested building an on-site office with a toilet unit. This way, she could greet customers properly, avoiding the awkwardness of taking them directly to their lodgings or, worse, to Lori and Callum's house. She yearned for control, seeing the potential in this job as a blank canvas with financial support.

Callum nodded thoughtfully, although he was a little distracted by Rory's antics from time to time. He led them down the hill and into an empty lodge. As small as it was, much like the one housing Jennifer, it had everything a person or couple might need. Tammy left Rory and Callum to keep themselves occupied while she inspected cupboards and checked every nook and cranny.

Pulling out her phone, she began taking notes, mentioning some decor ideas she had seen online. "Since it's autumn, it would be lovely to have wreaths in autumnal colours on the doors. Painting the doors in different colours would help guests find their accommodations in the gloomy light but more importantly it could also serve as a clever marketing strategy." Tammy nodded with a conspiratorial wink.

Callum smiled. "You know, I can get behind that."

He did little to dissuade Tammy from her ideas. In fact, he

spent most of the time following Rory around, nodding approvingly at almost every suggestion. "When can you start?" he asked as he walked her back to her car, Rory giddy and dangling with excitement over his shoulder.

"That depends. What will you be paying me?" Tammy bit her lip, hating money talks but needing to know what to expect. The job sounded like exactly what she wanted – a place to channel her energy, a chance to be part of something, to make her presence felt.

Callum chuckled. "Well, if you're up to the task, I'll be paying you quite well, considering I was trying to hire three people for the job. But if you can handle it, Tammy, I'll pay you well. Very well."

Determined to prove herself, Tammy held her head high. "If I can get this place booked up over the winter and market it in all the right places, then I'll hold you to that, Callum."

"Are you sure about this, Tammy? I mean, is Alan OK with all this?"

"He will be." She nodded resolutely, summoning the strength to share her exciting news with her husband. More money, but that also meant more work. He would likely see the downsides, but it felt right for her, her chance to show what she was truly capable of.

As the late afternoon sun painted the town's harbour in hues of orange and gold, Tammy strolled along the waterfront, Rory nestled peacefully in his pram. It was a cherished tradition, one that started when he was just a baby. She would watch the ferries, her mind drifting to the times when Alan was away on fishing trips. Weeks would pass, and the ache of his absence lingered, making it challenging for her to bid him a proper farewell. In those moments, Alan would playfully tease her about her downcast face, gently lifting her chin and enveloping her in his loving embrace. He was her everything, the finest man she had ever known, a beacon of joy, a light among men who always placed her before everyone else.

As a family nearby enjoyed fish and chips on a bench, Rory had succumbed to sleep, affording Tammy a moment of indulgent melancholy. She could sense an end for her and Alan, like a station at the end of the tracks. It was a clear path in her mind's eye, leading straight ahead with the certainty of her disembarking soon. Over the past year, their marriage had transformed into something she didn't desire – a breeding ground for resentment, competition, and a loss of respect. Parenthood had irrevocably altered them, and she had come to accept that. If Alan couldn't handle the change, perhaps she had chosen the wrong partner for life.

A tear trickled down her cheek, and she wiped it away absentmindedly. She questioned her reasons for clinging to the relationship – for her own sake or Alan's. She hoped the man she knew, buried deep beneath the layers of change, still existed.

Spinning on her heel, she made her way home. When she turned the key, Alan was there, waiting for them. He took Rory, kissing his forehead and beaming at him. Rory squealed with delight, tugging on Alan's nose. Alan tickled his underarms, encouraging more shrieks of laughter.

Tammy observed their interaction, acknowledging that Alan was a good father, taking pride in his son, but in a relaxed way. She, on the other hand, always felt like she was gripping tightly onto everything, staying in control, making sure Rory's every need and demand was met.

Alan led her through to their bedroom, sitting on the bed with Rory. "Did you take the job?" he asked, bouncing Rory on his knee, his gaze unmoving.

"Yes," Tammy said quietly, then straightened her shoulders. "It's better pay, doing something I enjoy … plus, you'll get to see Rory more." She nodded enthusiastically, although her tummy did somersaults.

Alan got up from the bed, jiggling Rory. "Well, better get your glad rags on then. I'll serve this guy some leftovers, then bath him. You get dressed." He nodded, giving no more away, but kissed her on the cheek.

"But … Rory?" Tammy said with confusion.

"I'll handle it; you just get ready. Have a shower, put on make-up – whatever you girls do before a date!"

"A date?"

Alan's mother had arrived after bath time, while Tammy was nervously waiting in the kitchen nursing a glass of wine. As quickly as Alan put Rory to bed, showered, scrubbed, and wearing a shirt Tammy had never seen, he took her out the door.

Their walk through the quiet street was subdued. Tammy pondered her new job but found no words to share with Alan. Entering the main street of Morvaig, they peered into Lori's shop, seeing it dark inside with the closed sign up. Waiting at traffic lights, Tammy's hand instinctively went to Alan's before they crossed the road.

With a smile, he took it and soon led her into a waterfront bistro. They were seated at a table adorned with a bouquet of pink roses. "Congratulations," Alan said, squeezing into the small booth seat, as Tammy sat opposite, savouring the scent of her favourite flowers.

"That's kind of you," she said, touched, but her words still came out stilted, expectant, a frostiness still shielding her. How could she ever relax?

A bottle of bubbly appeared, and with a pop she was handed a glass. "Are you sure about all this?" She wanted to look at her phone, just to check with Alan's mother if Rory had gone down OK. But she willed herself not to, then debated about pretending to go to the bathroom to glance at her phone there. Before she got up, Alan coughed and breathed out.

"I'm sorry." He looked down at the menu.

Tammy frowned. "Is it too expensive?"

"No, no!" He shook his head. Then, meeting her eye, he said, "I'm going backward. What you said this morning has been going over and over in my mind." He moved his hand in a circular motion, then rubbed his forehead. "I'm going backward? That kind of hurt, Tammy."

"I'm sorry," she said immediately. The last thing she wanted now was to recount all their fights just before a lovely meal.

"I just don't think I'm enough. I thought I could support my family, but I failed at that – now you have to take a job to help us out. None of this is what I expected." He met her eyes. "I'm sorry, Tam. If this hurts, I'm sorry – but marriage has been tough. It's been work." He shook his head, and she was alarmed to see his eyes turning red. He blinked, and a watery tear fell down his cheek, just when a waitress showed up to take their food order. Mortified, Alan waved her away.

"Like, we were happy. Weren't we? We used to laugh all the time. You used to laugh at my jokes, now I think you just put up with me. You're distracted. It's like when I speak, you're thinking 'I can't put up with this eejit.'" He shook his head, his eyes darting around the restaurant, his head dipped. "The look in your eyes sometimes … I just don't know how to get back to what we were. Things were easy then. I'm just worried, and I can't lose you. I'm worried you'll get this job, you'll realise you don't need me." He shrugged. "I mean, what's the point of having me around then?"

The waitress hovered around them, and Tammy knew she was likely wanting to listen in, and immediately gave her a wild eye to clear her again.

She reached across the table and rested a hand on Alan's. What could she say? She needed to be honest too. She felt the hard, calloused hand under hers. Her finger traced along his thumb knuckle, which had two scars. Alan's hands had always been big, working hands, plunging into freezing water, gutting fish, and now – at Callum's lodges – working with wood and any handyman duties. Those big hands held her when she birthed Rory, reassuring her; his strength, Tammy now realised, had been what she needed.

"I just feel angry," she blurted out. "I feel the pressure to be a great mum, to get a great job, to have everything I wanted. Now I don't know. All I think about is what I'm not doing. That I'm not enough for Rory. I'm failing at this motherhood thing. I have no friends – no one likes me, which means who's going to want to be near Rory?"

"What are you talking about, Tam?" He laughed, despite the sadness that clearly weighed on him.

"No one likes me. And that's fine – but now Rory is here …"

He waved his hand dismissively. "You're the most vibrant person I know; people flock to you."

"I'm getting sidetracked." She pushed his lips together. "I just find being a mum a bit overwhelming, like everything lies with me, I need to make sure everything is … perfect." She gritted her teeth, knowing what she had just said was part of the issue.

Alan shrugged. "It just will never be perfect, Tam. You got to let go of that a bit."

She shook her head. "I can't do that."

"I'll help more." He took her hand in his.

Tammy slumped back on her chair, exhausted. "I just don't know if I can let go."

"Let's try together." He straightened his back, and with

the other hand brushed his suit jacket. "And I need to make more time for my woman."

"Oh really?"

"Yes, because you are my queen. You're such a strong, capable woman, who could rule armies if you had the time. So I know this job will be a success because you are amazing. That's why I married you; I had to before someone else took you off the market!"

"You make me sound like a house!"

"Well." He shrugged. "You're my home."

Tammy shook her head, chuckling. Then got up, slid in beside Alan, and taking his face in her hands she looked into his eyes. Instead of looking away, he watched her intently. She kissed him, letting go of the tension that had been on her shoulders all day. Alan kissed her back, his hand resting on her shoulder, his gold wedding band grazing against her skin, reassuring her of their promise.

39

Rain drummed steadily on the tin roof above as Callum stood, soaked and vulnerable, in front of Jennifer at the Morvaig bus station. The curious eyes of onlookers fixated on the unfolding scene, turning the station into an unintended stage for a Highland Romance novel.

Callum's voice bore a thread of desperation as he pleaded, “I want to get this right, damn it.” The relentless rain and tense anticipation left him trembling.

It had been a spontaneous decision to confront his past, to throw caution to the wind and face the consequences.

Jennifer, however, remained sheltered beneath the tin roof, preoccupied and seemingly uninterested with her gaze fixed on the bustling street. “You had your shot, Callum,” she said, frustration colouring her tone. “I’ve been here waiting, and now you decide to show up?”

She was right; it had been a poorly timed confrontation on his part. Yet, he couldn't let her go. “I just need to be sure about all of this,” he implored, haunted by Lori’s last hurtful words still echoing in his mind.

Trust wavered as doubts about the paternity and Jennifer’s

intentions clouded his thoughts. Could he trust Jennifer after all these years? Perhaps she needed financial support, and this child might not even be his. The pain that realisation would cause in the long run for everyone involved weighed heavily on him.

"I just need—" he started, but Jennifer cut him off with a bitter declaration.

"I'm over all of this – I'll figure it out. Another man in my life is the last thing I need right now. I release you, Callum. You don't need to think about me or Matthew again." The screech of the bus coming to a halt mingled with the movement of people around them.

"Matthew? Is that his name? My son?" Callum asked, his voice trembling.

The revelation hit him with a profound force as Jennifer nodded solemnly, handing him a photograph. In the photo, a young boy with features mirroring Callum's own stared back at him.

He saw a young boy with nut-brown hair and bright blue eyes beaming with pride. He wore a mustard-coloured sports jersey and held a hockey stick.

This child was his, yet he didn't know him. So much could have been shared, but it was all torn from Callum's grasp. He would have given anything to embrace fatherhood.

"He plays hockey?" Callum asked, his voice numb. Around them, the bus driver loaded passengers' suitcases into the storage compartment beneath the bus. Jennifer nodded.

"There's no shinty there, just hockey."

He continued to study the photograph, taking in every detail of the child who was his but had grown up without him.

"Still doubt who his father is?" Jennifer asked, her tone softening.

"Are you sure you want me to get involved?" Callum

whispered. "His life will become uncertain, especially at this age …"

"His life is already uncertain," Jennifer replied, her voice heavy with resignation. "His father always knew he wasn't his. I never hid that fact, but we had other children, and he just accepted him. But now … now he wants a divorce. He despises me so much that he's prepared to reveal Matthew's paternity." Jennifer hesitated, her lips trembling as she looked away. "I don't want a divorce, but …"

The bus, a ticking clock, marked the moments slipping away. "Please stay," Callum pleaded, holding her hand, but she shook her head.

"I need to go. My flight …"

"I can take you to the airport. We can talk more," Callum offered.

She shook her head. "I need to go. I can't risk missing this flight. My mother is already waiting for me there. My husband … he's asked her to leave our home. I need to go and fix this."

The weight of the situation pressed on Callum. "But what am I supposed to do?" he asked, genuine concern in his voice. The prospect of losing touch with his son loomed large.

"You could maybe see him," Jennifer suggested, a deep sense of helplessness in her eyes. "When things settle down a bit. Would you do that?"

"Yes," Callum replied without hesitation, committing to a promise he hadn't fully comprehended.

Jennifer slowly melted away behind the blurry bus window, and with a final wave, she disappeared from sight.

Callum sat down on a small bench under the shelter, trying to process everything that had just transpired. The rain continued to tinkle on the tin roof, and he felt utterly overwhelmed.

"Are you OK?" came a voice nearby. His heart lifted for a

moment, thinking it was Lori. But instead, it was someone he had not spoken to in some time. His old friend Francesca stood under her flowery umbrella, concern etched on her face.

He could only muster a shrug, unable to find the right words to express the whirlwind of emotions swirling within him. For a while, they simply remained in silence, the rain providing a steady rhythm to their thoughts.

"The whole town knows my business!" he said, abruptly throwing his hands in the air. "I can just imagine them all licking their lips, spouting 'Callum Macrae, not the good guy you think – with bastards spread out all over the world'."

Francesca edged closer to him. "But you didn't know you had a child. Don't be hard on yourself, Cal Cal."

"Maybe. But it doesn't make it any less true."

Francesca placed an arm across his shoulder, and he felt like he had gone back in time. Her presence and comforting words after Jennifer had left the first time. She had stepped up as a friend, and now, despite everything, she was still here for him. For a moment, he winced at her touch, but the weight of sorrow and confusion bore down on him. He needed someone to rely on.

"I knew Jennifer. You knew we were friends when you guys were together," she said between breaths. "But *you* were really my friend," Francesca emphasised. "I have always loved you … as a friend," she corrected herself.

Callum hadn't fully caught her words; he pulled out the photograph of Matthew, his mind on the tough road ahead for the boy. He aimed to prove himself as a reliable, steadfast figure for him. But was he any of those things?

"She asked me where you were," Francesca said near Callum's ear gently. "I knew I couldn't protect you anymore. So I told her where you were."

Callum looked up, not entirely following the conversation. "Fran, what are you saying?"

Her arm remained across his shoulders. "I'm saying I love you, and everything I do is because of that." She took a deep breath. "Jennifer screwed up; you didn't deserve that. But I guess you should know now." She licked her lips quickly. "I kept in touch with Jen. I've been writing to her for years."

"You mean … you mean you knew I had a son?" He stood up.

"It wasn't my secret to tell." She raised her hands. "Jen had decided. I thought it was better to let you both talk it out yourselves. It was your business. I couldn't interfere; that wasn't fair. I wish she had never told me. But when you decided to get engaged to Lori, I knew you needed to know, before anything else happened, and things got really … complicated." She stood up slowly. "I'm sorry, Callum, I'm so sorry."

"What the hell!" He shook his head, wildly looking for something to kick or push. He found a loose stone, and kicked it across the road with such force it made it into the sea with a splash. "You knew all along! You knew I had a child and didn't tell me. Both of you kept such a thing from me, for what? To tell me when you think it's convenient for you both, when I was happy – about to get married to Lori!" He turned to face the sea breeze. He couldn't look at his old friend. "After everything, Fran, you still can't accept that I'm with Lori. Is that why you schemed for Jen to show up now?"

"This is not about me," Fran said tightly. "This is about your son."

"This is about everything, Fran. You, Jennifer, me, Lori, Matthew!"

She nodded solemnly.

"You've let me down."

"You needed to know before you married Lori. Callum, don't you see – she is not right for you."

"And what – you are?" he spat. "This is madness!"

"You needed to know about Matthew before you married. It would complicate things otherwise."

"Oh I'm sure, I'm sure it looks pretty good to you all now. I have land, a business, lots to take away from me."

Francesca shook her head. "Never."

"Did you come up with an agreement that if I left the land to Matthew, my son and heir, Jennifer would give you something?"

"No," Francesca said through gritted teeth. "But you can't see, Lori is not right for you. I bet she'd steer you away from that poor boy in New Zealand. She pushes you into things. She's making you spiteful. Don't you see, Callum? I've been here, the whole time – I didn't leave. What's to say she won't again?"

"What's all this really about, Fran?" Callum confronted her, his steps determined. "OK, we didn't invite you to our housewarming, and you weren't invited to the wedding. I'm sorry about that. But that's not Lori. That was me. I chose not to invite you." His fists clenched at his sides. "Something hasn't been right between us lately, and it's not what I wanted," he seethed. "Lori doesn't trust you, but she would never make decisions for me. She would welcome you, if it was what I wanted. And now I see she's been right the whole time. Keeping something like this from me for years, when you knew I was lonely. But you didn't tell me then, no, because I would've left to go to Matthew," he spat out bitterly. "You wanted me here, what for? To have me all to yourself?"

Francesca's face twisted with emotion. "Callum, please." She pleaded, tears glistening in her eyes. "You're so important to me. Your friendship is."

But Callum's resolve remained unshaken. He turned around, marching off into the rain.

40

Lori pressed the doorbell, her finger lingering on the button. The familiar sight of her gran's car outside gave her a sense of reassurance, but Lawrence's absence raised unspoken questions. Following a chance encounter with Flora Mackenzie on the bustling main street, Lori, armed with new knowledge, had made a beeline for her grandmother's house.

Flora, in her customary nosy fashion, had engaged Lori in seemingly harmless chit-chat, masking her true intent – to extract information about the wedding, Gran's new husband, and any other intriguing titbits. It wasn't until Lori walked away that the realisation hit her; she had unwittingly shared more than she intended. Gran would not be pleased when she found out. But Flora had confirmed that Gran had indeed been at her house all morning, and given Flora's reputation for knowing everything about everyone, Lori trusted the information.

Lori pressed the doorbell once more, her impatience growing. When there was still no response, she decided to let herself in as she used to. But to her horror, the door was locked. Something wasn't right. She skirted around the side of the house, through the narrow wooden gate to the back garden. There, Bracken came up to her, letting out two sharp barks, drawing attention to Gran, nestled on a lounger in the corner, concealed beneath a blanket. Lori's heart skipped a beat at the sight of her pale figure.

"Gran!" she cried out, rushing forward and shaking her by the shoulders. Gran lay motionless, strands of white hair cascading over her forehead. A second shake brought forth open, dazed eyes, focusing on Lori.

"Where am I?" Gran's voice carried a disoriented tone.

"You're home, Gran. In the garden. Are you OK? You had me worried!"

"How?" Gran rose slowly, Bracken whining from Lori's side.

Gran manoeuvred her legs onto the grass, stifling a yawn. A hint of amusement played on her lips. "What?" She shook her head. "I was having a nap." She chuckled, slapping her leg with unexpected vigour.

"You seemed out of it!" Lori retorted, her defensive tone betraying the concern beneath.

"So would you be after hosting another book club when it was meant to be Sally Henderson's turn."

"Oh." Lori glanced at Bracken, whose indifference was mirrored in his gaze. "I just … you locked the front door, which you never do!"

"That's because I wanted a nap, and that door has been all comings and goings. I haven't had a bit of peace. Lawrie has gone to the community committee meeting. I just couldn't face it."

"You never miss it."

Gran shrugged. "I needed to miss something." Rising slowly, she suggested, "Let's have a cuppa."

"Now I feel bad; I shouldn't have come in."

"Don't be silly – this house is always your home. And

I'm glad you came, even if it was through the back door!" With a playful wink and a slight limp, Gran led the way to the kitchen. Lori selected two vibrant mugs while Gran prepared the teapot. Muttering to herself, Gran scoured cupboards and, tapping her head as if jogging her memory, opened the fridge door, revealing a plate of scones oozing with raspberry jam.

"Lawrie puts everything in the fridge," she remarked, shaking her head lovingly. "Men."

"How is Lawrence?" Lori asked, aware that these moments with her gran were rare, usually happening when Lawrence was away.

"Great. He's keeping up appearances for me."

"So you said." Lori helped herself to a scone and sipped tea.

"How's Callum?" Gran's pale blue eyes scrutinised Lori.

Lori shrugged. "Good."

Gran ambled around the kitchen counter, cup in hand, and sat down. Stretching her back and rocking her neck, she turned to her granddaughter. "You're not very convincing. Do you want to talk about it?"

Lori sighed. "Not really."

They remained in silence for some moments, Lori finishing off a scone, only to grab another without much thought. She could never resist Gran's baking. "Will Lawrence be gone long?" she asked, her mouth full.

Gran smiled. "You don't like Lawrie much, do you?"

The unexpected comment caught her off guard, but instead of denying it, she shrugged wearily.

A light laughter escaped Gran's lips, and she quickly covered her mouth.

"We just never see you," Lori finally confessed. "Lawrence is nice enough, but I'm worried you've changed."

"We all change, Lolo."

"But I spent so long away from you, and I've chosen to

come back, to be with my family. To be with you, after all those years apart … I wanted things to be …" She shrugged again. "I don't know, different to this!"

"Things can manifest differently than what we want," Gran offered with wisdom in her voice. "You've to act how you see fit. What do you want to happen? Don't wait around for others to make it happen. If you want something, you do it," she said, not unkindly.

"I want to feel connected to you again," Lori admitted quietly, emotions tightening her throat.

"Well, what's to stop us?" Gran asked.

"You're always busy. Lawrence is here all the time. You're changing. Everyone is changing. Nothing is what I expected it would be," she confessed, surprising herself as the words tumbled out.

"We could never move on," Gran reassured gently. "We're family, we always will be. You've just to accept that it might be a little bigger now."

"I don't want it to be." Tears rolled down Lori's cheeks. "I never got to experience it."

"And that's something you'll need to bear. We can't stay static." Gran pressed her lips together. "I know it's different with Lawrie here, but he knows my family is the most important thing to me."

"Well, it's not to him," Lori retorted. "He won't even make amends with his daughter! What's to say you won't shut us out also?"

Gran sat back. "He mentioned his daughter to you?"

"At the hospital, he mentioned her. Said they don't talk," Lori recounted the brief conversation Lawrence had with her, his ambiguity piquing her curiosity even further.

Gran closed her eyes briefly, then looked sideways at Lori. "That's good he told you. He's mentioned it a few times since then. I think after his chat with you, it's been on his mind."

Lori circled a finger around the rim of her cup, the heat of the tea making her pause. "I've missed just sitting with you."

Gran pouted and placed an arm around Lori. "Me too. But I'm here. Don't keep looking back, Lolo. I'm here in front of you, encouraging you to keep going." She smiled. "How's the shop and the wedding plans?"

Lori let out a deep breath. "The shop is OK. Rhona is making it turn a profit. If it was left to me, I'd be doing nothing. The wedding is just taking all my energy, and I'm not particularly looking forward to it. I mean, I don't care. That doesn't sound right, does it? I should want to get married."

Gran's sad eyes met Lori's. "I'm sorry you've felt this way. I thought you were excited about the wedding."

"No one's showing me much enthusiasm." Lori shrugged. "Jean and Tammy have kept right out of things, and I guess I don't blame them. I've not been the most approachable person lately."

"They showed up when you needed them, didn't they?" Gran probed. "You sisters have a strong bond. Try not to be hard on them. You've had a lot on your mind too. Planning a wedding is not easy, especially with the groomsman working out his own problems."

"I just don't think I want to get married now."

Gran shifted in her chair. "Perhaps."

"You agree I shouldn't get married?"

"Well, what do you think? When you think of marrying Callum, how do you feel?"

Lori sat still, considering the question. Images of Callum washed over her. The moment she saw him at Tammy's wedding, the way he pulled her in close, making her breath disappear. And when they shared their first kiss as teenagers, by the rushing river after school. Callum always held her and looked at her with such certainty it left Lori tongue-tied.

"I want to marry him. But it doesn't feel right anymore. To have the extravagant wedding, with everyone there … I just don't know anymore."

Gran smiled. "I think you've answered your own question. Isn't that wonderful?" She squeezed Lori's hand. "And you are not alone, Lori Robertson. Never will you be. If anything, you have more people in your life now. It might not be what you envisioned. But it's life – our connections. And what we give to people. Like Lawrie, deciding to make that connection with his daughter after seeing what I have with you. And this child … Callum's child – will need your support too."

Lori nodded. "I'm sorry for everything, Gran."

"Oh wheesht." She waved her hand.

"I've treated you terribly." Lori edged closer to her, smelling her familiar fragrance of lavender and orange blossom. "You didn't deserve that. You want to be happy, and I've behaved like a spoiled child."

"You can't help how you've felt, Lori. A lot has changed." She smoothed Lori's cheek, pushing back the mass of heavy red curls off her damp face. "But you'll always be my granddaughter. My special Lolo."

The kitchen grew dim as the afternoon waned, but Lori treasured each moment with Gran, rediscovering their bond in the room's snug embrace, with Bracken nestled between them, snoozing contentedly.

* * *

Callum had been painting the outside banister that wrapped around the house when Lori parked, marching toward him with determination. "I've cancelled the wedding," she declared.

"What?" His voice rang in alarm, the paintbrush hovering in the air. "Why did you cancel it? Why didn't you tell me?" He placed down the brush, rubbing his hands on a towel, his gaze fixed on Lori. "Is it because of me? Because I have a son?"

"It's because it doesn't feel right anymore. To have a lavish wedding after everything. I didn't want it."

"But you always wanted to get married in a castle?" He stood close to her, his face serious. "I can't let you do that. I want you to have the wedding you want, the wedding you always dreamed of."

Lori smiled to herself, recalling her childhood fantasies of dressing up and pretending to marry in their garden with her sisters. She searched Callum's eyes. "I didn't want it. I want us both to have what we want."

"But this is important to you."

"Getting married to you is important to me, nothing else matters."

Relief filled his eyes. "I'm so happy to hear you say that, even after everything."

Lori gently pressed a finger to his lips. He looked down and chuckled, pulling out something from his pocket. "I would have cleaned myself up a bit if I'd known you were coming home, but I hope you'll excuse the paint." He led her toward their bench, overlooking their favourite view of the sea and the inner islands to the west. "I wanted to give this to you many years ago when I was a stubborn young lad with no money and too much ambition."

Lori smirked. "You'll always be those things to me." She caught his eye playfully and opened the box to find a beautiful simple diamond ring nestled inside. She touched the band. "It's perfect."

"You mean it?"

She nodded, and Callum carefully slid the ring onto her finger.

"Thank goodness it fits!" Lori said under her breath. "That's all we would've needed!" She giggled.

"It's meant for you. You were always meant to be my wife."

"Even after all the Jennifer business." Lori watched Callum, and instead of his usual flinch or change of topic, he looked her in the eyes.

"I loved Jennifer. But it was always you. I could never let you go. Even this ring found its way back to me, and I thank my lucky stars that you did too."

He touched her cheek, pulling her close, his lips pressed against hers. She folded into him, just as she always had. His woody smell, his days-old stubble, his strength. He would always be her first love.

She never failed to notice the tingles that lingered down her back, even now.

They sat side by side, the moon appearing behind a bright cloud. Callum touched her engagement ring, his breath close to her ear, and he kissed her hair. The nearby islands illuminated with tiny white dots through the gloomy light. The air carried the cool, fresh smells of autumn and Lori thought of autumn in New York, the crisp leaves floating in the breeze on her walks home. Then for the first time, she realised she hadn't thought about New York – about the buzz and potential parties she might be missing out on – in a long time.

Nothing else mattered. This was where she truly belonged.

Home pulled her back, and it was in these small, fleeting moments that it became evident. The shared laughter with Gran in the cozy kitchen, the warmth of Bracken's soft fur as she snuggled into him, Callum's comforting arm wrapped around her.

All the time she felt she had missed out on no longer mattered. She was here now, in the home she and Callum had built together.

They held hands, and around them, starlings fluttered, weaving through the young trees Callum had planted. She adjusted her gaze, watching the birds as they moved grace-fully through the air in pairs, spiralling downwards in a mesmerising dance. Their lively energy resonated with her. She knew it was time for the birds to depart this land soon for the winter, but unlike them, she would stay. In that moment, her imagination came to life. This house, though relatively new, teemed with life. From the birds to the trees, growing each day, she saw the potential for more. More barbecues, more parties, more laughter, and children playing.

Their house would become the home she had always dreamed of.

And it was up to her to make it so.

EPILOGUE

Lori's wristwatch echoed the erratic beat of her racing heart – an urgent drumroll preceding the life-altering decision she was about to make. Facing the swelling sea, a deep tremor coursed through her body. Nevertheless, she clung to the steering wheel, determined to ignore the persistent ache consuming her.

Today was the day she had to be here.

Waves surged forward, cascading over the sandy shore and assaulting her windshield with a burst of salty spray. Above her, the sky stretched out in a hazy canvas painted with delicate pink wisps. Her gaze swept across the horizon until it settled on the murky green expanse of the sea – the same sea that had already taken so much from her.

With a measured breath, she attempted to calm her racing heart, drawing on the techniques she used during panic attacks. Focusing on something larger than herself, she synced her breathing with the ebb and flow of the approaching waves. It was time, and there was no turning back. After all, it had been her idea. This decision would finally end the pain that had haunted her for so long.

Lori opened the car door and stepped out, her bare feet

sinking into the cold sand. The salty wind ran through her hair, and she smiled at what awaited her, embracing the unknown.

"You look beautiful." Rhona joined her, breathless, holding a bunch of daisies interwoven with wildflowers and ivy trailing down her gown. "But please put on some shoes; I'm cold just looking at you."

"It's already cold! I didn't want to get my white heels covered in sand," Lori scoffed, teasingly. "I'm a hardy Highlander, a little cold sand won't do a thing to me!"

"You sound more and more like your gran each day, Lori Robertson." Rhona shook her head disapprovingly. "Stubborn to the core!"

"I have a pair of wellies in my car you can borrow," Tammy offered, wearing a dress similar to Rhona's but with a more conservative neckline. Lori had custom-made three dresses, all in deep emerald-green satin, skimming their knees, with a ruffle tied across their waists. Seeing them against the brooding beach skyline, she was struck by the colours.

"Your feet are too big!" Lori playfully declared, following Tammy to her car. "Honestly, I'm fine in my bare feet. This will be over quickly."

"Oh Lori, you think the service is going to be quick?" Rhona said with mock sympathy. "That 'special person' you nominated will have us out here until nightfall!"

"Yeah, that was the risk." Lori scrunched her nose. "Don't worry, I'll give them my stare, and they'll know immediately to stop talking and get straight to the point!"

In a blur, Lori pulled into the wedding party, leaving her old self in the car, overcoming self-pity. It was up to her to make this the best life she could.

She nodded, taking a deep breath to steady her nerves. It felt surreal being on the beach that held such sorrow and fears. But it was beautiful. Open. The white sands stretched out, meeting hills and a tiny white croft house in the distance. It felt right, the place she needed to make peace with.

"I just need to clarify," Rhona interjected, raising her finger theatrically, "who's the leading lady in this bridesmaid ensemble, Lori?"

"You, Rhona, are the maid of honour." Lori chuckled, exchanging knowing glances with Tammy and Jean. They strolled toward the small crowd gathered under an archway adorned with white flowers, vibrant purple heather, and trailing greenery.

Lori stepped in time with Rhona, whispering. "My partner in crime, Rhonz."

"I'm so happy you came back to us, Lori," Rhona declared, gripping Lori's hand. "And that you're marrying your first love; it's so romantic!" With the confidence befitting a maid of honour, she squeezed Lori's hand and led the way.

As they approached the small ceremony, a trio of fiddle players serenaded from the side of the flower-draped archway. Lawrence, at the end of the aisle, fixed his sharp blue eyes on Lori. "My dear, you look breathtaking. Shall we?" She linked arms with him, and together they wove through the small audience. At the end of the aisle, standing in front of billowing ivy and ferns, was Callum.

In his kilt, grey tweed waistcoat, and jacket, he looked every bit the man she'd hoped to marry someday. It had always been Callum, even when she had planned to marry another. This was her moment, and everything about it clicked into place, almost like déjà vu.

Gran emerged, draped in one of Lori's custom opera coats, a deep blue mirroring the ever changing stormy sea beside them. Holding her head high, she waited for the music to fade before pronouncing over the waves, "We are gathered here today to witness and celebrate the union of Callum Macrae and Loretta Robertson. They have chosen to symbolise their love and commitment through the ancient and sacred ritual of handfasting." Holding a book but scanning the guests with confidence, she continued, "Now, if you haven't been to one of these before, this ceremony not only joins them in marriage but also binds their hearts and souls together in an enduring connection."

Rhona let out an "Aw!" and pouted, dabbing her eyes theatrically as she shimmied in front of Tammy and Jean.

Lori watched Callum, her heart swelling with pride. How she wanted to kiss him, to hold his hand. He caught her eye, winking playfully, and she relaxed a little. Her dress floated out into the wind, her ivory tulle from her headdress too. For a moment, she thought she might blow away on the breeze, until Callum's hand reached for hers.

Gran continued, eager to enlighten the wedding party, even though most had attended many handfasting ceremonies before. "The tradition of handfasting dates back centuries to a time when weddings were often held under the open sky. The couple's hands were joined and bound together with cords or ribbons, symbolising their union. Today, we continue this tradition as Lori and Callum come forward to declare their love and commitment." She placed a long strip of fabric across Lori and Callum's wrists, stitched together by Anne and Maggie using scraps from Lori's mother's sewing box. Gran gave a blessing over it, wrapping it around them tightly.

Even on the wide, open beach, for a moment, Lori felt the whole world was looking in. They kissed, cheers erupted around them, and the music swirled. She could feel her parents standing by, sense the support from her surrounding family on the beach, along with the love of her life. Finally, she could let herself feel at peace.

* * *

The night wove its magic around the lively gathering in Gran's garden, a gentle breeze carrying whispers of celebration. Chinese lanterns and fairy lights draped the scene in a warm, enchanting glow. Lawrence, with flushed cheeks from both entertainment and wine, reappeared, topping up everyone's glasses.

"I can't believe we're married!" Lori cheered, perched next to the dessert table, where Tammy had previously arranged a masterpiece. Only a few macaroons and a slice of wedding cake were left.

"That was a damn good wedding," Callum said, settling beside her and stretching out his legs with satisfaction. "Although, are you sure you're happy we didn't have the big, fancy wedding?"

"Absolutely!" Lori nodded, her eyes gleaming with pure joy.

"Well." Callum leaned in conspiratorially. "Maybe we'll throw a belated bash before we hit the road – let our hair down and invite the whole village!"

Gran, hovering nearby and ever the attentive soul, inquired, "Before you go?"

"Aye, we've decided to have a bit of a long holiday," Callum declared. "Now that Tammy's on board."

"And Rhona's got the shop under control!" Lori added with a twinkle of excitement.

Gran clapped her hands together in delight. "Oh, wonderful! Where were you thinking? Italy, Morocco, oh somewhere warm, I bet?"

"New Zealand," they both stated in unison.

"Well, I wish you all the luck and strength for that," Gran said soberly, raising her glass. "It won't be easy, but as long as you have one another, you're all the stronger for it."

To their surprise, she tapped her glass, commanding the party's attention. "You know I'm not one for speeches, and particularly since you've been listening to me drone on today – I'll keep it short." She chuckled. "It's been my privilege to be the silent observer of these two over the years. Sometimes when they weren't even aware!" She shot Callum a sly wink, eliciting laughter from the intimate crowd. "But I can say with all my heart that you both have been blessed to find that special someone. You know, the tradition of handfasting goes way back. It was custom for the couple to be married for a year and a day, a trial period so they could get to know each other better … a wise move for the woman, in case a more dashing lad strolled into town!" Gran held her glass high, undisturbed by the ensuing laughter. "But, in my eyes, you two have been handfasted for the last ten years … connected by an invisible thread, a bond that held you together until you saw one another again."

"Oh, stop, Mary!" Rhona interjected. "You'll have us all in floods of tears!" Laughter bubbled up once more.

Gran waved her hand dismissively. "Isn't that what I'm here for – to remind you all that it's never too late. From a woman who has lived a long, happy life, some things come back to you." She smiled lovingly towards Lawrence, standing by her side. "Anyway, I've done it again." She sniffed theatrically. "I can't make a short speech without blubbering anymore!"

"A short speech?" Lori teased, petting Bracken, who had appeared between her and Callum, asserting his presence.

"We wish you all the happiness in the world." Jean appeared by Gran's side, a glass in one hand, while Maggie held the other, standing together in support.

And Tammy, never one to miss out, chimed in, "We'll take care of everything here, go explore together!"

"Just don't be gone long," Gran cautioned with a playful finger wave. "And send us a postcard!"

Callum moved closer to Lori, but Bracken snorted between them. "What's Gran talking about, being the elder of the group? I think you've got a few years on her." He stroked Bracken on the nose.

"A hundred years old, I'd say in dog years," Lori said matter-of-factly, rubbing Bracken's velvety ear lovingly.

"Let's hope we grow that old together too."

"Of course we will, I have it all planned." Lori nodded.

Callum laughed, shaking his head. "Oh really?"

"Yup. Three children, a collie dog, and a holiday every year will keep us young."

"Three children?" Callum shrieked. "You've changed your tune!"

Lori shrugged, mischief glinting in her eyes. "Maybe."

"Well, we better start working on those three children immediately!" he said playfully, tucking a stray curl behind her ear. They leaned closer together and kissed softly amidst Bracken's protests and the cheers from family and friends around them.

WANT A LITTLE EXTRA?

Head over to www.clairegillies.com to receive a FREE download of Lori and Callum's high school meet-cute.

THANK YOU

If you enjoyed reading this, please leave a review on Amazon or Goodreads, and tell your friends! It really helps new readers discover my books.

Thank you so much lovely reader.

Claire x

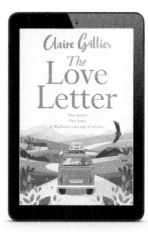

AFTERWORD

This book emerged during a profoundly emotional period for me. It became a sanctuary as I immersed myself in the world of the Robertson family upon returning to Scotland and reconnecting with my own kin after an extended stay in Australia.

In the midst of these experiences, I grappled with the essence of family and the inevitability of change. As I penned these pages, I consciously embraced life's simple joys, reflecting my personal journey of rediscovery.

Establishing a writing routine wasn't merely a task; it became a cherished part of my daily ritual, eagerly anticipated and joyously embraced. I found myself leaping out of bed, eager to delve back into the world of the Robertsons.

I sincerely hope that you find as much joy in reading this book as I did in writing it. Life is marked by constant change, but stories, like the bonds we hold dear, possess an enduring power to connect us to what truly matters.

Thank you for embarking on this journey to Arlochy with me.

ABOUT THE AUTHOR

Claire Gillies writes heart-warming, uplifting women's fiction set in Scotland. Having grown up in the Scottish Highlands, Claire later lived in Australia for several years, working in retail and creating her own fashion label.

Now back in Scotland, Claire resides in beautiful Inverness-shire with her family. She finds inspiration in her love of folklore, costume, and history, which infuse and shape her writing.

When she's not writing, she indulges in her love for costume dramas like Poldark and Jane Austen adaptations, by curling up on the couch with a cup of tea.

Claire enjoys connecting with her readers on a personal level. Sign up to her mailing list and grab some goodies at www.clairegillies.com

Join the conversation!

ALSO BY CLAIRE GILLIES

On the Edge

The Love Letter

* * *

Arlochy series:

From Scotland with Love

Threads of a Highland Heart

Printed in Great Britain
by Amazon